The Defender

By

Lloyd H. Muller

Also by Lloyd H. Muller

Family Tales and Letters
Old Ghosts
Section 5
I, Judas Iscariot
Days of Atonement
Heaven's Corner
The Wanderer
A Road to A Promised Land
Charlie
An American Miracle: The Making of a
Constitution
A New Start

Acknowledgements

Acknowledgements

Ever since I saw Billy Wilder's classic courtroom drama, *Witness for the Prosecution,* I have been fascinated by the genre. Throughout my writing career, I have been wanting to write such a story. This desire has been enhanced by modern stories of which two stand out as TV classics. One was *Perry Mason*, the attorney who always got his man while defending the innocent accused. The second was the original *Law and Order*. Here the prosecutor is most often Jack McCoy. Is it by chance that my Houston prosecutor's name is John McElroy? I'll never tell.

However, for writing this type of story, I had a basic problem. I'm not a lawyer and don't really know trial proceedings. I picked up a few tricks from watching my shows, but not enough to do a courtroom drama by itself. So, I concentrated on the characteristics of the characters. This proved to be my best choice because it permitted me to delve deeper into the conflicts facing litigators.

For prosecutors, the issue is convicting an innocent man. For defenders, the issue is defending people who will probably repeat their crimes if set free. How does one deal with those issues? This novel explores this question. Some just become inured in their jobs, and don't worry about the consequences. Others worry about them.

My hero, Bill Ginn, is a mixture of faults and strengths the way all of us are. He's neither all good nor all bad. He dwells on his success and laments his failures. He makes mistakes just as Charles Laughton did while defending Tyrone Power in *Witness for the Prosecution*. He also does some good deeds that I'll not describe Here. After all I don't want to spoil the story.

Anyway, I want to thank the creators of all the shows I have cited here. Without them as a guide, this story would never come about. Thank you all.

I now want to thank some important people in my life. First is my long-time editor, Karen Gardner, who has once again kept my writing straight. Next, is Peter White, my agent, who has taken a chance on this effort and offered it to the book market. Let's hope for a million sales. Finally, Dr. Russell Vacante, whom I have known for many years and with whom I have shared hopes and dreams about our stories.

Houston

Chapter 1
The Decisions

"Madam Forewoman, have you and your colleagues made a decision?"

"We have, Your Honor."

The judge turned to the defendant and ordered him to stand. He and his lawyer complied. When satisfied, the Judge said, "Please read your decision."

The Jurist opened a sheet of paper and read, "We, the jury, after having heard the evidence against the defendant, find him guilty of first-degree murder."

A murmur immediately rose in the gallery only to subside upon the rap of the judge's gavel. Members of the media shuffled from their benches towards the door. This had been a sensational trial involving an assassination of a state representative who had been probing into organized crime that was flourishing in Texas. The product of these enterprises was simple: drugs flowing north from Mexico. In addition to cocaine, the cartels were sending and receiving a new poison that would be known as fentanyl. This product could apparently induce a euphoria beyond anything provided by earlier shortcuts to ecstasy. Unfortunately, like an asp's sting, it was deadly. But its market was growing with customers wanting its flight.

When all was quiet, the judge returned to the actors who were playing an often-heard restaging of Hamlet's tragedy of decision. He said in solemn words, "Members of the jury, I thank you for your caring decision." He then turned to the district attorney and the plaintiff's defense attorney and said, "Because this is a capital case, the jury must decide upon a punishment for the defendant. You will return in two weeks and present your cases to the jury." Another rap of his gavel closed the day's proceedings.

For all intents and purposes, the defendant did not hear these final words. His face was white except for the gaping hole of his mouth that was an astonished gap of disbelief. His lawyer put his arm on his client's shoulder as if to encourage him. "Don't lose hope, we're not done yet," he murmured. Those words also didn't register with the client as a bailiff led him away.

The state's team remained seated to await directions of the lead prosecutor. Bill Ginn topped with inky black hair that often dropped forward like death's hood during his orations. His eyes added to this scene of doom with a dead blackness. Looking at them was to gaze into the eye of a black hole where not even light could escape. When he spoke, a resonant echo of hades could be heard. He was not a nice man. In no sense could one feel warmth. Cuddling with him would be hugging a cactus.

After a short minute of accepting congratulations from his team, he said, "Well, gang, we're half-way home. Now to hook him to a needle. Let's meet tomorrow morning to review our case and prepare for our presentation. We will also be needing to bring witnesses forward to testify about the destruction the prisoner brought to their lives. Enjoy yourselves this evening."

With that, the team left and the courtroom was empty.

Two weeks later, the courtroom was filled with the same players. Now the question was what the prisoner's punishment would be. It could be either death or life imprisonment. Both sides presented arguments. The prosecutor urged the jurists to pronounce death. The defense lawyer urged life imprisonment. Character witnesses were presented to amplify the pleas of the opposing lawyers. Instructions from the judge were given to the jurists as to how they should determine their decision. With that they were excused to deliberate.

The decision was not fast in coming. Death is a final answer that allows for no second guessing once it has been rendered. What if some error had occurred? What about the possibility of redemption? These and many other possibilities needed deliberation.

Finally, a note was delivered to the judge by the bailiff that a consensus was obtained. It was unanimous. Without unanimity, no decision was valid. The judge read the note, nodded silently, and ordered the bailiff to notify the prosecutor, the defense witness, and the prisoner to appear before him for the reading of the verdict.

When gathered, the judge turned once again to the forewoman and asked, "Have you made your decision and is it unanimous?"

"We have your honor."

Turning to the prisoner, the judge ordered him to rise and hear the decision. Clad in prison garb, the prisoner stood. He was about 30 years old, 68 inches high, and of stocky build. His face was twisted in anger but he said nothing while doing as he was ordered. His name was Giuseppe Bisognio. His legal profession was pizza cook. His illegal profession was soldier for the mobs around Houston.

The judge then asked the forewoman to read the jury's decision. She turned to Mr. Bisognio and looking squarely at him recited the words on the paper in her hands. "We the jury sentence the prisoner to life imprisonment."

The prosecution was visibly disappointed. The opposing defense team was overjoyed. The prisoner turned to Mr. Ginn and screamed, "I'm gonna get you! Mark my words!"

The bailiff took the prisoner firmly in hand and led him away. This trial was done.

Chapter 2
Daily Work

"Congratulations Bill. You nailed your first fish." The speaker was Bill's mentor in the office. John McElroy was his name, and a famous name it was. John had an excellent record, meaning he had tried and won more capital cases than anyone in the history of Texas. His office was lined with three rogue galleries. The first depicted the faces of the criminals he was trying. There were three faces staring at anyone who looked. The second displayed the offenders who were convicted of first-degree murder and had received the death sentence. These people were enduring their appeals processes. Twelve faces stared outward here. Finally, the third had just two faces; they had been executed. John not only attended them, but he also was certified as an attendant in the chamber. He delighted in showing a video clip of himself strapping a belt onto the arm of a convict while chatting about the fun they had had through the trial. Finally, he was waving "bye-bye" to the man while pulling the lever that started the flow of poisons. He refused to have two guards pull other levers to disguise who had pulled the fatal one.

As he once said on TV, "I just love putting people away. It's nice if they are truly guilty, but not necessary. As long as I win the case, that's all that matters." The media shrunk back immediately by calling him a psychopath. John didn't deny it. Perhaps he was, but he loved his work, and he was good, very good, at it. Texans in general thought he was a cool dude.

Bill smiled gamely and replied, "Thank you John. I couldn't have done it without your help. It was an excellent education. Now to my other cases."

"That's the way, my boy. Always looking forward to more opportunities. As we go through the appeals process for your victory, I'll keep you posted. Arguing before the appeals and supreme court justices is another art in itself."

"As work lets me, sir, I'll be in attendance watching you perform."

"As much fun as trial work is, the real key to success is with the appeals process. Here, you must know your law, its precedents, and how they apply to your case at hand. Often it's not exactly what is written, but how you present them. Knowing your judges is very important as politics come in here. Each justice is a politician elected to his or her seat. Voters decide whether they want progressive voices or constructive conservatives on the bench. You know some of them already. In this environment, debating skills are important. Some of these justices know their stuff, and your answers must be solid. Believe me, there is nothing more humiliating than being caught short on a subject."

"Yes sir, I know you review the Martin-Quinn scores of any judge you don't know. Less than a 0.0 score indicates liberal biases, and scores above them are conservatives. Among the progressives on the Federal Supreme Court is Justice Sotomayor whose score is -1.63. Samuel Alio's score is 2.59 making him the most conservative justice on the bench."

John brightened at the mention of the Martin-Quinn instrument. "You're right. I do. For example, one time I had to present my case before Justice Martin Scalia, who had the reputation for being a 100% hard-nosed conservative. As it turned out, he actually was not. Justice Clarence Thomas was consistently more to the right. This meant I had to present well-documented and cogent answers to Scalia's questions. They were thoughtful, and I had to think carefully before answering them. The far-right justices were easier; simple stock position answers were sufficient."

John relished his self-appointed role as a teacher. He was also good at it, and Bill listened carefully to his advice. Continuing with his lecture, John addressed the issue of constitutional law. "Bill, in these debates, the concern is not who done it. The trial usually has answered that question. Instead, the question is how the crook was found and how well he was tried. Did the cops do their job in accordance with both the Texas and U.S. constitutions? Did the trial process go in accordance with accepted standards of constitutional law? I know you have studied these documents well, but what you learned in school only scratches their surfaces. Past decisions affect present arguments. The biases of the justices are important in their interpretation of these laws. As Charles Evans Hughes said in 1907, 'We are under a Constitution, but the Constitution is what the judges say it is.' Again, the moral of this story is: know thy justices."

"Yes sir. As always, your insights are important. They finish what my law courses started. I just wish I could talk further but duty calls. I have a bunch of lesser crooks to deal with."

"You get on them, my boy, but never forget, any one of them could become bait for a supreme court appeal so treat them carefully."

"Yes sir. I will."

"But before you go, here's some real-world advice. The entire court proceedings from start to finish are not about justice or search for the truth. The opposing teams are there for a reason."

Bill was a bit confused and he asked, "Reason?"

"Yes, an important reason. They are there to win. Winning is what it's all about for them...for you. Here's an analogy. Tom Landry is a revered coach for the Dallas Cowboys. Why? Because he won. You lose lots of cases and you lose your job. So, it means you do what you have to do to win. Don't go to jail for it. That ruins your career. But push the ethics limits as far as you must to win. Got it?"

Bill rolled that last bit of advice over in his head and them smiled, "Yes sir. Got it."

"So charge my boy!"

Bill was not just fawning his boss. He meant what he said because John was a tour de force. He knew his stuff and was a veteran of many legal battles. He rarely lost. Bill had received an excellent education at the Austin School of Law that was associated with the University of Texas. It had the toughest acceptance standards in the state and its washout rate was high. Bill got in with some room to spare, and his record showed diligence in his grades. Upon graduation, he had clerked for a renowned Texas jurist for two years. From there, he was recruited by the Houston attorney general.

The prospect of being a litigator instead of a counselor had appealed to him. The prospect of courtroom battles against criminals seemed far more important and challenging than merely working for a corporate partnership. Perhaps he could have earned more money doing commercial law, but 100-hour workweeks devoted to improving the bonuses of senior partners left a sour taste in his mouth. As it was, he worked often 80 hours but it was more fun. Fortunately, Virginia, his wife, understood and accepted it all. "Just keep the paychecks coming in," was her only comment.

So, Bill forsook the financial lures of Wall Street and remained in Texas to work as an apprentice criminal litigator. Like all professions, he had to learn his trade. His schooling had given him intellectual tools; it did not give him street smarts.

Getting smart meant handling dozens of cases involving two-bit criminals. Most of them were failures. They couldn't succeed honestly, and they couldn't succeed as crooks. When caught, they knew they were guilty. Bill knew they were guilty. Even his court appointed defense attorneys, who were serving their own apprenticeships, knew they were guilty. The court schedules were crowded. Attorney calendars were crowded. Dozens of cases were waiting in line for justice. So, negotiation was the byword. Bill and his colleagues worked together in conferences negotiating pleas and sentences that would satisfy judges during allocutions. Once heard, and once the judges were satisfied that the perpetrators understood what they were doing, and that all procedures met minimum constitutional standards, the deals were accepted. Sentences were rendered. A swift bang of gavels ended the cases.

Cases of this nature almost always were non-violent. Drug pushers were busted. Prostitutes were hustled off the streets. Pickpockets were nabbed. DUI drivers stopped at a blockade. They were often repeat offenders well-known by the cops. Trials began when violence or the threats of violence occurred. Teenagers discharging a family gun and killing a sibling. A battered housewife stabbing her husband after being raped. A hold-up gone awry with a killer being brought to justice. These cases could not be negotiated. Full police investigations and trials were needed.

Television is full of crime and punishment shows. Some of them are actually pretty good. *Law and Order* and *NCIS* are two of the better-known examples. Crimes are committed leaving clues behind. Investigations are made, and eventually, people are brought in for questioning. At this point, no lawyers are needed. If any further information is needed, details to be evaluated, these people are released for possible testimonies at future trials. When persons of interest are brought in for questioning that could lead them to being charged, things become more serious. Such interviews are known as "custodial interrogations." If a lawyer is demanded by a suspect, all questioning must stop until one is present. That attorney may be privately hired, or if need be, provided by the state.

The provision of an attorney by the state does not occur instantly as one would think from the TV shows. Hearings are heard to determine whether the accused can obtain their own counsel or if a state-provided lawyer is needed. Once the determination that the state must provide counsel, an attorney is selected from a pool of public defenders or employees of private firms. Until such provision is made, the accused can be held in custody.

Bill remembered his first trial case. It involved a charge of assault committed during a drug transaction. His opposing counsel was a classmate from law school. Joe Brady was his name. A simple name, but its owner was brilliant. He was graduated first in his class and had already published several articles in various law reviews. Bill had prepared himself for his friend, but he needed help in deciphering a tangled series of precedents that pertained to this case. As usual, he came to John McElroy.

"John, have you minute? I have a question about my assault case."

"Sure. Any time. What's your problem?"

"You know my case. It's about a street corner peddler having an argument with his supplier. Words led to pushing and eventually, the distributor damn near killed his dealer. Not a good way to promote business, but that's another question among them. But could the distributor claim self-defense?"

"He's claiming the dealer swung first?"

"Yep."

"Try looking up reasonable actions. Is it reasonable to shoot an unarmed trespasser for breaking into one's home? Holding him with force until the police arrived might be considered a more appropriate action."

Bill nodded. "Particularly if the trespasser was found to be drunk and lost."

"Yep. That's it exactly. Self-defense is acceptable in Texas law, even to include "standing your ground." That is, Person A is sitting in a public park feeding the pigeons when he is accosted by an armed thug. Person A doesn't have to run. He's where he can be and harming no one. Therefore, his territory is "safe ground" where he can expect not to be molested. As long as a person is in safe ground such as a park or his own home, he may defend himself to the extent deemed necessary."

"Homes being part of the *Castle Doctrine.*"

This time, John nodded. "Texas recognizes both the Stand Your Ground and Castle Doctrines. It recognizes how rational decisions may be impeded in the heat of protecting life or limb. So, if you ever try a case in another state, review their laws carefully on these matters."

"So, the illegal environment has no bearing on this case, only the issues of assault, which, in this case, got someone beaten up."

"You got it. Keep me posted."

As Bill thought back on that time, he smiled at its outcome.

As the movie of this memory unfolded, John saw him later passing down the office hallway and asked, "So, how did it go?"

"Go?"

"Your trial, what else?"

"Not good."

"Lost it."

"Yep. My classmate, Joe, even in school, he could sell sand to an Arab or convince him the Sahara desert was being flooded. Yeah, he was good."

John clapped Bill on the back. "Welcome to the litigation world. Some days you win; some days you lose. Either way, it's past history. Keep on truckin'." John paused to rethink his answer. Then he spoke. "There's another lesson here. Juries are sworn to uphold the law, but like justices, they often have their own interpretation of what's lawful and right. In your case, they saw two thugs and one got thoroughly trounced. He undoubtedly got what he deserved, and that was justice enough for the jurors. So, the client got sprung. Let him show up again, however, and he can be seen as a repeat offender. Jurors are not as forgiving of these people. Incidentally, defense attorneys will try hard to keep past records of crooks from being presented. Ignorance of sins can lead to forgiveness."

Coming back to the present, Bill thought, *And now, I'm in the bigs. Murder trials, life, death, right, wrong. What a jumble.*

Chapter 3
Time for a Change

Six months passed after Bill's murder case. He continued to negotiate nuisance cases but newly recruited attorneys were picking more of them up. His cases now were bigger, more complex. One such case involved a county treasurer who had embezzled public funds for years. His technique was amazingly simple. The computer program rounded figures to the nearest dollar. The logic for doing so was sound. Over a period of time the plusses and minuses would even out, but meanwhile, accounting past costs and forecasting future expenses were simplified. Seeing this factor, the treasurer simply diverted the odd cents into his own bank accounts. A nickel here, a dime there, eventually over the years, he had stashed some sizeable savings accounts that led to profitable investments.

Then, one day, the computers failed and humans had to audit the county's accounts. As they did so, they included the cents and noted a consistent deficiency. H'mmm was their reaction. Something doesn't make sense. Further investigation showed the treasurer was living well beyond his legal means. One thing led to another, and Bill had the case. He won. John was very pleased.

When his litigation skills had improved enough, Bill was invited to witness appeals cases as John's second chair. Included was his murder case. Here he saw John's mastery as a legal scholar at hand. His debates were bravo performances. Bill did not just sit there watching a master at work. He was constantly researching points of law. At first, they were cued by John. Later, Bill began to follow arguments and was able to forecast what case details would be needed. Bill had them in front of John before they were cued.

Eventually, Bill was permitted to argue his first case. It was a relatively simple one. The constitutional issues were straight-forward. No new legal territory was being plowed. The defense maintained that the police had not recited the Miranda statement to a Spanish-speaking defendant in Spanish. In preparation for his argument, Bill reviewed his academic record. He was a high-school graduate who had attended Houston schools from kindergarten. When this information was presented, the justices quickly decided that no language deficiency existed. The English language Miranda presentation was judged adequate, and the guilty decision and punishment stood.

As time passed, Bill's doubts about the death penalty abated. He could see how good defense attorneys could keep miscarriages of justice at bay. In addition, he saw how appellate courts further minimized chances of executing an innocent person. Not that the system was fool proof. That assurance could never be given. But it was good enough to satisfy Bill. As a result, his enjoyment of trying people grew as his partnership with John expanded.

Homelife was another question. Even though both Bill and Virginia were wage-earners, there never was money enough to meet forecasted expenses. Both of them enjoyed their luxuries. The children were growing and in need of everything including attendance at a private school with an expensive tuition for their daughter, Susan. Virginia worked as an elementary teacher and earned $38,000 yearly. This was below the median because she had forgone a master's degree to enter work faster in order to support Bill through law school. Bill's salary as a prosecutor was $74,000. Neither job offered any promise of improvement. Dollars and cents, these wages didn't make sense.

This problem became glaringly apparent as it would when being invited by Joe Bradley and his wife, Mabel, over for dinner. Even though Joe was still an associate at his law firm, his standard of living was much better. Mabel was also a teacher earning the same salary as Virginia, so there was no difference there. Joe simply brought home more bread and it showed. Bill's car was a used Toyota. Joe drove a Volvo while sending his kids to the same school as Susan. If Joe were to become a partner, he would be driving Porsches while Bill's Toyota would simply be older. Virginia was quick to notice this possibility, and it became a source of heated discussion.

"Bill, I'm proud of what you're doing by making our streets safer, but facts are facts. If we want the better things in our lives, including good educations for the kids, we need more money. As it is, we're not saving a dime. What would we do if you lost your job?"

"We won't. Trust me."

"I wish I could. But look at the federal government. Secure jobs are being chopped by the thousands. If they go, will ours follow? You know how stuff trickles downhill."

"Yeah, 'stuff' stinks and we'll be covered with it."

These discussions were repeated until Bill decided to talk with Joe. One day, after a day's trial work was finished, they met at a nearby burger joint. With their hamburgers eaten, both men sat back to enjoy their cups of coffee. Bill took this opportunity.

"Joe, we've gone back and forth on this trial and several others. You win some, and I win some. I enjoy our battles. You're a good opponent."

"Kind of like the tennis games we played in college."

"Exactly. Nothing was personal, and the competition was fun."

"Yeah, those were the days."

"Well, they're still here except our court is in the court."

Joe smiled and nodded. "Yep. You're right."

Bill paused a bit. How to start the next stage of this chat? *Just jump in I guess.* "Joe, competition aside, how do you like your work?"

"I don't understand your question? What do you mean?"

"Well, I'm not exactly sure myself. But, without digging into details, you obviously earn more money than I do. But, what about the rest of it? Let me explain my situation and perhaps you will understand where I'm coming from.

"Like most of us who did well in law school, I thought about going into commercial law on Wall Street. But the thought of working day and night for the enrichment of a senior partner didn't sound like a lot of fun. So, I went into public law. I've had a lot of fun there. Our battles have really been like another round of tennis. I don't know about you but John McElroy has been my coach for our games. You know him, I'm sure."

"Yes, I do. He's a challenge."

"Well, he has been generous in mentoring me. I have learned so much from him. When I say that, I mean the whole thing. Doing research into the facts of a case, learning how the Constitution is applied to dealing with crooks, presentations...the whole thing."

"But?" Joe looked at his friend with a quizzical look. His eyebrows knotted in question.

"But yeah. Like you I have a young family that is generating expenses faster than the money rolls in. Government work means fixed salaries. There are no bonuses for doing a good job...you simply get another job to do well."

Joe looked at Bill carefully for a long time. Thoughts were rolling through his mind. His eyebrows rocked around. *This is a tough question. I'm earning the money, but can I stand the work?*

Bill waited patiently for an answer. He knew this was a tough question. *I'm asking him how he likes working for the firm.*

Finally, Joe started an answer. "Bill, We're talking about night and day. Yes, I do earn more money, but you can say you're working for the public good. It would be entirely possible that you could be trying a man who molested my daughter. Put him away and you have my deepest blessings. Frankly, that doesn't happen very often in defense work. Occasionally, you get an opportunity to play Perry Mason but not often. Most of my clients are scumbags, pure and simple. I know they did the deed as well, as you do. But they pay the hourly rates, and I get them off. Yeah, I know the Constitution demands everyone has their day in court, and it's a good thing. Certainly, no one wants to be thrown summarily in jail, but when that child molester is caught injuring some other baby, it's hard to yell yahoo when you win your case. You know damn well he'll just repeat his action."

Bill nodded knowingly. "Yeah, you're referring to the dude you got off. He was the son of a Texas oil millionaire?"

Joe's eyes sadly agreed.

"He got killed by an unknown assailant. John didn't press for an investigation. 'Let the bastard lie in Hell' was his response. Justice was finally done on a back street. I wouldn't be surprised if the judge, jury, and hangman were the girl's father."

Joe's silence answered loudly in agreement.

Bill then asked, "So, when you won the case, what did your partners say?"

Joe laughed sardonically, "Great job Joe. Here's your next case. Sound familiar Bill? But it's not that the office is evil. No one enjoys dealing with assholes. No, of course not. It's just that essentially, the firm is selling time."

Bill's eyebrows went up in surprise.

Joe continued, "You're surprised? You shouldn't be. The firm offers services but it charges by the hour. Win cases and more time is sold to eager clients. Lots of wins generate more sold time that brings bonuses to the senior partners."

"In short, Joe, selling time is the firm's business? No time sold means the firm goes broke." *Just like John told me, litigating is all about winning and losing.*

"Yep, you got it. The associates, who really do the grunt work, sell their time to the firm that is resold to the clients at profitable rates. So, their work needs to be good or they're fired. Do excellent work and maybe they'll be promoted to a partnership where the profits go."

"No guarantees though of a promotion?"

"Nope. None. So the associates like me work our asses off to generate enough profits to grab the brass ring."

Bill saw clearly how much their jobs were alike. It was a hoot to think about it. "So, really, you and I are in similar positions. We're both working for ultimate prizes and stuck in similar pay grades. Your quagmire pays more than mine, but it's fixed."

"That's it, my boy."

"I always knew you were smart, Joe. So, thanks for the lesson." Looking at his watch, he said, "And now I gotta get home to relieve our nanny and fix some dinner. Virginia is stuck in a long teacher's conference and probably won't get home until late."

"And of course, she'll be paid overtime won't she?"

"Of course. She wouldn't have it any other way. So Joe, thanks for your time and counsel. It's been most helpful."

"Any time. Now I gotta hie back to the office. I have a trial summary to prepare for a partner to present tomorrow."

Bill returned home to relieve his nanny. He had a lot to think about when his phone rang. It was Joe. His voice was hushed.

"Bill, one last thing. Associates who don't make partner eventually get fired."

"Huh? Why?"

"I can't talk long, but here's the jist. Associates do get longevity raises just as you do. However, eventually, their salaries become so high that its cheaper to fire them and hire new graduates."

"A revolving door. Is that it?"

"Exactly. Either I make partner by next year or I'm looking for a new job. Fun huh?"

"Oh yes. You're dancing I know. OK. Thanks for this. Now, get off the phone before you're fired today."

"Okay. Bye."

"Bye."

"Damn," thought Bill. *Here with the county, I'll always have a guaranteed job. Life in the private sector isn't all it's cracked up to be.*

The next several weeks saw him doing more research on life in the private sector. As Joe had said, Bill used his position on the hiring committee to see how many candidates were newly fired from local law firms. They weren't failures. Perhaps not next generation of Clarence Darrow, but they weren't idiots. Some of them had participated successfully in large legal actions. They were articulate and knowledgeable about the law. They were all his age or perhaps a bit older. Certainly, he could not leave his job to become another second chair at a defense table. Not at his age. It would probably keep him from getting a job anyway. He had worked long enough to earn a salary bigger than what tyros were commanding.

Taking a job at a law firm would definitely be a backwards move.

Another thing he noticed among these applicants was how few of them were criminal defense lawyers. Most of them litigated civil matters. A call to Joe prompted a second cup of coffee with Joe at the burger joint.

"Joe, I've been doing some research on young private sector lawyers." He related them carefully with Joe agreeing with his findings. Then Bill asked a question that had not been covered in their last discussion. "I saw how many of the candidates I reviewed had little or no criminal defense experience."

"Yes, that's right."

"This leads me to believe that your law firm and probably others do not spend a lot of time in this area. Is it possibly true that those criminal defense specialists don't become partners or perhaps only junior partners?"

"Why do you ask that?"

"Well, look at it. Civil action lawsuits can involve millions of dollars. Defending thugs is peanuts. So, where do firms go with their time? Civil actions. Those associates who bring in the bucks in civil actions will be preferred over equally skilled criminal defense employees."

Joe became a sad young man. He sat back in his chair, took a long sip of coffee, and then blew out a caffein breath. He had been drinking a lot of coffee lately during long hours of defending scumbags.

"Bill, you're right. In fact, I fully expect to be among those lawyers looking for a job with the county. There's just not enough rich people like O.J. Simpson murdering their wives to attract large firms into the criminal defense business. At best, it's a niche activity."

"Here's the irony, Joe. Crime is big business. The drug wars are costing the government billions. Even President Trump's legal problems are costing a lot. Estimates of $100 million in legal fees have been spent defending his various escapades. His crimes are not violent but they violate the Constitution as fully as O.J. ever did. Murder or fraud...which one hurts society more?"

"You're right Bill. But so what? We still need jobs to support our families."

"We do, and I don't know the answer. So let me work on it. Meanwhile, you defend the downtrodden young molesters. Your fortune will be the gratitude of millions. Just not in dollars however."

Joe laughed grimly. "OK, Mr. Law and Order. You continue to earn your millions protecting society from the likes of my clients."

With that exchange, they went their separate ways. Still, Bill kept thinking about how to earn money in the criminal defense racket. How did crime operate? How was it organized to earn profits? His studies offered some amazing insights.

First, the gangs, or cartels as they are known now, had a distinct chain of command. At the bottom were the Falcons. They were essentially covert spies providing information on police activities, rival gangs, and similar organizations. Next were the Hitmen whose duties were obvious. Bill had taken part investigating them under John's leadership. Lieutenants were regional managers of all activities in their territories. They reported to the Drug Lords who supervised their cartels. These names might have different names in other gang cultures. For example, among Italians, a drug lord would be known as *Il Caporegime.*

These officers in the various gangs buy, sell, and direct the operations of a wide network of independent operators. Among them are the drug producers who buy raw products, convert them to drugs, and sell them to contracted cartels. These relationships are often monopsonic meaning that through violence or simply market availability, the producer has no bargaining power.

What the buyer offers is what is accepted. This means that prices can be kept low for greater profit. Other players are distributors, street dealers, accountants, and money launderers.

Bill was surprised at the sophistication of the cartels' logistics systems. First, the American freeways are the principle routes for inland movements. They are filtered in all directions along well-developed corridors. Getting to these highways involves an ingenious system of transporters. Among them are "mules" who carry drugs in their suitcases or ingesting bags of drugs that will be vomited out later. Smuggling in cargo ships is another avenue. Recently, Mexican officials nabbed a couple of "narco-ships" or custom-built submarines. These latter carriers have become serious enough for the President to order Navy aircraft to bomb them. His justification was calling the shippers as terrorists. This operation was legally dangerous and could eventually trigger a regional war.

Above all, the element of trust was paramount in these operations. When he thought about it, what other sort of contract could exist? Certainly not paper documents that would be presented in court. Considering the reporting of so much violence, one would not believe how trust could exist among these gangsters. Yet, they rely exclusively on it. Of course, anyone who violates this trust could expect a short life thereafter.

In short, a successful cartel operation was not much different than a successful legitimate business supply chain. Numerous independent operators cooperate in fulfilling customer demand. The product was illegal. The logistics were hidden. The money exchanges were not publicly recorded. But lying in the shadows of corrupt politics and violence, people earned their livings selling ecstasy to an insatiable market.

Bill thought how narcotics is no different than Prohibition when Al Capone ran liquor through Chicago. People wanted their liquor and were willing to bet their lives on bad booze. Amphetamines, heroin, cocaine, you name it. People wanted drugs and were willing to spend their last dollar on them. Meanwhile the government is spending billions trying to close the floodgates of this torrent.

What I don't see are lawyers. Not too surprising I suppose, but these people do need them. I know. I have put enough of them away. Most of them have been street dealers who rely on court appointed lawyers, but bigger fish are occasionally brought to court. Joaquin "El Chapo" Guzman is perhaps the most famous of them. He is now in an American prison but not without representation. His sons are negotiating a plea deal with the U.S. Government and their lawyer has been Jeffrey Lichtman. He ain't doin' that for free. So, if Lichtman can earn his living being a lawyer for a crook, is there room for other lawyers? That may be something for Joe to research.

"Joe, can we meet sometime for lunch? I've got something I want to share with you."

"Sure. Absolutely. It's nothing with Virginia or the kids, I hope."

Bill laughed shortly and said, "No. Nothing like that. Rather, I've been thinking a lot regarding our last chat about our careers. Been doing some research as well. Now, I'd like to give you some thoughts. So when can we meet?"

"Today at the usual joint works for me."

"Good. See you there at noon?"

"Yep. I'll be there."

Bill arrived a bit early to find a booth where he could spot Joe and wave him over. It also provided a bit of privacy. When Joe arrived he saw Bill and come over.

Shaking hands, Joe asked, "What's up?"

"Let's wait until our orders have been taken and served."

When they were eating, Bill reviewed how their careers seemed to be mired with little chance of advancement and higher pay. Then he talked about his research into organized crime.

"Joe, I've been amazed at how the drug lords run their businesses. They're as illegal as three-dollar bills, but otherwise, they have the same issues of finding raw materials, finding producers, marketing their products, moving to customers, and balancing books. You name it. All the same as legitimate businesses. Really, they operate supply chains no differently than General Motors or Exxon-Mobile."

Bill let Joe finish his hamburger to give him time to consider what he had just heard. Then Joe asked, "Well, so what?"

"What I haven't seen are lawyers. Again, they're no different than your clients. Screw up and they get into trouble. Drug dealers, by social definition, have screwed up. They need the same lawyers as your clients. I know there are some lawyers doing work for them. My question is...well...um...is there any room for a couple of hotshot lawyers to represent their interests?"

Joe sat back looking like the proverbial deer in the headlights. "You mean, become crooks?"

Bill snorted. "No, if it were only that easy. Neither of us are smart enough to do that. We'd be caught in a New York minute if we tried...and I don't know about Mabel. Virginia would not stand for the idea of visiting me in jail. Seriously, just the opposite. We'd want to be legal to the nth degree both to keep the Bar off our backs and to survive working for the drug lords."

"H'mm. OK on the first part, but the second?"

"Think of it this way. The gangs do business with handshakes. No contracts allowed that would convict them. Trust is their glue. Someone screws up and bad things can happen, especially if it's intentional."

"Break the trust?"

"Exactly. If we worked for them as lawyers, we'd have to tell the absolute truth 100% of the time. Our opinions would need to be sound and given in good faith if we were to gain their trust. Miss that standard and we'd be the proverbial dead ducks."

"Which would truly ruin our careers."

"Quack, quack."

Joe sat back and thought for a long time. Bill's logic appealed to him. His career wasn't promising at the firm. It was too late to start again litigating civil law. Mabel was pregnant with their first child, which meant increased living expenses, and they'd pretty much lived up to his salary as a carefree couple. On the other hand, working directly for the mob meant high, really high risks. He hadn't defended any big-time drug lords, but newspapers described all too often killings associated with them. Before he'd agree to any association with them, he'd need to think about things.

"Bill, you've got a wild imagination. No two ways about that. Yet, your assessment of our careers is spot-on. But there are risks to be considered, and before I agree to anything, we need to know as much as possible what we would be letting ourselves into. So let me do my homework. Let me see what sort of market is open to us. Also, let me think about what our obligations to the drug lords would be. Once I'm satisfied, I'll get back to you."

"Great. I'll do the same thing."

Joe started his investigation by talking with a street dealer he had once defended. Amos Baxton was his name. He was a young Black man of cream color. Obviously, white men had visited his ancestry. He was also in jail pending a drug charge. Joe met him there. *Joe* thought Amos might be able to help him with his problems so he volunteered to defend him *pro bono.*

Pro bono work was often done by defense attorneys for various reasons. Law firms occasioned absences from normal caseloads when time permitted and perhaps by broadcasting a good public image.

"Mornin' Mr. Bradley." Amos's eyes were downcast, and his voice was soft. Sadness came off him like sweat off a horse. He was 19 years old with no future.

"Good morning, Amos. You got busted again? I just got you off a couple of months ago."

"Yep. My luck. But I ain't got nothin' else goin' for me. I got no education or trade."

"Not even your high school diploma?"

"No sir."

This was an important admission. Young Black men with no diploma were not hirable. That piece of paper told bosses whether an applicant had anything to offer. Joe asked, "What happened with you? I know you're smart enough."

"I dunno. I was tested once and told I had dys...dyslex...somethin' wit' my eyes."

"Dyslexia?"

"Whatever. Yeah. If you say so. Anyway, I never really learned to read. But that don't mean I'm dumb. I can do numbers in my head no problem. Just tell me what I got to figure, and I can do it. Go on, try me."

"OK. You got 32 ounces of smack that you want to cut by 30%. How many ounces would you have to sell?"

Without missing a beat, Amos answered 42 and a half. Joe thought, "Damn, I'd need a calculator to do that."

"OK, Amos. You proved your point. How far did you go in high school?"

"Tenth grade."

"But you think you could pass a GED exam?"

"Can't read. Get it?"

"Yeah, I get it but here, let me see if it could be read to you."

A short googling gave the answer. It was yes. A candidate would need to submit a request with justification and if accepted, the exam would be given by an oral reader.

"Apparently no one ever told you that GED's can be read. With your dyslexia you're effectively blind. So, let me arrange things for your exam. But two things I need from you."

Amos brindled. *Always a catch.* "What is it?"

"Relax. I asked for your case when I heard you were here. You're not a bad kid. Just someone who's trying to survive. Am I right?"

"Yeah. That's it."

"You don't carry either?"

"Nope. Carryin' just creates more problems. Guys that do have to use 'em and that leads to serious prison time."

"Don't use it either?"

"I have but no more. It's a sucker's bait. I just sell it."

"That's what I thought or otherwise, I'd never have taken your case. Now, if I can get you off and arrange for your GED, what will you do with your chance?"

"Whaddaya mean?"

"Just what I said. I don't want to see you here again and that means stop dealing. That means you still got to support your mama. How you gonna do that? What kind of work can you do?"

"Not much, Dealin' is all I know."

"Well, without a GED, you're goin' nowhere. So, again, I'll help you find your way off the streets."

"Are you serious? No one's ever made an offer like that to me."

"Serious as sunshine. What will you do or what can you do? You can't join the Army with your record. They won't take you. So, it's something else."

Amos didn't answer. It was obvious he didn't have an answer to a question no one had ever addressed. That was all right with Joe. He didn't expect one so he said, "Amos, you needn't answer me now. That's OK. But when I come back, I want some thoughts from you about it. That a deal?"

"Mr. Bradley, ain't no one done nothin' like this for me so I gotta ask why you doin' it?"

"Good question. I want two things. One is to get you straight. Frankly, you're not cut out for drug work. You got a better chance in something legitimate, and I want you to get that opportunity. Second, I want information."

"'Bout what?"

"Who's your supplier or better, his wholesaler. Now relax, you're not going to be a snitch. I'm not working for the cops. I'm a defender. Remember? I just need to talk with them. No action will come of it. I'll make sure they understand this and that you're a stand-up guy."

Seeing Amos becoming anxious at giving information, Joe said, "Look. I'll let you introduce me to them. You can call ahead, or whatever you want to do, and assure them I'm not a fake. Actually, I'm hoping it'll be a good deal for them as well."

That assurance let Amos relax a bit. He replied, "Ooookay. But let's get me out first."

"I wouldn't have it any other way."

Later that day, Joe called Bill and asked if Amos could be released without charges. When asked why, he related Amos's background and the deal he made with his client.

"It's pro-bono work for a kid who's trying to support his mother with damn few resources. He doesn't use drugs nor does he carry. If I can get him out and through the GED program, I think we can save him. Also, he agreed to introduce me to his suppliers. These guys will recognize I'm a good guy trying to do right by one of their people and hopefully, they'll talk to me. This'll give us the information we need."

"This is not the normal course of justice I generally take, but since you're such a nice guy, I'll do it. It'll be fun not sending someone to jail."

Two hours later, Joe got a call from the jailer saying Amos was free to go. Joe met him at the exit door and piled him into his car. From there, they drove to a nearby McDonalds where they had burgers and cokes. Amos was smiling from ear to ear.

"Mr. Bradley, ain't no one ever done this for me. No sir. You won't never regret it. I promise."

"I know that Amos, but let's talk about how you're going to keep your promise. You need to find a legit job that supports you and your mother. Then you need to study for your GED. You're good, but it's a tough exam. So what's your plan?"

"I been thinkin' 'bout that, and I think I can get a job hustlin' stock at the corner grocery store. It don't pay much, but with Mama's disability checks, we can squeak through."

"Amos, this really makes me happy. I believe you can do it. Just remember, if something comes up that throws you in a bind, call me first...at once...don't wait. promise?"

"Yessir. I ain't gonna screw this up."

"Now about studying for your GED. Who can read and talk to you?

"My mama. She's smart and reads good. We both know how to use the internet to study things we don't know."

"Good. Get that job and tomorrow I'll bring some GED books for you to use."

"Yessir."

Joe took Amos to the store and waited outside while Amos applied for a job. A few minutes later he came out with a smile and thumbs-up. "I got me a job. I'm on my way. Thank you again, Mr. Bradley."

Joe smiled and replied, "You're gonna see a lot of me until you get where you want to be. That's a promise."

The next day Joe brought the GED books to the store where Amos worked. He introduced himself to the owner explaining how he kept Amos out of jail with him promising to get his life straightened out. The owner introduced himself. He was an elderly gentleman with gray hair that was cut closely to his scalp. Over his nose were a pair of glasses. When he smiled, a gold tooth shone. He was wearing faded chino pants and a plaid shirt. His shoes were heavy duty brogans.

"Yes sir. I'm Paul Jackson. I've known Amos since he was a pup. He's had a tough life what with his daddy gone. Where he went no one knows, but the upshot has been a hard time for Amos and his mother."

"Would she want to meet me?"

"I believe so. Alma is a good woman. She knows this is a rough neighborhood with plenty of temptations for a young boy. Whether she knows Amos got busted...I don't know. But any help getting Amos started right will be most appreciated."

"Well, I'll ask Amos, and when he wants to introduce me, I'll meet with her. Meanwhile, here's my card. Please contact me any time, and I mean any time day or night, if you see where I'm needed. I really want Amos to succeed."

Mr. Jackson shook Joe's hand warmly. "Yes sir. I'll do that. Meanwhile, thank you so much for what you're doing. Not many people would do so. It lifts my heart to see it."

Joe left Amos pretty much alone for the next several months. He would give encouraging calls and cheer Amos's efforts. But otherwise, getting his new start going ultimately depended on Amos. Making an application for an oral reader did take up some time but it was eventually set. When Amos was ready he'd take the exam. Finally, one call brought a changed voice.

"Mr. Bradley. I done it. I got my GED diploma."

"Whaaa?? Oh wow, this is great news. Where are you? I want to take a picture of you with your diploma. My wife and I are expecting a baby son soon, and one day when he complains about his schoolwork, I want to present you to him as an example of how hard work can bring success. You'll be his role model."

Amos spoke softly. "I dunno about that. Mama and I did work hard for the exam and I got it. But without you I'd still be another street dealer trying to stay out of jail. Yes sir, I'd like for you to come over and meet Mama. She knows about you and wants to meet you as well."

The next day, Joe went to the house where Amos and his mother lived. It was clean but worn. It needed paint and repairs indicating a lack of money. Regardless, that would come in time with continued work by Amos. His knock on the door was answered by a tall woman in her mid-forties. Her coloring was like her son's: light cream. Her face showed signs of a hard life while her right hand held a cane showing a disability. But she still had a dignity. She wasn't broken.

"Yes sir?"

"I'm Joe Bradley..."

"Oh my! Do come in. Please excuse my rudeness. Not many men come by without somethin' bad on their minds. Amos told me all about you, and I am so happy for him. He's a changed man."

Joe went into a house that was spotlessly filled with worn furniture. As he was led to his chair in the living room, he looked left and saw a dining room table filled with study materials.

"Yes, ma'am. I'm also proud of Amos. He was coming close to getting in trouble when I met him. But there was something about him...perhaps you, now that I've met you...that said he was a good kid. Now he's a better man with a future."

"He does, thanks to you."

"But let's not forget what he has done for himself. You and I, we just helped. For that help you gave, thank you."

Mrs. Baxton smiled broadly.

Just then, Amos came in, saw Joe and for the first time gave him a huge hug. That just made Joe's day. He saw this young man as something other than an avenue to bigger drug dealers. Amos was a future for himself, his mother, and who knows?

After pictures were taken and hugs exchanged again, this time with Mrs. Baxton as well, Joe asked if Amos could chat with him alone. Amos nodded. He understood the second half of his bargain.

"Amos, when we first met, I told you how I wanted to meet with your handler and his distributor. I stayed off your back with this request. You were busy doing the right thing. Now that you have a future, it's time. With your new plans in life, you can introduce me to them from a strong position."

"How so?"

"Think about it. You quit the streets to study. You've succeeded. But, at the same time, you can thank your handler for the support he gave to you when you needed money for supporting your mama. He can't argue with that. At the same time, your success gives me support in dealing with your handler. He will know I'm not a snitch. I'm not a cop. I'm who I say I am...just a lawyer who has done some good in his neighborhood."

"I think you're a bit over the top, but maybe it'll work. I know he won't shoot you. I always had a good in wit' Mr. Maxwell, he's the distributor here in Houston. So, let's see."

With that, Amos did see Mr. Maxwell. He didn't call because of fear his line was tapped. Dealings with the drug world are done better on a face-to-face basis. But an arrangement was made for the following week at the J Town Bar.

When Joe arrived, Amos was waiting. Together they went into a seedy bar filled with TV sports screens. Rock music was blaring. The air smelled of stale beer. A couple of pool tables hosted some games. Several faces looked up at this white man walking in, but when they saw it wasn't a sting or a bust, they relaxed and resumed their play. Amos led the way to a back office.

Shutting the door behind them, Amos said, "Mr. Maxwell, I'd like you to meet Joe Bradley. He's the guy I told you about. Who got me through to my GED. Joe, this here's my distributor, Mr. Maxwell."

Mr. Maxwell nodded to Amos to scat. Amos did so saying only thanks. Joe was offered a seat with a wave of a hand. Mr. Maxwell surprised Joe a bit. He was anything but the flashy stereotype of a drug dealer. Instead, he was slim, conservatively dressed in a quiet blue sport coat and gray slacks. Black, well-shined shoes shod his feet. His desk was as neat and clean as he was. A well-organized man thought Joe.

"Well, what can I do for you?"

"First, let me introduce myself to you so you know who I am. I'm Joe Bradley, a defense lawyer who got Amos sprung from a drug rap."

"How did you do that?" Mr. Maxwell was stone-cold with few words. His eyes were dead flat. He was not a man to be trifled.

"Simple. I have a friend who's a prosecutor. I told him I wanted to help Amos. I also told him that Amos could bring me to you."

Mr. Maxwell stiffened just slightly but it spoke volumes. Don't jack me around.

Joe continued, "I know this is a meeting like you've probably never had before, so I'll be straight to the point. My friend, Bill Ginn, and I are not satisfied with our futures. He's going nowhere working for the county, and I'm going nowhere working for my law firm. So we've been talking about starting a partnership representing people like you who want to stay out of jail. We would do so by representing your interests just like any other lawyer represents the interests of their clients. Now my question to you is simple. Is there room for people like us wanting to do business with you? Incidentally, I'm willing to do a strip search to show you I'm not wearing a wire."

Mr. Maxwell grunted a laugh. "If you had one, I'd have known it already, and you'd be regretting it. No, I'm meeting you solely because of Amos. I've had a lot of kids working for me, but Amos was a different dude. He was absolutely honest. He dealt only enough to support his mama. He would not take a bag more than what was needed to put food on the table. His financial dealings with me were accurate to the penny. One time, he lost a couple of bags, and you know what? He immediately contacted me with the details. Then he swore he'd repay me from his earnings. It took some time, but he was good for his word. Now believe me, he'd have paid me one way or another, but the fact that he was so honest and earnest about it made the difference. Then when he told me about you offering him a chance to get off the streets, you know what he said? Amazing. Hard to believe. First, he thanked me for the opportunity I gave him to support his mother. Then he explained where he wanted to go and asked me for my blessing. Can you believe that? Thanking me and asking for blessings? Upshot? The only reason you're here is because Amos swore by you that you were straight."

Joe nodded slowly while replying. "I expected as much. Without someone vouching for me, the best I'd get here is a beer if I paid for it. So, here's my pitch. I'll leave you alone for as much time as you need to check me out. Also, check out Bill Ginn. I'm sure you know people who have dealt with him. Then when you decide you can trust us, we'll meet again. If you can't trust us, say nothing, and we'll understand. Is that fair?"

Mr. Maxwell said nothing but simply blinked his eyes. Joe knew it was time to leave. He rose, offered his hand, which was refused, and left.

After taking Amos back to work, Joe called Bill to make a lunch appointment about his meeting with Mr. Maxwell.

"I'm telling you, Bill, this guy is the coldest man I ever met. I've defended thugs before, but Maxwell is in a class by himself. He really scared me. But strangely, he's an honest man. He didn't back away from anything I said about his being a criminal. Furthermore, he honors integrity. The only reason I got to see him was because Amos endorsed me. Why was Amos believed? Because he reported a loss of drugs to Maxwell and then accepted responsibility for the loss by paying for the cost."

"So what was the upshot?"

"I invited Maxwell to check us out. If he likes us, we get an invite. If not, well, nothing."

"No answer is an answer."

"That about sums it up. But if we do get an answer, don't BS him. He'll smoke you out in a second. Whether we live long thereafter...maybe we'd do better to live in the South Pole."

"OK. Joe. We know what we're in for. We'll need to get our act together."

Chapter 5
Decisions

By this time, it was apparent to Bill and Joe that their spouses must be brought into their plans. Following through on them would mean giving up their secure jobs for a high-risk venture. The upside, however, would be the prospect of higher salaries. They would certainly need good answers to the questions Virginia and Mabel would be asking. Their ideas did have one advantage and that was a lack of commitment from Mr. Maxwell. This meant no final commitment had been made, and their plans were only tentative with time for more investigation.

Bill waited until a Saturday when the kids were outside playing. He had held a family barbeque with their favorite food of burgers, hot dogs, and baked beans. Virginia was relaxed from a full tummy.

"Virginia."

"Yes Bill."

"The kids are quiet, and we need to talk."

"About what?"

"Changing jobs."

"Changing jobs? To what?"

"Representing crime figures in court and perhaps act as counselors depending on what I can sell to them."

"Them? Who's them? You've actually contacted some mobsters?"

"Just one, a Mr. Maxwell. He runs a couple of bars that front his drug business."

"What on earth would make you want to represent him?"

"Money. Simply money. Working for the county is a dead-end proposition financially speaking. I can be another brilliant John McElroy sending all sorts of crooks to jail, but I'll not be earning a dime more than what I'm getting now. So if we want more income, I gotta go where it's found."

"Do you think you can get it from them?"

"I think so. Being illegal, they need lawyers like me who can keep them out of prison. Staying out of prison means long-term employment at commercial rates. People won't like me for what I will be doing but, you know what?"

"What"?

"The Constitution says someone has to do it, so why not me?"

Viginia didn't waste a minute thinking about Bill's question when she said, "Bill, do your homework. Be sure you're getting what you want and if it works out, let's go. We like to live high, and we want the best schooling for our kids. I know Joe works commercially where partner bonuses are the key word. If you can make it happen for us, let's do it. Just keep me posted, and let's review the numbers as they become known to us."

As Bill and Virginia were contemplating this opportunity, Joe and Mabel were doing the same thing. He outlined the facts about his career and prospects as Bill did and how it entailed quitting the firm and working directly for gangsters. The reason for the change was the same: money. Mabel thought carefully before answering.

"Is this what you really want to do?"

"What do you mean?"

"Well, working for the firm has been all about money, making rain, with resulting bonuses for the partners. Social welfare is of no importance to them. The Constitution demands their services, so it's legal. But, morality is not a factor, only ethics as written in the canons. Working for the drug lords will be all of this except on steroids. Does making money alone light your fire? Is this what you dreamed of in law school?"

Joe laughed as he thought of himself in law school with dreams of being a modern Perry Mason. That dream got blown away long ago. For every guiltless client, he dealt with dozens of people with legal problems. Some were big, and others were small, and they all could result in penalties.

"Mabel, at first, I did believe in the Perry Mason show. But that lasted about a week at the firm. Since then it's simply been doing something I was good at, for which I earned a good salary. But that alone is not enough. You know criminal law is a sideline with the firm. I probably won't make partner. Criminal law doesn't generate large fees. So, working with druggies closes an avenue that will always be closed. But to be honest, does this prospect of fronting for drug lords float my boat? The money would be good but otherwise, I can't say that it does."

"What does then?"

"Well, until recently, I didn't really think about these things. My work was simply what I did. Until..." and here Joe paused.

"Until?"

"Well, you know that boy I've been talking about."

"Amos?"

"Yes, him. When I think about where he has been coming from, the hurdles he's overcome, and the new path he's created, I'm just amazed by his abilities. Why, Mabel, do you know he's decided on going to Jr. College and studying vehicle mechanics. When he finishes he'll get his Automobile Service Expert - ASE certificate. With that, he has steady employment that can bring a solid income that will support a life impossible to imagine in the ghettos."

Joe's eyes lit up as he thought about these prospects for a young man he'd hardly known several weeks ago. Mable saw it, and she asked, "Joe, does this offer you a future where your criminal law background can be put to the dreams you once had?"

Slowly, Joe admitted how this idea intrigued him. He then went on to point out its problems. "Helping youngsters is appealing. Exciting really. But will it pay our bills especially with a baby due?"

"It's a girl, Joe. I just found out today."

"Oh wow! A girl! But can I save kids and give her what she needs?"

"Joe, we'll probably take a financial hit following your dreams but if we plan on it, maybe we can make it work. The important thing for our little darling is not treasures but love. If we can give her that, she'll do all right. It'll be tough, but yes."

"Mabel, you've always been my anchor. With it, let me think about everything. Do my homework. Perhaps talk to the firm and see what they say. Maybe they'll support this crazy idea of helping kids. Probably not. But let's see. Meanwhile, start thinking of a name for this little one."

With that, the young couple hugged, settled back into their lawn chairs, and dreamed of possibilities.

While waiting for Mr. Maxwell to decide what to do with Bill and Joe, they continued to learn as much about the drug trade as possible. The first thing they saw was how each region of the U.S. had different problems. Transportation was a big issue. The longer the haul, the higher the delivery cost. So, for Houston, sitting on the border with Mexico, transportation was fairly cheap. Mr. Maxwell would deal with the Mexicans. Seattle on the other hand might find suppliers in Canada or China. Competition was another issue. Wars among the cartels were always possibilities. Among the Mexicans, there were only a few places along the American wall where mules could pass through with a reasonable chance of success. Controlling the access to these outlets became an important issue. The gang that owned them could sell their products to the Americans. So, the owners protected their realms fiercely.

The products being sold also had their individual differences. Heroin and cocaine were Latin American products that were absolutely illegal. Growing poppies and coca plants had to be done where the police could be controlled, that is corrupt. American officers generally did not deal. So, these drugs came from Latin America for Mr. Maxwell. Up north, perhaps Afghanistan would be a better source. Marijuana was another issue.

This plant had long been harvested in the States. It was also a growing agricultural industry with the advent of so many states permitting its use either for medical or recreational uses. Colorado, for example, offered plenty of Mary Jane for anyone wanting it, and it was legal. The federal government still banned it, but when the state legislatures decided that it was good business, the Feds be damned. Consequently, smuggling marijuana from Mexico slowed measurably. Texas still banned the drug, so Mr. Maxwell still bought a lot of Mexican pot. But, what about going to legal producers in the states? Now there was another opportunity.

The drugs from Colorado and elsewhere were fairly well controlled. Their quality was fairly consistent. So, logically, buying American pot made sense. It was still illegal in Texas, but that was no change from before. What was different was how it could be easily shipped and offer a higher quality high to the buyer. This would be something to discuss with Mr. Maxwell.

Joe participated in all of this research being done by Bill, but he was also looking elsewhere. Mable's question kept running through his head, "Is this what you really want to do?" The more he thought about it, the less he wanted to work for professional gangsters. Bill was right. They were just businessmen trying to earn a living selling forbidden products to people who were anxious to pay for them. He could also see how public opinion about drugs was changing throughout the country. The 18th Amendment prohibiting alcohol didn't work. It only provided opportunities for people like Al Capone. Likewise, prohibiting pot only provided employment for Mr. Maxwell. But as long as these drugs were still illegal in Texas, being a legal beagle for him was still just something to do for the money. *Is that why I became a defense lawyer? Was I just dreaming about Perry Mason? Is it possible to do good by representing bad guys?* He had to keep looking.

Eventually, he came around to the Harris County Public Defenders' Office. He had known colleagues who worked there. Their caseloads were filled with the same people that he defended. A big difference was he only took people who could afford the firm's rates. That was not the case with public defenders. They would handle cases like Amos but by policy.

Amos was a pro bono case for him and so, their contact was really just a stroke of luck. If he were to open a private office to defend them, he still had the practical problem of feeding his growing family. His clients would still have to pay, which was something that Amos simply could not do. He could not expect support from Mr. Maxwell either. Street dealers worked at their own risk. That was simply an accepted part of the job. While Mr. Maxwell deeply appreciated Amos's integrity, it didn't go further than that. Street dealers were expendable. *These kids need more than simply catching lucky breaks.*

Joe decided to investigate the Public Defenders' Office. He found it staffed by lawyers like him who were trying to do right. They represented anyone who could not afford their own attorneys. That meant they caught really bad guys as well as those just scraping by. *No other resources were being devoted to the causes of illegal behavior. *Wow! This ain't seen in the firm. If there's no money there, there's no honey. And they don't care about the consequences of who they defend and who falls through the cracks. Making rain was their only concern. Maybe, just maybe, these public defenders might care about their clients.*

Finally, as he promised Mabel, Joe asked for an appointment with a senior partner of the firm. Travis Morgan was his name. He was also Joe's main director. With him, Joe always believed he could talk as openly as he could with anyone.

After taking his seat, Joe outlined his position in the firm. "Frankly, sir, I really don't see any future for me or my family here at the firm. The possibility of my making even junior partner seems dim since criminal defense is not a big money stream."

Travis sat stoically through Joe's monologue. He was trustworthy enough as a mentor but only to the extent that it benefited his bonuses. After hearing Joe out he said, "Joe, you're a good lawyer. But your values are not those of an ambitious associate who is aiming for a partnership. And you're right, criminal law is a sideline here. Corporate litigation is where the money lies. Finally your dreams of helping people are good for Sister Teresa, but she doesn't pay the bills. So, in conclusion, while I appreciate your desire to do good, yeah, you're right. You need to find another job that provides family security as you save the world."

"Thank you sir for your candor. I'll be acting on it."

With this information, Joe came home from the office with a lilt of joy in his voice. He had called Mable earlier to ensure she had set her issues aside to provide time to talk. She could tell it was both good news and something important.

"OK, Joe. I'm here. You're here. What's on your mind?"

"It's a continuation of our earlier discussion about what do I want to do."

"And???"

"After talking with Travis, I think I'll apply for a job as a public defender for the county. It'll take some time for an opening but I'm sure I can stay on at the firm long enough to make it happen. Once it does, then I won't be working for rain but dealing with people like Amos who need a break. Here's the best part, we won't have to worry about feeding our little one. The salaries they pay are roughly what I get at the firm. They won't change much...only raises for seniority, but they're enough for our needs. How does that grab you?"

Mable looked at her husband. He was happier than she had seen him for a long time at this chance to "make a difference." This difference was always on the lips of every law student she had known in school. Now Joe was getting his chance. He would be working for the greater good rather than simply a paycheck.

"Joe, I'm really excited about all this. I'm sure there will be times when you'll be defending no-good-nics, but you've been doing that already. So, no change there. Now, from what you've told me, you'll have a chance to help some good-nics. Let's do it."

Joe took Mable in his arms and gave her the longest and warmest hug.

Shortly thereafter, Joe and Bill held their how-goes-it-meeting at the burger joint. Joe was obviously full of good news, and Bill asked, "OK Mr. Music Man, what's on your mind?"

Joe related the decision that he and Mable had made about working for the Public Defenders' office. "I've gone over there and filled out the paperwork. I'll be having an interview shortly and assuming I pass it, I'll start working there when a spot opens up."

Bill didn't react much. He just sat there thinking about what effect this could have on his chances of working for the mob. Finally he asked, "You're sure about this?"

"Yep. I know this is where I belong as a lawyer." He then related his relationship with Amos and how it had directed his decision. He followed that up with his discussion with his mentor, Travis Morgan. "Taking all this in consideration, it's the right choice. I'll be able to help someone instead of working for a paycheck."

Bill nodded in understanding. "Joe, even in law school you had a streak of being a do-gooder. But not every client will have a happy ending like Amos. Will you be burning yourself out in frustration when your clients are repeat sad sacks?"

"Good question. It's one I've thought about, but here's the point. What am I doing at the firm? Defending mostly wealthier clients who have no intention of falling into the straight and narrow. What's my angle there? Giving them the opportunity to being repeat clients for the firm. Additionally, on a practical note, you know I'll eventually be fired from there because there's no partner room for me. But working for the Public Defender Office gives Mable and me financial security. No, I won't be making a lot of money, but as long as it's secure, that's enough. We've talked about it a lot and we'll make it."

"What about defending someone like a child molester and getting him free? Can you handle that? Could you defend someone who molested your daughter?"

"I wouldn't be assigned to that case."

"You're evading my question. Every father's daughter is your daughter. Could you tell him his daughter's molester got sprung?"

Joe sat back at that question. It was an honest question...one that every defense lawyer hated to confront. Bill waited patiently for a reply. .

"Bill, I suggest you ask yourself this same question. It is one that every defense attorney must confront. This will eventually include you. Look at things this way. As a prosecutor, your job is to put molesters away for as long as possible. Society's safety depends on your ability to do so. You also have an out that defense lawyers don't have."

"And that is?"

"A review process. A prosecutor gets one bite at the trial apple. Win it, and his client faces jail time. The defense lawyer must live with it through the review process in hopes of springing his client. When he succeeds and then hears of this same client being brought up again, he knows he was at least partly responsible for this tragedy. He'll live with this guilt for the rest of his life. Now, when the prosecutor wins, an automatic review process starts. An erroneous decision by a jury can be overturned. The process takes time, and often years pass before justice is properly done. But it's not final except in death penalty cases and even there, the review process is excruciating. Every syllable uttered in the trial is evaluated for righteousness. So, ultimately, prosecutors don't carry the burden of a wrongful decision's consequences that a defense lawyer does."

At this point, Joe looked carefully at his friend's reaction to his statement of facts. Finally he asked, "Bill are you ready to assume the burden I've been carrying throughout my career? That's what you're considering."

Bill took a long sip of his cold coffee as he mulled Joe's question in his mind. Finally. "Point taken. Frankly, it's one I hadn't really considered. I need to think about it. When I have an answer for myself, let's meet again and review it. OK?"

Joe sat back, relaxed, and took a sip of his cold coffee. He smiled and said, "Bill, that's a deal. But here's a joke that happened to me when I was confronted with this problem."

Bill sat back and smiled. "Make me laugh Joe. I need it."

"One day, a prospective client came in about his son who was being accused of molesting the daughter of a neighbor. I really didn't want to handle it because from the evidence presented, I was certain I could win the case, and the kid could go on screwing young girls. So I talked to my boss and he solved the matter immediately. He said I should tell the client the firm's fee would be $1,000 an hour. The client almost fainted. Suffice it to say I didn't get the case. It was dodging the bullet, but I let some other poor lawyer handle the morality of the case."

Bill didn't laugh but pondered the implications. "Joe, in the P.D.'s office, you won't be able to do that. If such Is case is assigned to you, you gotta take it. Are you ready to bite that bullet?"

Joe sighed and said, "Yeah, sadly. I'll have to do so. The Constitution says I must. But nothing stops me from talking to the client about getting psychiatric help when he's sprung. In that regard, if I were the defense lawyer of a convicted rapist I might advise him to accept castration as part of a plea deal. There was a recent case in Louisiana where a guy accepted the deal as a means of being able to leave prison. If given such a case, I would also advise the client that if he is sprung, he is never to approach my wife or daughter. If he does, I'll shoot him in the balls before I kill him. Then I'll turn myself in."

Joe was dead serious. Bill shook his head. Here was a side of a man he had known for years yet was never seen before. Joe was dead flat in this declaration. *Joe. Wow. You've solved that problem about morality and the law.*

A week passed when the friends met again for their ritual lunch at the joint. Joe led off by saying he had gotten an unexpected interview and job offer. He immediately took it and submitted his resignation at the firm. It would be effective as soon as he finished up his immediate trials and passed off his remaining workload to another associate. Other than Travis Morgan, the partners were initially surprised at this turn of events but when Joe explained his reasoning, they understood and wished him well. "In reality it meant they didn't have to fire me and pay a separation fee. It was a good deal all around. Very amicable."

Bill reached out and shook Joe's hand to wish him well with his decision. In retrospect, it was not surprising as he had heard about it through the office grapevine. As for him, he was still waiting for a response from Mr. Maxwell. But if a good offer were given, Bill was willing to take it. About the molester issue, he offered some long thoughts.

Essentially, he would be representing an illegal business that needed Constitutional protections as much as any other enterprise. Therefore, the chances of representing a molester was minimal, which Bill admitted was a serious concern. Yes, he could see the probability of defending a murderer who most likely was a professional hitman.

"After all, if street dealers shoot each other, that's no concern of a drug lord. Only if they brought pressure on him would he be concerned. A skilled hitman was another matter. If he was to attract good shooters, he needed to offer loyalty and protection. I would be that protection in court. And since all of these issues involve personal acceptance of the issues from buying street drugs to international smuggling and distribution, I don't really care about any of the people. The relationship is not the same as defending a molester killing an innocent child. This being the case, I'll do my job well and let the chips fall where they may thereafter. Really, my biggest problem would be pissing someone off who will hire the hitman today whom I successfully defended yesterday."

Joe grinned and said, "Always a hitch to every decision isn't there?"

Bill laughed and said, "Yep."

Chapter 6
A New Defender

The next several weeks were uneventful. Bill and Joe clashed over some minor cases involving teens. One was a hit and run driver. The other was a drunk driver. Fortunately, no one was injured, but the boys were brought forward, found guilty, and sentenced.

As Bill prosecuted these cases, he thought about what he was trying to change in his life. *I'm hoping to sit at the other table. If it's an important case, John will be sitting where I'm sitting now. It'll be strange by using what John has taught me against him. I wonder how he will take it? Will I succeed or does he have other tricks up his sleeve? Well, time will tell.*

By now, several months had passed since his interview with Mr. Maxwell. Bill was becoming a bit discouraged about his prospects with the gangster. Then, his phone rang.

"Bill Ginn speaking. May I help you?"

It was not Mr. Maxwell's voice that answered. "Mr. Ginn, this is Mr. Maxwell's son, Travis."

Bill's heart took a start. *What now? His son?*

"Yes sir. How may I help you?"

"Would you be available for a meeting with Mr. Maxwell this week?"

"Yes I would at his convenience."

"How about this Wednesday for lunch?"

"Wednesday, at noon?"

"Yes, that would be fine."

"Where might we have lunch?"

"At the Texas Ranch House. Do you know where it is?"

"I do, and it will be a good place."

"Then we will see one another there."

The line went dead.

Bill checked his calendar, and fortunately, he had no cases, and his paperwork was up to date. So, he requested personal time for the afternoon. It was granted without question.

Wednesday came, and Bill left the office for his lunch. He was a bit anxious. This meeting could change his life. But who would be there? Mr. Maxwell or his son? Travis did say only, "we." Does that mean no meeting with his father? Lots of questions.

When he got to the restaurant, he found it empty except for a man about 30 years old. He was dark-haired, obviously fit, and dressed in a dark, blue suit with a white shirt and a red tie. His table was empty except for a cup of coffee. Assuming the gentleman was indeed Mr. Maxwell's son, he went over to introduce himself.

"Mr. Maxwell? I'm Bill Ginn."

It was Travis. He stood up, offered his hand, and said, "Hi, Mr. Ginn. I'm Travis. Please take a seat."

Taking a seat, Bill replied, "I'm glad to meet you. Please, call me Bill."

The waiter came over immediately. He had obviously been told what to do when Bill arrived. He placed menus before each man and departed.

Bill asked, "I've never been here before. What do you recommend?"

"How hungry are you? Their portions are large here."

"Not really. Something light would be enough."

"Then I would suggest the tacos."

"Tacos it is."

The waiter came and took their orders. While waiting for their tacos, idle exchanges were made until

Travis asked how Joe liked his new job. Bill responded brightly and with sincerity,

"He really does. He and I talked at length about the prospect, and he had thought carefully before taking it. But being able to help people such as street kids is very satisfying."

"Didn't he work as a defense lawyer before?"

"Yes, he did, but it was for a private firm that could not devote much time to helping kids. Here he has more opportunities to do so. This difference is important to him."

"I see."

Bill's reaction to this exchange remained positive for Joe but inside he had thoughts. *This was a subtle message. Duh! Mr. Maxwell has eyes and ears. I hear you as well as see you.*

After their meals were served and he was assured privacy was attained, Travis led off. "Bill, this obviously is not a social occasion. My father has given your earlier meeting a lot of thought. He is a very cautious man for obvious reasons. During that time, he watched you and Joe. He was actually pleased to see him take the PD job. It means he knows who will be defending his troops. Believe it or not, maintaining trust with them is very important."

Yeah, since no written contracts can exist between them, trust is their only glue.

"I understand that completely. After I had flunked out of college, I joined the Army and did a tour in Afghanistan. It was dicey at times there, and only our trust in each other and our officers kept us together and alive. So, yes, I do understand trust. Unfortunately, in business, I often find that missing. Sad. Bad business as well."

Travis nodded. "Bill, my father does want to offer a job, but he wants to be sure you still want it, and why. If he's satisfied, and he believes you, you have it."

Bill thought long before answering. *Think carefully here. Don't try to BS this man. He and his father will smoke me out in a second. Be honest. If he likes what I say, then I'll have it. If not...then remain a prosecutor. But don't lie to him. That could be dangerous given my job of putting his guys in jail.*

"Travis, your questions are real, and I've given them a lot of thought these past months. So here goes. If they meet Mr. Maxwell's idea of who he wants, then we have a deal. So, first. Yes, I want the job. We'll have to discuss what it entails, and I have some ideas that he should hear."

"We have time so let me have them."

"We both know that besides his bars, he sells drugs that are illegal. As a prosecutor, I understand that. I've put some of his people in jail. So, as a defense counsellor, I know what my opposition would be if I defended Mr. Maxwell's people."

Travis just nodded, and Bill continued. "A smart lawyer will keep Mr. Maxwell's people, or in worse case, him, from being convicted. A better lawyer will keep them from being tried in the first place. Think about it. If someone goes to trial, their time is not being spent on earning revenues. It's wasted in a court. So, I'm suggesting that my time for Mr. Maxwell can be better spent analyzing his business practices and keeping him inside the law as much as possible. Then, where the boundaries are broken, give counsel on minimizing risk."

Travis's eyes lit up at this prospect. Bill noted it as he continued. "Now what does that mean? First, it means that I will never lie to Mr. Maxwell. I will tell him the truth even if it's what he doesn't want to hear. Again, think about it. If I recited only good stuff, how can he trust me?

I'd just be leading him down a primrose lane to a conviction. So, it's the truth or nothing."

Bill waited a second and then asked forcefully, "Are we clear on this?"

"We are. Go on."

"Next, I will not take part in the planning of any specific operation. That's a real no-mo for lawyers because then I'd no longer be a counsellor but a participant in a crime. I'll be disbarred and sent to jail, which would really ruin my day."

Travis laughed at that prospect. "What can you do then?"

"Before any operation is planned, I can advise in general terms. Actually, I'd hold lectures and seminars talking about the law, how prosecutors get evidence, how people got caught in past convictions. These discourses would be aimed at promoting team efforts among your father's management team. With this information, you and your father can close your door and do your thing. But you will be doing so knowing how to do it with the least risk. Now, regarding anything legal, of course I can sit in during any planning activity."

"How much would your rates be?"

Bill replied quickly. "It's far too early to discuss rates. Obviously, I'm in this for the money. We all are. And we'll get to it in due time but for now, it's more important that Mr. Maxwell be satisfied with what he'll be getting. If he isn't, then talking money is a waste of time. If he is, then we can negotiate a workable pay and working conditions contract. Any question here?"

"Nope. Good answer. Wanting money is one thing; greed is another. You know, a friend of mine who is an investor once told me about the market, 'Bulls make money; bears make money; pigs get slaughtered.'"

"Oink, ugh!"

At this point, Travis looked at his watch and said, "Bill, this has been a good meeting. I'll be getting with my father and telling him about it. I'm not promising anything. He makes up his own mind according to his instincts, and they have been dead right for the past 30 years. He won't move fast, but you will hear from him with a firm decision. OK with that?"

"Works for me. So, thank you for your time."

Shaking hands, the two men paid their lunch tabs and departed. Bill then went home to think about what all had been said and to talk with Virginia.

That evening, after dinner and putting the kids to bed, Bill related the essentials of the meeting. Virginia listened carefully. Her reaction was what he expected.

"Bill, this is a decision we're making with a lot of risks. But if they work out, our financial future will become a lot brighter. It does mean we'll be dealing with people we wouldn't be caught otherwise meeting at a skunk fight. So, taking care will be the name of the game."

Virginia sat back and reviewed what she had just said. Then she began to laugh. Bill wondered what the joke was. Finally, she answered his unspoken thought. "This is so funny, we'll be making good by doing bad. That is, we'll be helping people to greater addictions that I wouldn't wish on my worst enemy. God help anyone who tries to peddle them on our kids. But here's the irony. The law demands that someone do this, and we have the opportunity to take advantage of it. So, let's go with it and let other people worry about moralities."

A week passed when Bill's phone rang. Again, it was Travis.

"Bill, this is Travis again. Could you make time for a meeting with my father?"

"Sure. Let me get my calendar to see when we both have some open time."

An appointment was quickly established. It was to be held at Mr. Maxwell's office where they had first met. When the hour arrived, Bill found himself being led back through the seedy bar to Mr. Maxwell's office. Inside, Mr. Maxwell was sitting behind his desk. He gestured for Bill and Travis to take seats. His cold demeanor had not changed from before. He was beautifully attired, but the clothing simply surrounded an iceberg.

Mr. Maxwell led off. "Mr. Ginn, Travis related the gist of your discussions. Frankly, I like what I heard. Above all, your demand for freedom to tell the truth impressed me. I get so many bullshitters feeding me stuff I think I'm in a dirty barn. But that I can't stand. My continued success in my business demands care...attention to details. Some, or perhaps many of them are not pleasant, but they must be attended. Therefore, I need honesty in their presentation. I also understand your need to avoid presence in a planning session. If you're disbarred, then who would be my lawyer?"

Bill nodded silently and waited for Mr. Maxwell to continue, which he did. "So, Mr. Ginn, how much do you want to be my counsel?"

Bill repeated his earlier position on pay. "Mr. Maxwell, I'm pleased you want to advance our relationship but as I told Travis, now is not the time for discussing salaries. You need to hear my ideas about avoiding trials. You need to know how much time we will be spending advancing your business. You should know the details. Then, and only then, can you make an informed decision as to what I will be worth to you. I also suggest you have Travis do some research on what a good mouthpiece earns. Like you, I'm here to advance my financial interests, but haggling is not my cup of tea. I only want what's fair. So, let's just say for now that we together, get to know one another, discuss plans, and when you're satisfied, make an offer. If it's marketable, I'll take it as is...on a handshake. Is that fair with you?"

Mr. Maxwell's eyes opened in wide surprise. Here was the first time he had shown the slight spark of emotion. He said, "You mean that's it? You invest your time talking about a new partnership and then you'll take what I offer?"

"So long as it's fair, yes."

"Well, I'll be damned." Turning to his son, Mr. Maxwell said, "Travis, can you believe this? Here's a guy who could go to a fancy law firm and haggle for a million bucks just sitting here and talking about being fair."

Returning to Bill, Mr. Maxwell was smiling. "Son, you have blown me away. After years of dealing with grifters trying to skim my last buck, here you sit asking only for 'what's fair.' This is a new experience for me."

"Well, get used to it. My father was a career Army officer, and he always told me never to lie and give whatever I do 100 percent. That's the way I learned to operate."

Mr. Maxwell extended his hand and replied, "Then I believe we have a contract. Travis, work with Mr. Ginn here to develop a schedule when we can meet and develop his ideas. Then, when the issues are understood, offer a financial package. At that point, he can accept it and proceed to tell the county that he has a new employer."

Bill took Mr. Maxwell's hand and said, "Thank you sir for this opportunity. I'll work hard to ensure it is not wasted."

Leaving the office, Bill and Travis went to another office where they developed a working schedule during evenings and when Bill could take vacation time. Both agreed this time period would not be long. Then a final offer could be made and accepted. That night Bill and Virginia went out to dinner to celebrate.

Bill and Travis negotiated for a week's time until a final proposal was sent to Mr. Maxwell for his approval. Bill had kept Virginia appraised, and she did her homework to determine what was needed to support the impending expenses of their children. School tuition was a big factor. The final package focused on the program that Bill envisioned for keeping the police at bay. Meanwhile, Travis investigated the average hourly rates and annual incomes of corporate legal partners.

Mr. Maxwell reviewed the package and liked what he read about doing business as legally as possible. But he could not meet the annual income rates corporate lawyers expected. "Travis, I like what you've brought to me. However, I have a couple of questions. One is whether you trust Bill?"

"Pop, yes I do. Bill is painfully scrupulous. His answers were well thought out and researched. Furthermore, he constantly asked me to double-check everything he said. I did, and he was solid. I also believe he will demand the same of you when you get advice from him."

"H'mmm. A lawyer wanting to be double-checked. I wish my doctors were as humble. But, yeah, he's being smart. I will never be able to say that he double-crossed me."

"More to the point, Pop, before you make decisions, and I know I'm preaching to the choir here, you gotta know the details. They will always kill us if we don't take them into account. So, Bill's emphasis on double-checking him is important. That tells me we can trust his faith and reliability. He won't do anything that will endanger his license to practice law, but he will be an effective counsellor."

Mr. Maxwell nodded with satisfaction then continued. "Travis, can we afford him?"

"Do you mean as an exclusive lawyer with no other clients? The answer is no. His hours in the beginning will be high as he reviews and proposes changes to our operations. But they will be an investment for the long-term health of the company. Thereafter, when things are going smoothly, then our requirements will drop. After all, a clean operation means no problems to be litigated."

""And when that time comes, how much of his time will we require?"

Travis blew his nose and replied, "I estimate about 30 percent, maybe more, maybe less."

"But a significant amount of time that would attract him?"

"Yes."

"Have you discussed this prospect with him?"

"We have, and he accepts it. Actually, it would be to his advantage."

"Why's that?"

"Simple, he could not be accused of being a planning mouthpiece, He would be a counsellor to anyone needing his services. One thing, though, and this really attracted me."

"What's that?"

"We are not the only game in the region. If he gets a large offer from a player, he would have us vet that person. If it's coming from a rival we don't like, he'll refuse their business."

"Damn, what loyalty."

"He's giving it, and it is important. Still, he's smart. Trustworthiness on his part is crucial if he wants to stay alive. He knows this."

"Still, you say he was a military brat, and he talked about his word being his bond?"

"Yes, that's right. Apparently, he has no qualms about the business we do, but his personal integrity is important to him. He'll keep his word if it kills him."

Mr. Maxwell laughed at that conceit. "If he doesn't keep it, he's dead. If he does, other gangs will kill him. Seriously, though, it does mean we'd need to protect him."

Travis spoke slowly now. "One thing Bill did suggest and that was to make nice with the other gangs. He's not being a wimp, but his ideas do make sense. Collectively our products and services are in demand. Insatiably so. What this means to him is that there's enough to go around for everyone. What is bad for business is the publicity that comes from gang wars. Politicos have to keep an anti-crime face for the voters if they want to stay in office."

Again Mr. Maxwell laughed, even harder than before. "So the biggest crooks need a mask of righteousness. But, again, Bill is dead on. We've never done this, but like *The Godfather* movie's meeting of the families negotiating who does what, cooperation makes sense."

"And we have our lawyer and they have theirs. That keeps everyone alive."

Mr. Maxwell reviewed everything that was said one last time. Finding nothing alarming, he blew out his breath and said, "Ok. Travis. I think we are making a good choice with this man. Make the offer."

The next day, the offer was made and accepted. That night, Bill and Virginia celebrated again. The following morning saw Bill submitting his resignation at the office. His mentor, John McElroy, immediately came to his office wanting to know what was happening,

"John, I'm glad you came in. I want you to know what's happening and why."

"I'm listening."

"The answer is simple. I can make more money being a defense lawyer than I can as a prosector."

"That means you'll be defending scumbags."

"No more than the PD's do."

"Can you live with successful outcomes?"

"If you mean worrying about scumbags who will do the next day what got them into trouble, the answer is no. Not in the least. What they do on their time is not my problem as long as I'm not abetting them."

"Some of them might involve kids."

"Yep, and that's the parents' problems. In my case, if a pusher came in needing me, the first thing I'd tell him is leave my kids alone if they are smart."

Nothing was said for a long time. Finally Bill continued. "Look at it this way. You need criminals to prosecute. Without them you'd have no job. Without them, I'd have no job. Besides, I know you like prosecuting because of the charge you get putting people behind bars or when possible on the table. You need crooks for this reason."

Slapping Bill on the back, John laughed to say, "Yeah Bill, that's right, and we both know it. Tell you what. Beat me in a court battle on a big case, and I'll buy you a beer."

In turn, Bill said, "Seriously, you've been a wonderful mentor for me. You set high standards that I've followed and will follow. Yeah, eventually, we will meet in front of opposite tables, and it'll be a good fight."

John laughed. "Bill, yep, you have been my best student. You've learned well. But don't think I taught you everything I know. So let's take the rest of the afternoon off and have a beer."

"You're on."

Chapter 7
Getting Started

The next several weeks were hectic. Cards had to be printed. Bill joined *LinkedIn* and the local chamber of commerce. He ran an advertisement in the local newspapers. It was certainly eye-catching. Hiring employees would have to wait until some money came in.

Virginia actually wondered whether it was an appropriate style of advertising. Bill replied, "It's not, and that's why I'm using it. In the old days, lawyers were not allowed to advertise when they hung up their shingles. Since then, most legal advertising is very somber and business-like. Well, I'm a defense lawyer trying to crowd into a packed herd of mouthpieces. So why not? It's funny and does draw attention."

It did work but unfortunately most of the callers were low-lifers who didn't have a dime to their names. Bill referred them to his friend, Joe. One such low lifer Joe got stuck with. The guy's name was Anthony Rapozzo, and he was charged with a murder rap. Apparently he saw Bill's ad and called him. As Bill described it, "This guy calls me and hires me. I gave him my pitch about being honest. so not only does he lie to me about the rap being a capital one charge, but he forks over a bum check. So I throw him out of my office with instructions to call the P.O. office."

Joe replied glumly, "Yeah. Thanks. Now I gotta defend him."

"Maybe John McElroy will get him to prosecute."

"Wouldn't bother me a bit. You know how John loves to hang these guys."

In fact, John did get him and now there's another picture hanging from his rogues gallery. Everyone agreed that John did a good service for the community.

If the client was young and broke but with potential for getting right, Bill particularly emphasized Joe. He cited how Joe was passionately interested in getting the lives of young kids turned around. "He won't just defend you through a turnstile at the courthouse. He'll work with you towards a good future. I will warn you, however, don't jive him. Screw with him, and you'll find yourself in jail so fast you won't know what happened and know what? It'll all be legal. So be square with him, and he'll help you."

It wasn't long before Joe called. "Bill, I'm getting contacts about kids needing help."

"Yep. I'm sending them to you if I think they're worth saving."

"Well, thank you. I appreciate it. By the way, your ad's cute. I like it."

"Glad you do."

Travis just roared when he saw the ad. "It's the funniest, and most honest ad about shysters I've ever seen. My father laughed more than I've ever seen him. He's normally pretty tight, but this rocked his boat. So, when can you come in? I've tried to let you have some time, but now we need to start making plans happen."

"This coming Monday at 8:00?"

"Sounds good."

Bill worked with Virginia over the weekend. She listened to his opening pitches, critiqued them, and added some insights. She was always good in this way. She was objective, impersonal, and had good ideas. She was a sounding board that Bill relied on whenever an important decision was to be made. Had been since they met in college.

Bill was already at the bar's entrance door when Travis and his father showed up, and they were on time to the second. *It's not good to keep Mr. Maxwell waiting.*

"Good morning Mr. Maxwell, Travis."

The father was silent but Travis replied cheerily, "Here he is Pop, Mr. Guilty and he's deep in sin."

Mr. Maxwell smiled briefly and said, "Shall we go in, have a cup of coffee, and get down to business?"

They did.

After a brief bit of small talk, Mr. Maxwell opened up the business at hand by asking, "Bill, you've had a lot of time to think about what can be done to keep me out of jail. I know you've talked to Travis at length. Now, I want the details."

"Yes sir, I have. So here it comes."

Bill waited for a second to ensure total attention, then he started. "Mr. Maxwell, when I was in the Army, we always planned backwards from our objective. That was not always an easy task. What were we supposed to be doing was the crucial question. Answering it then generated accurate estimates of what operations and logistics requirements should be. A bad estimate about goals would screw everything afterwards up tighter than a granny knot that would always let us down. And, for you, just staying out of jail isn't a good objective."

Mr. Maxwell's eyes raised in question. "Really? I thought it was."

"Yes sir, staying out of jail is important but it doesn't lead to effective planning. It's a tactic along the way that will enable you to provide a solid future for yourself and your family. By contrast, establishing strategic goals for your business is always your starting point. Define them, and the rest will fall into place given careful work."

"H'mmm. Never thought of things that way. You have my attention and curiosity. Please continue."

"Mr. Maxwell, your drug business is very good. You've got a good income from it. But the question is: what can you do with it? You can't report it to the IRS. You can't go to Merrill Lynch and ask them to invest it. At best, by itself, you can only hide it. So I ask you, what good is it? Trying to make money that you can't use is not an adequate strategic goal."

A long silence followed. Mr. Maxwell sat quietly by. Travis anxiously looked at his father trying to decipher what was on his mind. No clue came forth, which was really what Bill expected. With that, he continued.

"Actually, you have been doing a good job answering that question by operating your bars. They provide enough honest receipts that keep the police, the feds, and the IRS off your back. But don't kid yourself. They know what you're doing. They just haven't been able to get the goods on you well enough to convict you."

Mr. Maxwell nodded in agreement as Bill continued. "The ultimate objective for any drug business should be to get out of the business. Use it to fund your bars until they're self-sustaining well enough to meet your continuing financial goals. Then, when they are, your drug businesses will have done their job. At that point, it'll be time to go legitimate where you can't be tagged. Now I know your next question will be how? So, let me continue."

Mr. Maxwell blinked slowly to do so. Bill then described how he could establish accounts in an offshore bank. It would be disguised with code numbers and covered with the banking's commitment to *omerta,* Italian for silence.

"I know from Travis that you've already been doing that. So, here's the kicker. You, along with others whom you trust, will start a local bank. Call it the Neighborhood Bank where it's advertised as dedicated to the community's well-being. It'll be entirely legitimate with bank examiners looking at the books. You will use this bank to obtain loans for more bars and another idea, smoke halls that I'll discuss in a bit. These enterprises will also be legitimate even to carding every customer. But you will get them through legal loans from the Neighborhood Bank that gets its investment funds from your offshore accounts. In effect, you will be borrowing from yourself. You will repay these loans with interest that will be tax exempt. Then when you have built up enough bars to meet your financial goals legally, you will sell your drug business to whomever. It'll take time to trickle your offshore money through the Neighborhood Bank, but it will be syphoned into good investment opportunities for your cached money that you want to bring to the light of day. And it's all legal or otherwise, I wouldn't be sitting here talking about it."

Mr. Maxwell slapped his knee and said excitedly, "Damn, I like that. I really do. It works toward an achievable goal of taking care of my family. Travis, make sure you reward Bill handsomely."

"Yes, Pop."

"Thank you sir."

Actually, Bill had other ideas for the bank. First, however, he wanted to learn more about the retail drug business. So ,he called up an expert: Amos.

A hesitant voice answered Bill's call. Amos was moving ahead with confidence, but he was still a street kid and new voices were suspicious until proven otherwise.

"Amos, it's Bill Ginn here. I'm a good friend of Joe. Actually, I was the guy he contacted to get you sprung from your last bust."

Amos became receptive. "I'm glad to meet you sir. Yes, getting me sprung has given me a new start in life."

"That's wonderful. Joe saw something in you that told me to give you a chance. Since then, I have referred other young people to him for the same reason. Some work out. Others don't, but Joe's always trying. So, how are things going for you now?"

"Great Mr. Ginn. Joe has continued to help me with my studies. He actually did some car repair when he was a kid and understands the basics. That means he can explain the technologies that are used today to fix them."

"How so?"

"Today's cars are computer driven and most of my study books emphasize them. Here's where my reading problems come in. I guess you know from Joe I never learned to read good. It's getting better, but it's still a bear. Joe can read the books and explain what they mean. When I hear it, I got it. My first exams have gotten good grades. I talk to my professors about my reading problem and most of them will help me there as well. They don't tell me the answers, but they do talk to me about understanding the questions. A couple more exams and I'm hoping to find a mechanic's job somewhere. It'll just get me low pay 'cause I can't do everything, but it'll be better than what I got, and it'll only get better."

"Amos, that's wonderful. Now can we meet somewhere soon? I got some ideas about getting other guys off the streets, but I need to learn more about life selling drugs."

"Yes sir. If it gets kids off the streets, then I'm your man."

"How 'bout this Saturday?"

"Noon, my house?"

"That works for me. See you then."

As scheduled, Bill showed up and knocked on the door. Amos answered and showed Bill in to introduce him to his mother. A few minutes were spent on introductions and how Bill got to know Amos. When Alma heard how he got Amos out of a bust, she was almost moved to tears,

"Mr. Bill, ain't no way I can thank you enough. Most cops would have let Amos just rot. But you was different. Now my Amos has himself a future without always lookin' over his shoulder."

"At that time, ma'am, I was with the cops, and it was not often that I had the chance to do something nice for a change. Now, I'm a defender like Joe, and I'm here to see if I can keep other kids from being rounded up and sent to prison."

Hearing this, Alma turned to her son and said firmly, "Amos, you hear that? Now you h'ep this gentleman any way you can. Hear me Boy?"

"Yes Mama. I does."

With that Amos and Bill went onto the porch with Cokes in hand. Bill then laid out his ideas. "Amos, I'm not here to stop the drug trade. That's not gonna happen. You know it, and I know it. People want their highs."

Amos nodded in sad agreement as Bill continued. "Now here's my thought, How can I get guys like you off the street is what's buggin' me. In order to answer that question, I want to know how you did your business. I don't want names or dates. You'd be reluctant to tell me for fear of becoming a rat. But you can tell me without using names, how did it work. Where did you sell? Who were your customers? How were sales actually made? How could you know who to trust? Things like this. You OK with this?"

"Just so long as I don't have to rat nobody out, I'm good."

Amos related how he started as a look-out. He was almost thirteen, and Alma's ailments were worsening. She had lost her job as a scrubwoman and had become reliant on disability retirement. These checks hardly met her monthly bills. Amos wasn't doing well in school and at his age, he had no legitimate skills, so drug dealing was the answer. It was a common industry in his neighborhood and one where being young and still able to roam the streets late at night was an advantage. His job involved scanning potential sales spots for cops. Usually, they were easy to see. Try as they might, something usually betrayed them. It might be the way they walked...alert, on guard or the opposite,,,,too casual. Real customers with experience knew well what to do, and they moved with confidence. First time buyers, usually college kids out on a spree, moved with uncertainty but not fear.

"They's usually too dumb to be scared, Often they's drunk on booze and lookin' for somethin' with a better high."

Continuing on, he emphasized how trust was the important issue. "Did I know the person?" was his constant question. "Actually, I got busted twice, and it was with two users who were busted by the cops. They was peddlin' a bit to friends, and one thing led to another leading the cops to them. So in exchange for a dropped charge, they ratted me out. I knew them from many sales and nothin' about their behavior set me on alert. So, there you have it, and you know the rest."

Bill asked, "Did you always buy from Mr. Maxwell?"

"Not directly. He had runners delivering to me. But I knew where it came from. He always had plenty, and he was always honest so long as you didn't try to screw him."

"You never delivered?"

"Nope. I didn't have no car, and that limited my range of operation."

"And it was always cash and carry?"

"Yep, Sometimes when there were lots of people around and the lookouts couldn't spot everyone, a sale would be a two-step operation."

"Meaning?"

"The customer would pass his cash to one person and then pick up his stash from another person standin' in a near-by alley. That reduced the risk of getting caught. If a cop saw a cash payment, the two guys could say a debt was simply being paid. Which, when you think about it, was the truth. You gotta pay for your drugs don't you? Ain't that a debt?"

Amos laughed at that thought. "In debt even before you get the stuff? Ain't that somethin'?"

Bill chuckled in agreement. He then thanked Amos and offered to help him anyway he could.

"Thank you sir. I hope it don't come to that, but I'll always remember you and Joe with kind thoughts."

Back home at his office, Bill thought long and hard about what Amos had told him. It was now obvious why Amos got caught. As much as they tried, open marketing was porous. Cops could always find these dealers and bust them. Then, from there, it was just a daisy chain to their distributor. Eventually, Mr. Maxwell would get caught and be tried. Knowing John's prosecuting skills Mr. Maxwell would do time, and he'd lose a good client. What to do?

This question remained on Bill's mind for a number of weeks. The answer was elusive. It was something that should seem obvious but like a will-o-the-wisp, it kept flitting away. Not that he brooded over it. Lots of other distractions interfered such as defending his first case. It was a simple DUI without any injuries or damages. The client simply got caught in a speed trap. He was doing 45 in a 35 zone. Fortunately he didn't have any prior convictions, and he got off with a fine. Bill suggested afterwards to leave the car parked and take a taxi next time. A promise was made. Whether it would be kept was something to be seen, but the client paid his fine and Bill's invoice for $300. Bill would have to defend a lot of drunks at that rate to equal what he earned from the county, but it was a start.

It wasn't until he saw Virginia placing an Amazon order that it hit him. Of course, sell by mail order. That would eliminate open market selling, Mr. Maxwell would hire a few delivery agents who would bring the drugs directly to a customer's doorstep or some other trusted place. Orders could be placed via PayPal that would be connected anonymously to the offshore bank account. When payment was received, a delivery order would be placed and made.

Clearly, these transactions would need shielding from eavesdroppers, aka cops. How that worked was a mystery to Bill. He needed a young hacker to guide him. Better yet, Mr. Maxwell needed this expertise. So, he contacted Travis with his idea. After vaguely offering a better retail sales plan to peak his curiosity, they agreed to meet in Travis's office the following day.

Bill led off with his idea with a caveat. "Travis, as always, I can't be part of any detailed planning you do with your drug business but as a counselor, I can talk about ideas."

Travis agreed by saying, "Right. Whatcha got?"

Bill explained how his prosecuting experience showed him how street dealers were an inefficient and dangerous way of selling drugs. Travis agreed fully and waited for the second step. Bill then said simply that Travis and his father should study Amazon's delivery system. "From a personnel standpoint, you could eliminate a lot of people and replace them with a few, highly trusted and intelligent, delivery agents. "You see them all the time, those brown bread wagons stuffed with goods to be delivered to their customers' doors. Just study it, and think about it, and then let's talk later about your conclusions."

Travis was never one to keep a blind man's watch. He understood the possibilities that were being suggested. Bill then indicated that three things were needed. "A fleet of innocent looking vehicles. They don't need to be large. Your cargo is very small. But they must be inconspicuous. Secondly, you need a money transfer system such as perhaps, PayPal. Third, you need security for your electronic communications. "There's a lot here for you to digest so take your time, Talk to people in this business as well as computer nerds who can offer security ideas. When you're done, then let's talk again."

Travis smiled broadly and agreed to do what his counselor had suggested. Bill went back to defending DUI clients.

Several weeks later, Travis called to say that he had discussed Bill's concepts with his father. "He was delighted with it. The whole thing. He reduced his personnel issues with their risk of being caught and ratting out. His customers will certainly like the door-to-door service with the reduced risk to them. It'll take some time to make all this happen. Finding a good security person will be a critical issue. He'll need to be someone we can trust. If he can set up our security system, he can crack it."

"You got that right. So, take your time and find the right people. Among your street dealers, find the ones you want to promote into your new organization....yep, people will be your biggest challenge."

While Travis was restructuring his father's business model, Bill continued with developing his defense business. He found that it was similar to a surgeon's practice. People sought surgeons when something needed cutting. Once done, once gone. But happy patients told their friends. This was what Bill needed to cultivate.

Doing this cultivation meant he had to visit the police stations around town looking for likely clients who were sitting in jail. He had visited them many times as a prosecutor but as a defense lawyer he saw things from an unfamiliar perspective. Before he saw a routine that was comfortable. Now he saw it from the prisoner's eyes. Why was paperwork lying around? Easy. To facilitate prisoner management. Telephone calls were loud and inconvenient as they interfered with prisoner processing.

On the other hand, it meant that information was simply lying around...exposed to anyone who was curious. The question was who would be curious. Anyone with a need to know. Snoops, that's who. Snoops...h'mmm. That brought back memories of COMSEC, communications security, that were the bane of his military life. What's said here, stays here. Loose lips sink ships. Loose lips can also prevent repeat clients from going back to jail.

Who could be a good snoop? That was the important question. Just like the advice he gave to Travis. Find the right people. They couldn't be obvious. Blending in was important. They didn't need to know what was important. That was the job of an analyst. Being able to gather raw information from loose paperwork, idle chatter, and loud phone calls.

The answer came when he was talking to John about a case. A janitor entered John's office without knocking and began his morning clean-up routine. The waste basket was emptied, and ash trays were cleaned. John didn't even notice what was happening as he continued his remarks with Bill about a case. The janitor had been doing these mundane tasks so long he wasn't even noticed. That was it! Janitors became the perfect snoops.

Bill didn't say anything to Travis about his idea. It needed to be developed. So, while he did business, he watched. Where was trash paper taken? To dumpsters. When were they collected? After duty hours. Did anyone supervise these activities? Not much. Were the dumpsters left alone? Pretty much. Listening to telephone conversations was another issue. Information there was not to be collected like paper. It had to be collected in the janitor's head. Who could absorb random information through the day and remember it? Who could be the perfect tape recorder?

Again, the answer came by chance. One morning, Bill stopped by Joe's office to talk shop. It was a normal thing to do. After all they did have a common purpose in life...to defend people. During this visit, Joe commented on how much improvement in reading skills Amos was enjoying. "You know,, Bill, when I first met Amos, he could hardly read. But with practice, he's really getting better even through his dyslexia. More to the point, what he's reading is making sense to him. He can remember it, whereas before it had to be explained orally for him to remember it...."

Bill's mind started drifting from Joe's joyful success story. There had to be an answer to his snoop question. Who would be a good snoop? Finishing his visit with Joe, he continued on with his business. It was very routine letting him do it on autopilot... letting his active thoughts mull over Joe's observations. No answer through the day. None at night while he was listening to Virginia chatter about her day. He had some difficulty getting to sleep what with the question still running loose in his mind.

It hit him at 2:00 a.m. Of course, the perfect snoop had to be illiterate or nearly so. Amos couldn't read, so he learned to listen. Literate people remember what they read; illiterates remember what they hear. Janitors didn't need to read to do their jobs. Show them what to do with good explanations and, with good hearts, they became good janitors. Better janitors became excellent snoops.

By now several weeks had passed. Travis was making good progress with the reorganization project. Bill had clarified the details of his project snoop doggie idea. Now was a good time to lay it on Travis.

"Travis, I'm happy you're making such good progress because I can now blast you with another idea. Ready for it?"

Travis smiled broadly and said, "Shoot."

With that, Bill described his ideas. "Of course, I can't tell you what to do, and I never want to know the details, but this is my advice for the day. Use it as you will."

Travis just beamed at the prospect of knowing what the police were planning to do before they could execute their counter-drug operations.

Bill now cautioned his client. "Here's an important point. Select the snoops carefully. You want them to be clean when they apply for jobs with the contract cleaning company. They can be from the streets selling drugs, but they must never have been caught. Selling drugs can be an advantage because they will understand better what you want. But, again, they must have clean records and two, they must be trustworthy. Loyal to you and your father."

Travis nodded in understanding. Then Bill smiled and said, "Travis, have you ever thought of starting your own housekeeping business?" He then winked and said, "Just think, doing well by doing good."

Travis just smiled.

Chapter 8
Ascent and Dissent

The next six months were very successful for Bill's new law practice. He was able to lease an office, hire a secretary, and a new graduate from law school who was studying for his bar exam. What was most gratifying was the decline in drug busts. Mr. Maxwell was delighted. His businesses, both legal and illegal, flourished while the risks he had once accepted as "part of the terrain" had almost disappeared.

Even his former mentor, John McElroy, had noticed this decline in drug arrests. As he commented to Bill one afternoon, "You know, Bill, since you became a private attorney, the number of drug busts we've made have dropped almost to zero. Is there a connection?"

"I hope so. As I look at the drug business, it is just that, a business, and not a very good one at that. I tell my clients, if they're dirty, get clean. Concentrate on their other stuff. Drug money probably paid for it. Now use it. Get a return on your investments in time, risk, and money. Then I put it this way. I'm your defense lawyer. You get busted, and I'll defend you. But that's all a waste of time and money. Especially money 'cause I'm gonna charge you."

John agreed skeptically. "It's a good approach, and I applaud it. But you and I both know people still want their drugs, and somehow they're getting them. The question is how."

"I agree. People are being supplied. How, I don't ask. Doing so could make me appear as a conspirator instead of a counselor. Also, it's safer. What I don't know won't hurt me. So I don't ask. I preach my message and do my job."

"Good on you Bill."

John did authorize investigations, but he didn't find anything. Mr. Maxwell was his big target, but nothing. When forensic auditors searched his books, they were straight to the penny. When detectives crashed his bars, no warrants were requested. They were treated as professionals doing their duty. Nothing. When Travis was trailed, it was through a land for any man, Come to work, deal with suppliers, check inventories, remind bartenders to card everyone...even his father. Laughs. Nothing. Boring.

Eventually, other drug lords heard about Mr. Maxwell's success. They began to hire him as a consultant. Bill's message was exactly as he told John. Then, as if seeking confirmation, he told them to talk with Mr. Maxwell. His consulting fees grew with each visit, Virginia enjoyed the money, and the kids attended private schools.

Next came a lawyer's dream: TV interviews. Somehow, a staffer of a local station learned of Bill's relationship with Mr. Maxwell, a reputed drug lord. They wanted an interview that was full of gossip.

The host, Jane Evans, was a drop-dead gorgeous lady of indeterminate age. She did have credentials from a well-known university so Bill was satisfied that he was dealing with intelligence rather than simple beauty. Virginia approved. "Anything to generate business, my love."

"Good morning everyone. This morning, we have as our guest, Mr. Bill Ginn, once a county prosecutor, and now a mouthpiece for the mob. Good morning, Bill."

"Good morning. And for your audience, I gab, you listen. After all isn't that what mouthpieces do?"

Audience laughter.

"So, tell me, Bill. Why the change from prosecution to defense work?"

"Simple money. I enjoyed my work with the county, and especially with Mr. John McElroy." Turning a serious face to the camera, Bill intoned, "Mr. McElroy is a serious defender of the community. He's totally honest in his dealings with any accused person but very effective in prosecuting any wrongdoer. He taught me so much and even today, when we are opposing counsel, he still teaches me lessons. So, thank you John for everything."

"Wow! Kudos from a defense lawyer to a prosecutor. Now I've seen everything."

"No, really. That's not a proper attitude. Our Constitution is clear on this matter. Everyone, absolutely everyone, has an absolute right to proper trials. Otherwise, we'd have tyranny. So, yes, John and I are good friends, We fight in court for our clients and then go away as friends after the dust settles."

"But you left county work because of money?"

"It's not difficult. I have a growing family, and I want the best for them...especially the kids. That takes money, and what I was earning wasn't enough. So, I went into private practice. It's not at all uncommon among litigators."

Jane pressed on, "But does it bother you when you defend a client who you know is guilty and will repeat what they have done?"

"You mean murderers and child molesters?"

"I've prosecuted bad guys, but as of yet, I haven't had to defend any."

"You're evading my question,"

"No, I'm not. I described my situation." After a moment's reflection, Bill continued, "Listen. Our world is not perfect. I'm not Perry Mason where his clients are always the good guy. O.J. Simpson is a great example. He ultimately got sued for murdering his wife, but he did beat the criminal charge. Our system of law creates a paradox. Politicians today have been defended by lawyers who know their clients are working to destroy the very laws that protect them. So, I hope I don't have to defend a truly bad guy, but if I must, I'll do it and not miss a bit of sleep as a result. Does that answer your question?"

"I suppose so, but I could never be a defense lawyer."

Bill snorted, "And could you live with yourself if you successfully sent an innocent person to the needle?"

Jane had no reply to that.

Seeing he had made his point, Bill then described how he works as a consultant to his clients. "Some of them may have illegal operations..."

Jane interrupted him, "Care to name any?"

"No I won't. For the same reason, you wouldn't want me to name you as one of my clients."

"Can't argue there."

"Thank you. To continue, if a client may have illegal business, I try hard to persuade him to give it up. Get clean. As far as I'm concerned, being tried is a waste of time and money. Trust me, I would be taking his money defending him. So, why not be straight and develop a clean business?"

Jane smirked by saying, "All of which is to say that you earn your money by dealing with evil."

"Isn't that a bit cynical for you? Perhaps hypocritical? Yes, I do earn money by dealing with evil. Again, this isn't an Eden where evil doesn't exist. That means that if it were Eden I've have no job and neither would you as a reporter of wrong doings. The police would have no jobs catching bad guys. At least I preach a gospel of going straight. Do you?"

Jane now looked glowingly into the camera and said, "Great question, but now my director says we need to take a break."

After the ads, Jane returned to her interview. "Bill, you do have some level of involvement with the drug industry..."

Bill did not deny Jane's statement by remaining silent. The cameras carefully recorded this silent assent.

She continued, "Given your professional duty to defend drug dealers, what do you think about drugs?"

"Do you mean as a lawyer or personally?"

"Both."

"As an officer of the court, I am obliged to abide by the law even as I defend dealers. If someone gets caught and convicted, then it's off to jail for them. Without laws, we would have chaos with people doing exactly what they want without regard in the slightest for the consequences."

The cameras caught Jane nodding in agreement. "And personally?"

"Now that's a different story. If the choice were mine, I'd legalize the recreational use of all drugs?"

Jane's face showed surprise. "All drugs?"

"Yes."

"Even fentanyl?"

"Even fentanyl. Look at it this way. It's a drug people want and will buy whenever they get a chance. It's their choice. Just like a free-climber scales sheer cliffs for the highs. Make a bad decision and someone dies. Right now, one's legal and the other illegal."

Bill waited for the camera to finish panning the audience's reaction to his opinions. Some were pro while the rest booed and turned thumbs down. Then he continued. " Now I will rant a bit about some hypocrisy. Big Pharma developed and promoted oxycontin. It has enjoyed huge sales with physicians being their pushers. Unfortunately, their patients become hooked on the drug and eventually turn to heroin when their prescription runs out. So, the Pharma CEO's get bonuses for selling the drug that causes patients to buy heroin that sends street dealers to jail."

Bill then turned to the audience and asked rhetorically, "Anyone have an answer to that?" It remained quiet.

The rest of the interview continued with an exchange of banalities until the next celebrity was introduced to explain why he hadn't stopped beating his wife. Bill meanwhile was ushered from the studio with the producer's thanks after which he returned to his wife.

Virginia greeted her husband with a broad smile. "Got that little hussy, didn't you?"

"I did indeed. It couldn't have gone better. I've advertised myself as a Lone Ranger, wearing a mask while being righteous."

"So what's next?"

"Believe it or not Mr. Maxwell wants to convene a conference of all his people and even some competitors."

"Competitors?" asked Virginia incredulously.

"Yep. You heard me. Mr. Maxwell is a foxy old fellow. If he can get everyone working together and avoiding gang wars, then no noise can be heard that will attract Ms. Glamour or the police."

Virginia understood. "So no news for the public is big news for him and the drug industry?"

"You should be a detective my dear."

The next month, the conference was convened. It wasn't too large with about 50 men in attendance. To look at them, they would fit into a meeting of salesmen for the Pilsbury Dough Boy. They were courteous to one another. Some even exchanged family news.

Travis was the master of ceremonies. "Gentlemen, thank you for coming here. My father has thought long about hosting this meeting and he is gratified that you have come. The meeting will have two parts. One will be focused on why people get caught. It's usually because of silly errors that needn't have happened with a bit of care. Our lawyer, Bill Ginn, whom you all know, will be conducting these sessions. They will emphasize question and answer. Perhaps some role-playing during planning processes and executions. Meanwhile, Mr. Maxwell will be hosting a meeting of his closest associates. He's hoping some good strategic planning and looking for new opportunities will come of it. Any questions so far?"

None were heard.

Travis continued, "We'll have some opening remarks now from Mr. Maxwell. He's older than most of you here and has seen a lot of things come and go. Now, he is seriously thinking about retiring. He'll be talking a lot about that prospect because he believes it's the way all executives here need to consider. So, with no further ado, may I present my father, Mr. Philip Maxwell."

Polite applause.

Mr. Maxwell came up to the podium. He was wearing a grey, double-breasted pin-stripe suit. His shirt was a faint blue base with a white starched collar. A darker blue tie draped down his chest. Small golden cufflinks peeks from his wrists. His oxford shoes were spit-shined to a mirror finish. He was the epitome of an elder statesman.

Bill was surprised at how eloquently Mr. Maxwell spoke. For someone as taciturn as he was, Mr. Maxwell was a very good speaker. He led off with thanks for everyone's attendance and then confirmed that shortly he would be retiring from the business.

"I'm doing so for several reasons. It's time. I've been in the business for a long time and through it have been able to fund some lucrative bars and smoke shops. They are now producing enough money to meet my needs and those of my children and grandchildren. They will also be a base for further growth that will be entirely legitimate. Think about it. Aren't our families the reason we do all this?

And all of this was produced from money earned through drugs. For me, the drug business has done its work."

Heads nodded on cue.

"So, it's time for this generation to step down. I will be selling my drug business to the highest, qualified bidder. None of my children will be permitted to bid so it'll be an open opportunity for everyone in this room. These bids will be conducted in the same closed fashion that the government uses for doing business. I will be asking for a representative from each of you to oversee these procedures so that everyone will know what's happening. Keep it honest and avoid gang wars, which are the bane of our industry. Specific instructions will be sent out to each of you, but for now, any questions?

None were heard and Mr. Maxwell noted it by remarking, "When we are *en camera* conference there will be opportunity given for questions.

A sense of relaxation permeated the room.

Mr. Maxwell continued. "Gentlemen, a second reason for retiring is to allow the next generation to meet its destiny. What do I mean by that? The younger people have different ideas that are not impeded by how things are 'always done.' They have new ideas. I say this from having recently hired Bill Ginn as my counselor, *consigliere* for our Italian friends, who showed me how our business can be operated like any other enterprise for better profits and less risk. You have seen some changes in our operations on the street. I, for one, sleep better at night as a result of his insights. So, the question arises, why not let the next generation run things while we old-timers enjoy our retirement? Why not indeed, and that's why I'm selling."

Mr. Maxwell continued on for the next quarter hour forecasting what he sees in the future. He described in clear terms how Houston's retail drug operations were no different from selling gas. Exxon sells gas. Sunoco sells gas. There stations can be across the street from one another and no one gets excited. There's plenty of business for everyone. No need for fussing exists for anyone."

After Mr. Maxwell finished his keynote speech to polite applause, Travis invited everyone to the bar for a break and then afterwards to the dining room for lunch. From there, the seniors would retire to a smaller conference room for talks. The remaining attendees would go to a larger room for seminars.

Bill headed the seminars. It was an interesting experience for him, and his comments caught the attention of his audience, some of whom were indeed "made" bad guys. "OK gentlemen. Let me introduce myself. As it might be said in an AA meeting, I'm a reformed prosector."

Laughter tinged with irony.

Bill continued, "Yes. That's right. But not to worry, Mr. Maxwell is now my employer. I am his counsellor and now as your observer of why you get caught. As a prosecutor I worked with the police and here are things they look for."

Audience attention became very focused.

Bill spent the afternoon telling the men in front of him how small things such as wearing distinctive clothing while on the job can be identifiers by passers-by, how sloppy bookkeeping can make forensic accountants very happy...the discussion went on. Along the way, he encouraged questions, comments, and discussions among themselves. At the end of the afternoon, he ended his session with these remarks. "Gentlemen. This was a good seminar I believe. I hope you noticed how I dodged questions about specific events both past and future. It was done with a purpose. As a lawyer, I can't engage in such discussions because that makes me a conspirator with you. I l would lose my license if caught and go to jail.

Imagine that...a defense lawyer going to jail. But as a counselor I can advise and if you get caught, defend you. Now, from all this, you have come to know who I am and what I know. If you need my services, then I'm happy to serve."

A warm round of applause followed until Bill made a final comment. "As you know, Mr. Maxwell is retiring. He's doing so at my suggestion of getting out while he can. I make the same suggestion to you. When legitimate business brings home enough money to support you and your families, get out. Be clean. My defense bills are expensive and for you, trials and prison are a waste of time. I'm sure you will agree with that."

There was absolute agreement.

A few minutes after Bill finished his seminar, Mr. Maxwell's meeting was finished. After meeting in the bar for a chaser, Travis invited everyone again to the dining room for a steak dinner. At its conclusion, Mr. Maxwell made a few closing remarks of thanks for everyone's attendance and the conference was closed.

Bill, Travis, and Mr. Maxwell returned to the bar for a night-cap and a review of the day's events. Their drinks, interestingly, were cokes. Bill had listened to his host's order and followed suit. It was obvious that father and son were complete teetotalers. *Do as I sell, not as I do.*

In general, Mr. Maxwell was pleased with the results of the conference. His business would be transferred to others without a gang war. No publicity there. He was also very complimentary about Bill's TV performance and the feedback received from his seminar. His final comments were words of warning about several attendees.

"Bill, I like you and want to see you succeed without getting into trouble. Avoid Jake Jones and Smiley Smith. They have no honor and will sell you down the sewer in a heartbeat."

"Thank you sir. I'll take your counsel."

Mr. Maxwell now stood indicating the day's activities had come to an end. Without comment, he and Travis departed for home. Bill did likewise.

When he got home, Bill saw how Virginia was awake. She had an empty gin glass on the coffee table in front of her. She was not a happy camper. This was a surprise and a let down from the euphoria he had enjoyed during the day.

Bill made the mistake all married men make. He asked Virginia what's wrong.

"Nothing."

He then made the second mistake all married men make. He said, "You've got me fooled."

"Oh Bill, you just don't understand."

"Understand what?"

"Never mind."

Bill knew this night would not be fun. *Damn, just when things were going well.* "All right. I don't understand. So, when you're ready to clue me in, let me know. Right now I've had a long day, and I'm going to bed."

"Ooooh 'mmm. Okaaay."

Bill took his shower, put on his pajamas, returned to the living room, and saw Virginia still sitting there. "OK. I know I'm just a dumb husband but give me a hint at what's bugging you."

"You should know."

"Well I don't, and you're not helping by sitting there with a martini glass, a cigarette, and stewing while expecting me to be a mind reader. And smoking, when did you start smoking again? Virginia, what the hell's going on?"

Virginia turned toward her husband and started to cry.

Bill now made the third mistake that all married men make by saying, "Oh dear, stop crying."

Now the waterfalls made Niagara Falls seem like a brook babbling, which made Bill's brewing anger boil over. "Virgina, again. What the hell's going on?"

"I'm so lonely."

"About what?"

"Everything."

"That helps me a lot. Any details that you'd like to share?"

A long time passed while Bill sat glaring at Virginia until she finally turned to him and said, "You're gone all the time and now my friends won't talk to me...not after that awful TV show you put on."

"I thought you approved of my performance. And don't talk to me about being gone a lot. You knew beforehand I'd be putting in a lot of hours getting my practice going. Besides, if you might remember, I spent a lot of hours away as a prosecutor. Listen, you can't have it both ways. Earning the money we want takes time and energy."

" I know. I didn't or don't. I don't know."

"OK. I get that. I'm gone, and your friends think I'm a mobster. Is that it?"

Reaching for another cigarette, "That's it, basically."

"And when did all this start?"

"After your interview. Then everyone knew what you did for a living."

Bill snorted angrily. "And now they're dumping you for being a mobster's moll. Well, what do you want me to do about it? By the way, I'll bet Betsy Jones is leading the charge about my interview."

Virginia sniffled. "Well, she really thought your remarks about legalizing drugs were horrible."

Bill replied sardonically, "Yeah, Ms. Mary Jane."

Virginia snipped back. "What do you mean by that?"

Bill snapped in return, "Get off it. You know full well what I mean. Every time we've visited her house, I can smell the marijuana she's been smoking. Yeah, criticizing you because I defend the mobsters she buys her Mary Jane from. And now, you're joining her by buying liquor by the gallon. Just what planets do you broads come from anyway?"

"Well, at least try staying home for a change. The kids are wondering where you've been."

The picture now began to clear for Bill. "Yeah, I agree. I've been on the road these last six months, but it's been what I've had to do to get my practice up and running. And it's been working in case you haven't noticed. We've got the kids in good schools, which ain't cheap. We're making double payments on the house and our student loans, which will make us debt-free well ahead of schedule. So, what's the problem?"

"I thought when you left the county things would get better with more money coming in. Well, they haven't."

"So you want me to return to prosecuting?"

"No. We can't afford that."

"Then what the hell do you want? Virginia, again, you can't have it two ways. Right now, I'm working like hell to get one thing done...our financial security. It takes time. And about your so-called friends. You always called them duds before. Now you think they're important? Virginia, what do you want? Tell me, and maybe I can do something, but it ain't workin' now."

The discussion, if one could call it that, lasted until well into the night. Virginia wanted something, and Bill couldn't give it. Nothing was understood or settled before they went to bed. There was a large gap between this married couple.

Chapter 9
What To Do

Bill returned to work the next day. It wasn't as much fun as it was yesterday. Virginia's change completely confused him. It was so sudden. From celebration to this. *Here I talk to her about leaving the County and starting my own practice. She was all for it. Keep the money rolling in was all she said. So, what did she expect anyway? Perry Mason? Come on. She knows the world is full of bad people. What did she think prosecutors do all day? Sit around and smoke cigars? No, I put bad people away proving that bad people live in this world. She also knew from Joe that lawyers defend these bad guys. So. if I became a prosecutor, what would I be doing? Women, I don't understand them!*

Bill fussed about the office through the morning until 11 o'clock when he called Joe. "Joe, Bill here, Listen, Virginia's got me upset about things, and I need a good ear to hear me. Can we have lunch today?"

"Yeah. That'll be good. It's been a long time what with the changes in our careers. The usual joint at 12:30?"

"That'll be great."

"See you there."

At 12:30, Joe walked in and came over to Bill's booth. It had been a long time. Joe thought, "Bill's looking tired. Starting a new practice is like getting a mile-long freight train moving. Yeah, he's tired."

Shaking hands, Joe sat across from Bill. Both men remained silent until their orders were taken and served. Once their burgers had arrived, they started chatting about what was new. It was just stroking, and both men knew it. Finally, Bill said, "Virginia and I had a fight last night. She's not happy with things. I'm gone too much, and her friends think I'm a mobster and are apparently dropping her. What the hell is with her anyway? Women..."

Joe thought a bit before replying. "Yeah, Mable didn't like my being a defender. She's still not wild about it with me defending for the County. Same issues as when I worked for the firm but with more financial stability. But she tolerates it. She also liked at first my efforts to reach kids,... Amos...until it got to be too much for her. I was gone too much was her complaint."

"Welcome to the club."

"We had a couple of good fights about it. I wasn't facing being fired as I was at the firm but otherwise, that was the only thing she liked about my being there."

"So, what happened?"

"Well, I would continue being a PD, but trying to save every kid who came my way stopped. This gave me more time at home. We had a little girl you know? Betsy is her name."

"Virginia told me. Congratulations. I'm sorry I forgot about sending a card or getting with you all to celebrate. Things just got away from me."

Joe shook his head and said, "Yeah, I know. Life's a bitch sometimes...."

"And then you marry one."

"Come on. It can't be that bad."

"Well, if it isn't then I'm facing a good substitute. I'm stuck. I made my move into the private world, and I gotta work to make it a success. Get that money. You left it for government work, which left you able to cut back on your hours away from home with no loss of pay."

"Yeah, I see what you mean. That is a big difference. By cutting back I've been able to spend more time with Mable and Betsy. It's a happier home."

The friends continued to talk a bit more about things. Mostly it was Bill with Joe listening. Finally, with a glance at his watch, Joe called it quits. "I gotta get back to the office. Bureaucratic rules you know."

"How well I know. Anyway, thanks for listening."

"That's what friends are for. Any time."

Life continued. Bill worked, and Virginia was remote. It led to more futile arguments. Finally, he said, "I can't stand this change in you, so I made an appointment with a marriage counselor. Maybe he can show us something we're missing."

"If you say so, dear."

On the day of the appointment, Bill left the office early to fetch Virginia. She climbed into the car without saying anything, They rode in silence to the counselor's office where they checked in for their appointment,

"Doctor will be out shortly. Please have a seat."

A minute later Doctor came out with an extended hand and introduced himself. "Hi, I'm Jack Powell. Please, let's come into my office."

They went into a comfortable room that was devoid of anything business-like. Easy chairs and a davenport were placed around a table. In the corner was a pot percolating. Coffee in hand often made things easier with stress. Dr. Powell was tall and lanky. He wore chinos, a bright sport shirt, and loafers. His hair was thinning a bit with a receding hairline. A pair of reading glasses sat on his widow's peak.

With a casual wave of his hand, he offered seats and then asked who wanted coffee. Bill did. Virginia was silent. When everyone was seated, Dr. Powell waited for a while until unspoken words became tense. He then asked, "I imagine you're having marital problems, or you wouldn't be here. So, who would like to lead off?"

Virginia sat mute. Her eyes were glazed. Bill looked at his wife hoping for some response. Nothing. Finally, he led off with a short history of his employment change, how Virginia had been happy with it until several weeks ago when they had a fight." It seems she's not happy with my work defending bad guys. It seems I'm away too much for her, and she's losing friends who accuse me of being a gangster. Well, I'm not. I'm doing a job that is demanded by our legal system and for it, I'm being paid very well, which was her demand when I proposed leaving the County as a prosecutor."

Turning to his wife, Bill growled, "Well dear, what the hell did you expect? Bring in the money was all you said, I'm doing that. If your so-called friends can't handle that, then maybe you need to find other friends. Particularly those friends who patronize the dealers I defend."

Virginia only said, "I want my friends."

Dr. Powell asked her if she would be happier if Bill returned to the county to his old job where there was less money. Virginia replied, "That won't work because our kids are in private schools with expensive tuitions."

Bill broke in, "There you have it. I'm a trial lawyer...what I've always wanted to be. I'm 35 years old and too late for starting into something else. Take another job and guess what, I'm at the bottom of the pecking order earning peanuts. No schools for the kids. So I catch hell about that. Win or lose, I catch hell."

A sudden thought occurred to Bill, and he went silent. Then, almost jumping up, he yelled, "Virginia, the kids have been avoiding me lately...not being warm like they used to be...have you been bad-mouthing me?"

Viginia sat mute. Now, Bill was standing with fists on his hips. "Damn it woman, answer me." No answer.

Dr. Powell then said, "Virginia. Bill asked a question. Can you answer it please?"

Viginia hesitated. She had never seen her husband this angry before. She cringed. In a weak voice she said, "I only explained how you had a new job."

"Bull shit. You told them I had a new job, and it was making you sad. I was the reason for your being lonely. Also, I've noticed martini glasses around. How many bottles are you drinking now? One...two?"

"I've had a few."

"A few? What's a few? Looking at how you're gaining weight, you're looking like a drunk sow. Oink, oink. And your face, see those blood veins? They don't come from drinking water."

No answer.

Dr. Powell broke in to keep the meeting under control. He was seeing a family explosion that was probably long overdue, but when Bill was still venting, he let things ride for as long as the couple only talked or perhaps...Bill mostly yelled. At the end of the hour, he called a halt with some soft words. "There's a lot of confusion between you two, and unfortunately, it's affecting your kids. A lack of real talking may be the root cause of all this. If I might offer a suggestion, take a weekend off with your kids with a babysitter, talk, make love, with the goal of becoming reacquainted."

Bill rejoined, "Good idea, Doc."

Virginia said nothing.

Good for his word, the next day Bill found a beachside motel for the next weekend. Fortunately, it was off-season, and the crowds were gone. They would have solitude to think and talk. He was actually looking forward to this break. He had been working hard and was gone a lot, so a break would be good for them.

Virginia did not object.

That next Friday, Bill took off early from work, picked up Virginia and kids, and headed to her parents who would do babysitting. Virginia didn't go into details as to why they wanted to be away, and they didn't ask. Virginia had already been complaining about his life, and they understood their need to be away.

The motel was an upper-class establishment. The room was large, completely equipped with TV, refrigerator, coffee pot, large sauna tub...the works. The dining room was quiet and offered an excellent menu and service.

Each ordered their favorite meal. Wine was served. Virginia downed her first one and ordered a second one. As the courses were served, Bill ate heartily while Virginia just pecked at hers while ordering another wine. Little was said until Bill asked what she thought of Dr. Powell. He's OK was her reply. When he asked how teaching was going, fine was the reply. Bill paid the tab, and they returned to their room.

Once there, each got ready for bed. There was only a single king-sized bed. Bill was careful to request it in hopes it would bring Virginia back. She had been sleeping separately since their fight. She did share this bed but resolutely on the far side. Bill sat up and turned on the light.

"Virginia. We came here to try and resolve problems. Lying there like a frigid log isn't helping things. Now do you want to deal with our problems?"

"If you say so."

"What the hell does that mean?"

"Simple. If you think we have problems, then I guess we do."

"You don't think so though."

Turning to Bill she said tersely, "Frankly no. Find another job that brings in money, and I'll be happy."

"Simple as that, eh?"

"Yes. Good night, Bill."

The rest of the weekend continued. Nothing as far as Bill was concerned. He didn't like it, but he did take advantage of the silence to do some thinking about things he would have dreamed even a week ago.

Well, this idea of a weekend was a bummer. Viriginia's attitude sucks. She wants to the benefits of money but not its responsibilities.

Responsibilities?? A light glowed in Bill's head. He began to think about their courtship. He was a returned veteran trying to get back into a school routine that was set for younger kids who had no concept of killing and dying. Sleeping was still a problem with him. Dreams of battle would erupt with the whoosh, boom of mortars coming in. One night he dreamt he was paddling a canoe down a river of blood. He recalled his buddies surviving a tough patrol only to get stoned. Afghanistan's biggest export was poppies, the heart of heroin. It was available. Even when he was awake, sudden sounds would have him hitting the deck even when he recognized the noise as harmless. So he stayed awake, studied, and his grades rose.

Eventually, Bill applied for law school and to his surprise, he was accepted given his early grades. Why law school? Business didn't make sense. Medicine? No way. He'd seen enough blood. Computers? They were the coming thing but learning how to code? He could hardly speak English let alone recite code. So, law school it was. He could earn a good living with it.

It was during his second year in law school that Bill met Virginia. She was finishing her undergraduate program in elementary education. She also was president of her Tri-Delta sorority. Very popular. Lot of boys hung around hoping for a chance with her. She had only one thing in common with them and that was parties. She loved her parties. Still, she was smart and got her grades without too much effort.

It was actually at a party where he met Virginia. He had been invited by another girl. It was boring. The girl was just a ditz. Then Virginia came in. Like an angel. Her hair was blond. Her figure was hourglass. Her eyes were blue. Bill wasted no time.

He left the ditz and walked over and said, "Hi, I'm Bill Ginn, and I want to meet you. Care to dance?"

Virginia already had a couple of drinks and was slightly irresponsible. Enough to say, "Yeah, big fellow, why not?"

It was during their third tune that Bill asked her for a date. "Young lady, I'm a heroic soldier who has seen hell, and now I'm seeing heaven. May I have a date with you?"

"When?"

"As soon as possible."

Taking another sip of Seven and Seven, she said yes but "Only if you kiss me now."

Bill recalled that kiss and smiled to himself. *It was a good one. Led to a lot more.*

The kiss indeed led to a lot more. Bill and Virginia became an item. She took him home to meet her parents. It was a stiff affair but accepting. Bill was a soldier. That was good in her father's eyes. Solid American stuff. He was becoming a lawyer. That meant a comfortable living for her daughter in her mother's eyes. So, upon completion of the school year, Virginia was graduated with a teaching job in hand. Bill had what he believed would become a calm and quiet family life. Armed with ignorance, they got married.

Bill shook his head at this image and thought, *Calm and quiet. Then why am I sitting here in the dark with a drunk? What did I miss?*

As he thought back on the images that had floated through his head, a common thread appeared. It was women. Virginia was always surrounded by women. She wasn't gay. Her enjoyment in bed denied that. But his wife drew her energy from her friends. Always had, always will. And now she's losing them with nothing to replace them but a bottle and cigarettes.

Duh! So now, she's married to a mob shyster and losing her friends and she wants me to change? At this late date? Just when the money is rolling in? Well, Virginia, you may want your friends but not at my expense or the kids. If changes must be made then they must come from both of us.

Monday, he called Dr. Powell and told him about the weekend. Bill thanked him for his time and insight as it helped him immensely. He then asked for a bill to be sent to his office.

The next several months continued with no change. Virginia was drinking more than ever. Bill thought about pouring all liquor down the drain. *But what good would that do? Drunks will get there booze somewhere. At least at home she's not driving to get drunk.*

Eventually, Susan and George came to their daddy and asked, "Why is Mommy so sad?"

"I wish I knew," was Bill's sad reply. "Why? Is she doing anything?"

Susan's eyes were filling with tears. "She's always drinking. Sometimes when we come home she's lying on the couch unconscious. Bottles are everywhere. Doesn't she love us anymore?"

Bill took a handkerchief and dabbed her eyes. It was the hardest thing he had ever done. *What answer can I give her?* As he was thinking he saw George sitting back just trying to be brave. *Poor kid. Being a brave boy. What a mess.* He could only give them hugs.

The next day, he called Virginia's parents. He needed help. *I can't take care of the kids and earn money at the same time. Together, Virginia and I could have handled my work, her work, and what the kids really needed...love from both parents instead of hate between two adult children.*

When he got to the home of his in-laws, the door was open. Frank and Martha Krupka were waiting for him. They were a solid couple who had worked hard together to meet their life's problems. It wasn't easy for them, but they did it. At 60, they were devoted to each other, their daughter, and their grandchildren. Bill's relationship was more formal. Not much affection was ever exchanged, but they approved of him in general terms. "Virginia could have done a lot worse," summarized their feelings toward their son-in-law.

Bill didn't waste time with small talk. Frank and Martha would have seen it as a waste of time. Directness was their MO. "Frank, Martha, I'm here asking for help."

He got murmurs of sure, anything.

Bill continued, "Virginia has gone off the deep end, and I think it's time that you take our kids."

Shocked expressions faced him. They expected problems but taking the kids? What's this? Bill went on to describe what home life was like with their daughter becoming a drunk. "I'm sorry to call it like this, but that's the only way to describe Virginia. She's becoming a serious drunk. I'm amazed she's held her teaching job. Now, I did take her to counseling and to a long weekend at our counselor's advice. No go. No response. Virginia does not talk to me in any way. Believe me I've tried. Maybe you can make her get straight."

Stuttered words of so sorry...we didn't know...of course we'll take the kids...they need to be protected. Bill, then sat there and said words he'd never expected to say. "Frank, Martha, I've got to get out. I can't deal with Virginia like this. I've got to meet my responsibilities as a father to my kids by earning an income. That takes time from them. They need love and attention." With that he related his talk with Susan.

Frank and Martha were shocked to their souls, but they told Bill to go home, pack up the kids, and bring them over. That he did. Next he phoned Brian Smith, a divorce lawyer whom he had known through the years.

Brian had an open spot in his calendar the following Wednesday, and Bill grabbed it. While waiting for it he did a lot of thinking. *Change jobs she said. Make more money and I'll be happy she said. So, what am I...an ATM? If so, then I'm out. What's really sad is how she never noticed the kids were gone until I told her where they were.*

When Wednesday came, Bill was in Brian's office. Brian offered his client a seat and started to ask the usual icebreaker questions when Bill interrupted him to say, "Brian, this will be simple. I want to divorce Virginia and further, here are my terms. Virginia can keep the house. I'll continue paying my half of the mortgage. The kids need their home. Second. I'll pay the going rates for child support that includes half of their school tuition. Virginia can support herself and the kids from her teaching salary. That's it. No argument. Virginia will not be expecting this, and I want to use surprise as a weapon to get her agreement signature. Once gotten, the petition can be submitted for the usual 60-day waiting period. There will be no changes permitted during that time. Once the 60 days have passed, I want the divorce."

Bryan was stunned. He had handled a lot of angry divorces before, but this case was so cold...so calculated. He stuttered, "Bill, Bill, I'm a bit overwhelmed. Are you sure?"

"Yeah. Just make it happen as soon as possible."

"OK. You'll have your agreement for signature this Friday."

"Great."

Upon leaving Bryan's office, Bill went to a realtor to find a small furnished apartment, A half-hour there and he was a new leaseholder. Returning home, he went through his personal effects to decide what he needed to take with him. Some he could take to the office now knowing Virginia would not notice their absence. Others he noted for packing on Friday afternoon before Virginia returned home from school. Then he went through estate and legal papers for the same purpose.

Friday came and his divorce settlement agreement was prepared, ready for signature. He signed under his name immediately. After paying Bryan, he then returned to his house and removed everything that he needed. By noon, everything was transferred to either his office or new home.

When Virginia entered the house, she saw Bill was sitting there. "What brings you home Bill?" was her question as she lit a cigarette and went for the gin bottle.

Bill stood up, went over to his wife, reached into his pocket, brought out the divorce agreement, and said, "This is the last time you'll see me here. Please sign here."

Taking the agreement, Virginia asked, "What's this?"

"Simple, to use your word. It's a divorce agreement."

"What? What are you talking about?"

"Are you daft? A divorce agreement. You see dear, you told me to find a new job that pays more money. I thought about that and decided that was exactly what you needed to do. So, this lets you do that."

"What? What? A new job? I'm a teacher."

"You are now but when you're divorced you can take on a new profession."

"What? A new profession. What, for God's sake, are you saying?"

"For a smart girl, you certainly are dumb. With a divorce, you can be a whore and find a rich guy with no job to support you."

Virginia reached out to slap Bill, but he gently caught her hand. "Think about it. You only wanted money from me. You got it, but you now want more than me and that's your friends. With this you can tell them you threw me out or whatever...but I'm out. O-U-T, out. Now sign here."

Virginia began to cry, but Bill did not offer his handkerchief. He simply offered her his pen. "Now please sign here. You'll be better off. You won't have to share this house with me. You can have it as well as the kids. I'm paying for both of them. Now sign here."

Virginia was completely broken by shock. Crying like a baby, she took Bill's pen with a trembling hand and signed the agreement. Taking both back, he placed them in his pocket and left without a word.

While on his way, Bill's cell phone rang. A screaming voice pierced his ear. "You bastard. You goddamn bastard…" Bill simply rang off and continued to Bryan's office. There he left the agreement. Bryan saw him with the receptionist. Bill told him what had just transpired.

Bryan listened and then said, "You know, Virginia can get a lawyer who will say you ambushed her into an unfavorable divorce."

"So? That's why I hired you. Make this happen."

The next 60 days indeed saw Virginia try to weasel out of the agreement, but Bryan was a junkyard dog and ate her lawyer like a bone. He didn't have a chance. A signed agreement was a signed agreement, cut and dried.

The judge reviewing the agreement saw that everything was kosher. He turned to Bill and asked if he was satisfied. Hearing that it was, the same question was addressed to Virginia. She looked like a truck had hit her. She also smelled of booze, but she agreed. Gaining agreement from both parties, the judge pronounced the divorce final.

Bill left without saying a word to Virginia.

Las Vegas

Chapter 10
Expansion

The next several years were ones of growth. Without having to worry about Virginia or the kids, Bill was able to concentrate on the law. As his case load expanded, so did his litigation skills. But his improvement was not merely due to more practice in courtrooms. Mr. Maxwell had shown him how the drug business was just that: a business. So, he went back to school and got an MBA degree through night school. Finance and business law courses became very important. The more he knew about those subjects the more he understood Woody Guthrie's old song about Pretty Boy Floyd. The words went like this:

> Yes, as through this world I've wandered,
> I've seen lots of funny men.
> Some will rob you with a six-gun,
> Some with a fountain pen.

There was another advantage to be had from fountain pen artists, they weren't as likely to use their guns on him. They would also be able to afford appeals of guilty pleas and that made it rain for lawyers.

Actually, business had begun to grow enough that moving to a state with lower taxes seemed logical. He liked Texas well enough. He didn't have to pay state income taxes, and it provided enough business for the moment, but more was better. A large firm with lots of associates and paralegals appealed to him. Why work in only one state? Crime was everywhere; growth meant chasing it. Or perhaps, even better, was having clients from everywhere chasing him. So, in addition to studying business, he studied for bar exams elsewhere. Those states that accepted Texas certifications on a reciprocal basis were a joy. Do the paperwork, and the application was accepted. The question would be finding a good center of operations.

The more he looked, the more Nevada attracted him. Its violent crime rate of 2.89% well exceeded the U.S. rate of 2.64%. The state also enjoyed a booming growth of standard businesses but also those that were illegal elsewhere. Mr. Maxwell, what did I tell you? Finally, Las Vegas had a population of 2 million people with Lake Tahoe adding another 430,000 residents. Real estate prices were not bad, which meant he could buy land for both living and office space. Checking his taxes, he would definitely save money since state income taxes were not levied. Yes, Nevada was becoming ever more attractive.

Moving there meant he should do it sooner rather than later. If he were to establish a large office in Houston, it would become harder to move. Logistically, a small move was easier than a large one. This being the case, he pursued his Nevada Bar Certification. He did not intend on leaving his Texas practice behind. Rather, he looked for a relatively senior associate around town who was ambitious to make partner in a hurry. That he could offer. What Bill wanted was that person with ambition and talent. He had to win cases. Don't worry about justice. That was for someone else. He wanted the skies to rain money.

As he was pursuing his change of venue, Bill learned that Virginia was selling her house. Great. That meant no more monthly payments. A closing appointment was established for him, Virginia, and the new owner. Although Bill had given the house to Virginia, he retained joint ownership. Hence, his presence was needed at closing. Virginia would keep the proceeds from the sale. Bill was just happy enough to get out from underneath his share of the mortgage.

When he arrived at the lawyer's office, Virginia was already there. Bill was almost shocked at the change he saw in his former wife. When he had married her, she was a very attractive woman. Some would say she was gorgeous. Now he saw a chubby, blowsy, female with rheumy eyes. They said she had aged a lot. Faint red veins lined her cheeks. A faint sour odor followed her, and it wasn't perfume. Virginia was a drunk. Later, the grape vine told him she had lost her teaching job, and she had to find cheaper quarters. The kids were now being cared for by her parents. That information he had already known when he was told by Virginia's lawyer to send his child support payments to them. Bill wondered how long the money from the house sale would last. *You've come a long way Baby.*

The sale transaction took only a few minutes for the papers to be signed, and the check passed to Virginia. At the end of the transaction, Bill smirked, "How are your friends Virginia? Are they staying with you?" She simply looked at him with vague, unseeing eyes.

Something about this meeting set off bells in Bill's mind. Up to now, all communication between him, Virginia, or anyone associated with her was routed through his lawyer. He had never once spoken to her or seen the children. They were a closed chapter in his book. But, what the law demanded and what Bill saw could be two different things. He couldn't imagine what, but clang, clang, went the bell. It prompted him to call his attorney.

"Bryan Smith speaking."

"Bryan, this is Bill, and I have a request to make."

Bryan, by now, knew that Bill didn't ever waste time with explanations. He replied simply, "Sure, Bill what is it?"

"Please send a note to Virginia through her lawyer that I am very concerned about her decline. I suspect that it might be alcohol but whatever, I am urging her to seek help before it's too late."

Bryan also knew that Bill didn't mean a word of what was to be sent. It was simply a self-protection statement in the event he was charged with creating her drunken stupor. So, he simply replied, "Sure. I'll have it out by the end of the day. Do you want a copy?"

"Yes. Please. I appreciate this."

"Bye and take care."

"Bye."

It wasn't more than a few weeks later when Joe Brady called to tell Bill that Virginia was in an auto accident.

"Joe, thank you for letting me know. I've been expecting something like this for several weeks...actually since I saw her at the house closing. How bad was it?"

Joe's voice went grim. "Very bad. She killed a little girl, then resisted arrest, and was found to have a blood alcohol reading of 4.0. She was really smashed...out of control. She's struck out."

"When will her trial be held and who will be her defense?"

Joe gave the expected trial date and the name of Virginia's defense lawyer. *Thank goodness it isn't Joe. I'd feel terrible for him having to defend someone who was once his friend.*

"Anything else Joe?"

"No. I'm really sorry about all this."

"It's painful for everyone. As things stand now, the kids don't have a father and now they don't have a mother. Fortunately, her parents are caring for them. If Virginia's convicted, it'll be a long time before she gets out."

"You're right," responded Joe. "She'd need a Houdini to pull her out of these charges."

The two friends talked a bit more about their daily lives. Then finally they agreed it was time for other things.

Bill called John McElroy to ask what Virginia's status was. He couldn't go into details, but he did confirm what Joe had already told him. Bill wanted to know when the trial would be held, and John guessed it would be next month. "The evidence is already there, and even her lawyer said it was not a complicated case. When I know, I'll let you know, and Bill, I'm truly sorry all this had to happen. You had a beautiful wife there."

"At one time...but thank you John."

As it turned out, John's guess was accurate. The trial was scheduled for the next month, about six weeks. Bill took this time to think about what all this meant. He was really torn. He had been a prosecutor and if it were anyone else, he'd want to throw the book at Virginia. He was also a defense lawyer who had defended clients with similar charges. He consistently lost them. At best, he was able to get reduced sentences. Finally, he was a parent who hadn't seen his kids in more than a year. The girl's parents would never have a chance again. So, where did this leave Bill? In the middle of a muddled circle. His mind twirled around like a carousel. Round and round with no end in sight.

So, what is the cause? How do I understand what's involved? What's really the question? Yeah, what is the question? What's the answer? What's involved with both the question and the answer?

Was it a desire for money? Virginia never made bones about it. She talked about sending the kids to a private school. That took lots of money. But more than that, she liked money. So do I for that matter. But would money alone drive her to drink? She always liked her martinis but before I became a defense lawyer, she wasn't a drunk. When I did become one, she was getting money enough to satisfy her.

Friends. She discovered she needed friends. But what sort of people were they? The type who would accept her for herself? Apparently not. They were judgmental. Oh, they were that. So why did she want their acceptance? We never talked about it. Or rather, Virginia wouldn't. She only repeated how she wanted her friends. They certainly have dropped her as her condition deteriorated. But, with me out of the way, she could have met their conditions for acceptance. Why did she continue to drink herself into oblivion?

Bill pondered the questions of money and friends. The more he did so, the less he understood. Money, friends, and booze just didn't come together. If there was a connection, he probably would never make it. But were they the important questions he was facing? What about the dead child? Her parents?

That little girl. She's gone. Mine are gone from my life. Virginia took care of that, and I didn't fight hard for them. So, that's on me as well as her. Anyway, they're gone from both of us. I wonder if they'll even remember us beyond vague images when they're older? Hold up. That's not relevant to the dead girl. Her parents will never see her grow up, have birthdays, squealing at sleepovers, boyfriends, all of the events that mark raising a child. A terrible loss that can never be filled. Having another child might help but they'll always feel robbed. Someone's drunkenness robbed them. Virginia's drunkenness robbed them. H'mmm. I think I'm on to something.

Robbery was something Bill understood. He had prosecuted some thieves, and he had defended some. He was good at both, and it provided an earning, But either way, Virginia killed that innocent girl, which was something she ultimately had to live with.

Virginia. Virginia. Virginia. Who are you? Do you even know? Fighting with an officer immediately after taking a life. Did she, does she, understand what had just happened in her life, the girl's life, the life of her parents? If fighting is a clue, she probably didn't. Does she even now?

I don't know since I haven't talked to her. Either way, regardless of what the law or lawyers say, she is responsible for the death of an innocent girl.

Responsibility always meant doing what was right. His parents always drilled that lesson into his head. Prosecutors try to hold people to that standard. Defense lawyers try to help them evade it. That was the law, and a good one for preventing tyranny by the government. Look at John's bragging about not worrying about sending an innocent person to the needle.

As long as the evidence fits, I don't care about innocence. I could send the wrong person to death. Doesn't bother me a bit. Just like me. I can't worry if a repeat client kills someone after I get him off. But the client knows. If he or she's psychotic, these questions don't matter. If not, then they must live with their decisions to act. Act? Act? Decisions?

There was the connection. Decisions and actions. One must decide to do something. Virginia decided to drink. Why? That question wasn't answered long ago. There isn't an answer that can be found. But she did decide to drink that day. She did decide to drive while intoxicated. She could have taken a taxi. But she decided to forego choices of not drinking or not driving.

That's it. The girl may have run out into the street without thinking. That could have been a fatal decision on her part as someone else could have been at the wrong place at the wrong time while driving completely sober. That sober driver couldn't make a decision. That driver would be investigated and if found sober and driving properly, would have been exonerated by the law. But Virginia had choices, and she made bad ones. She had control over what she would do. The girl died. Simple as that. Virginia was responsible for her part of the fatality.

Regardless of what the processes of law may say, Virginia had killed someone through choices of her own making. Regardless of what anyone will say, if Virginia is a human with a bit of decency, with any empathy for the girl's parents, she is obliged to atone for her wrong. Sin may not be an appropriate word; one must be religious for that, and Virginia was not religious. So wrong is the word for her, and if she is to regain a moral righteousness for herself she must atone for her wrong.

That's the answer. Virginia had choices. She made tragic ones. Therefore, for her own sake, not the law, for herself, she must atone for her wrong.

Bill now knew what he must do. It would be the hardest thing he would ever do, but the cards had been dealt, and they must be presented to the judge for proper action. However, the judge needs to know why it must be done, and Bill could, would tell him why.

The phone rang. "John McElroy here."

"John, this is Bill, and I need to talk with you. May I come to your office this morning? It involves Virginia. I'm having a crisis of conscience to use a trite phrase."

"Sure. How about 10:30?"

"Thank you."

At 10:30, Bill knocked on John's door. John looked up, saw his colleague, and waved him in. He asked how he could help.

"Thank you for seeing me on such short notice. But, I have a request."

"And that is?" John suspected Bill wanted leniency for Virginia. He had faced similar requests in the past, and he rejected them flat. But, this was different, and it would be difficult saying no to someone whom he knew so well.

Bill knew this, and he went straight to the point to relieve John of the pain of saying no. "John, I'm here to ask if I may testify in behalf of the prosecution during Virginia's sentencing."

"Whaaaa??" John let out a long breath of relief. He was a bit confused however. A husband asking to testify for a wife? That was a new one on him.

"Bill, I'll be frank. I've never gotten a request like this. But why?"

Bill gave a long answer to John's simple question. It involved all the soul searching he had been doing since the accident. It boiled down to taking responsibility. Virginia had failed that test. Bill's test was coming, and he was damned if he would fail it. He must tell the judge why his wife needed prison time.

"Bill, I have never heard anything as heart-felt as your story. I can only imagine how your decision has torn you apart. But yes. I'll have you there. To ensure that you get your chance, I'll take this case for myself. Yeah, as I think about it, I need to be there. I want to see justice, with a capital J, done. Honestly, you've got courage that I've never seen before in all my years on the job."

Bill thought a while about John's appraisal. John could see turmoil in his friend's face, so he waited. Finally, the answer came to Bill, and he said, "I was an Army brat. A career Army brat. My father would always snap at me when I tried to weasel out of something I did wrong. He would always say, 'Yes sir, no excuse sir.' Then when I was in Afghanistan, death was a daily caller. I had to bury seven of my troops one week. My decisions were like a courtroom. They were either right, or people died needlessly. Consequences were absolute. Writing letters home to families about the death of a son or husband is something I hope you never have to do. After doing so, I had to ask myself, "Did I do wrong? No excuses. Did I do right? Don't know. So, here I am. Did Virginia do wrong, and I see that girl's face in my dreams. No excuses. No legal jockeying. Did she do right? The judge needs to hear this story."

John was as hardboiled a man as they came, but he had to wipe his eyes at Bill's judgement of himself, his wife, and life.

Virginia's trial came and went. Bill attended each day. She was tried for three offenses: manslaughter, driving under the influence (DUI), and resisting arrest. Manslaughter was obviously the worst offense as it carried a maximum penalty of 20 years Driving while intoxicated can bring a year's jail time plus fines and loss of license. Resisting arrest can bring other penalties. Altogether, Virginia could be facing a lot of time in prison.

The trial droned on to the jury's review and decision. That process lasted about three hours. Virginia was convicted on all three counts. She did not react. She looked toward her parents with vacant eyes that appeared not understanding what happened. Bill wondered if she was drunk.

The penalty phase started a week later. The defense asked for the time to prepare a plan for leniency. When convened, the judge opened with a statement that summarized how the jury had found Virginia Ginn guilty of involuntary manslaughter, driving while intoxicated and resisting arrest. Before rendering a penalty, both sides asked if they had anything to say. The defense said yes and was granted time to present a case for leniency. Expert witnesses were brought forth who testified how alcoholism was a disease over which the afflicted suffered daily through its consequences. Virginia did not choose to testify. Her eyes told everyone why.

When the prosecution's turn came, John stood and introduced Bill, who would act as his witness. The judge nodded his approval, and Bill stood and began to speak.

"Your Honor, thank you for allowing me this time to render an opinion on this matter. You know who I am as I know both the prosecutor and the defense lawyer. They are both good at their jobs and are honorable men.

Together, they fulfill the promise of the Constitution for a fair, open, and speedy trial. I too have sat in both chairs and presented cases like this one before you.

"Personally, I was once married to the defendant and had two children by her. We know each other well, and I'm sure she is surprised to see me here testifying for the prosecution. I am also acquainted with the parents of Jessie, whose life was tragically stolen from them. I have never had to suffer their loss, but I am positive there are holes in their hearts that time will never heal.

"All of this means that I am in the middle of a circle surrounded by people whose positions I have filled at one time or another. It is not an enviable place to be, I can assure everyone. But here I am, and after all the legal processes are said and done, I want to bring us to the nutshell issue confronting Virginia. What responsibilities must she bear? I mean her personally, not what the law says, but what she must bear for causing Jessie's death. Our legal traditions have asked this question since biblical times, and it consistently says that it must be met, and when wrong is done, atonement must be rendered. Such is the consequence Virginia must face in light of the decisions she made that have led to her conviction for manslaughter.

"You must render a partial answer to this question by the imposition of a fair penalty. Right now, having been convicted of three crimes, she is facing more than 20 years in prison. What term she gets is entirely your decision, and I will accept it. But, afterwards, what atonement can she make to Jessie's parents? That must be her decision.

"To provide a proper place for her to make her choices, I recommend she be given maximum sentences with possibilities of parole. During that time, society will be rendered safe from repeat offenses by her. She will also have time to review her life and seek help. Prisons have AA programs and counseling services. If she takes advantage of them, as I hope she does, and shows herself steadfast in reform, then I recommend she be accepted for parole at which time she can offer herself to Jessie's parents. Perhaps they will offer forgiveness. I don't know. That will be their decision to make. But for Virginia to become a righteous person again, she needs to go through the process I have suggested to you. Thank you Your Honor."

There was a stir in the audience that resulted in a gavel's banging for order. The judge excused himself to review the statements presented to him. After an hour's absence, he returned to the courtroom to announce his decision.

"Virginia Ginn, having been found guilty of manslaughter, driving while intoxicated, and resisting arrest, and having heard from both your defense and the prosecution, I sentence you to maximum, consecutive terms of imprisonment as prescribed by law. I strongly urge you to follow the words of your husband. They are well worth your time. This case is closed."

As Virginia was led away, she turned to Bill and yelled, "You bastard!" The guards pulled her through the exit door before she could continue. Bill got up and met with Jessie's parents who thanked him for his words. They also said they would pray on the hard task before them. Forgiveness is always hard and especially so for the killer of their daughter. Bill urged God's blessing on them. When he left them, he bumped into Virginia's parents.

Her father, Frank Krupka, a heavy man who smelled of stale tobacco, said, "It's sad about the girl, but may you roast in hell for what you did to our daughter."

Bill replied evenly, "I just hope you don't raise your grandchildren to be another set of Virginias."

Chapter 11
Settling In

Following Virginia's conviction, Bill was anxious to leave Houston. Reviewing his finances, he saw how things would be tight for a year or two. However, his taxes would be lower, and he made a good bargain with a buyer who was a senior associate wanting to make partner. Jackson Schmidt was that man. He was a thirty-year-old who actually was Joe's replacement. Like Joe, he saw early how his chances of making partner were nil. But he had established a good record around town as a defense attorney, and Bill was confident he would be leaving his practice in good hands. Their bargain had two stages. The first would have the revenues divided in half. When Jackson had things under control, he would buy the practice. That strategy meant each would have a good starting income.

Once that issue was settled, it was a simple matter of cancelling his condo lease, hiring a mover, finding another condo in Las Vegas, and moving in. Like his new start in Houston, he worked out of his home at first. Mr. Maxwell put him into contact with colleagues he could trust. Others he advised Bill to avoid like the plague. He did repeat his convention gig that allowed him to meet and evaluate the attendees. Mr. Maxwell was right. Bill met some men who were simply not good client candidates. They would have him defend them and then sting him for his fees. In all cases, Bill did not go into any long-term relationships. It was simply defense as needed. Perhaps later, when he knew better who was trustworthy, a relationship as business counsellor might be established. Otherwise, patience was the word.

His early cases were typical small crime defenses. There was one case that was actually funny. A fifty-year old man came in needing urgent help. This case went as follows.

"Mr. Ginn, I'm Jerry Gleason, and I need your help."

"That's why I'm here. What seems to be your problem?"

"Statutory rape."

"Ugh." Bill looked at his client. He was middle-aged, a little pudgy, well-dressed, and obviously educated. Why he had to buy his sex was something hard to understand. He certainly had money to afford a wife. But perhaps not. Anyway, going forward, Bill said, "Please give me the details."

Jerry had recently been divorced from a woman who cleaned him out. Moreover, he did not want any sort of continuing relationship. Marriage was out. Furthermore, he had no girlfriend and never had one. Infidelity was not the issue. Incompatibility over petty things like who would walk the dog or clean the house was the splitting ax in his marriage. Jerry had a poor lawyer, and it cost him. So, one-night stands became an affordable alternative for his needs. Apparently, that was another incompatibility factor: he wanted, and she didn't.

Jerry continued." I was in a bar one night over at the Venetian Hotel when this lovely young thing came in obviously looking for trade. I started a conversation by asking if she would enjoy a drink. She said yes, and things progressed from there. Her name was Bunny Smith, *Of course it was*. She was 24 but looked younger. Being a dirty old man not wanting trouble, I asked for her ID. Everything matched. Her driver's license, employment card, you name it. Even her prostitute's work card. So, we agreed on a price and place. Both were accessible so I agreed. We went and did. The next morning a loud banging on the motel door woke me up, I answered to a loud, burly, man who claimed I had raped his darling 16-year-old daughter. Furthermore, what would I be willing to pay to keep silent."

"Badger game."

"You got it."

"Not good. Judges don't like badger games, but they also come down hard on older men preying on young girls."

Jerry agreed, but he did smile a bit as he reached for his cell phone. It was obvious he was not making a call but retrieving something. Bill wondered what that might be. It turned out Jerry had taken photos of the girl's ID documents.

"Something just told me to take these shots and while Bunny was hopping off to dreamland, I got up and did my deed."

"Now that really helps. It shows you took reasonable steps to determine the girl's age. That will help your case. But, to help it, here's a gambit. Let's turn her into the police."

"Police? Are you sure?"

"Well, we will charge her father with pimping an underage girl. Prostitution is legal here, but they must be adults. Your photo of her work card showed your intention of dealing with an honest working girl. How this father got these documents is anyone's guess, but your case is in the bag. When the police hear of this, they'll give you a medal and Mr. Pimp time in jail. The girl? Well, that's another story for someone else to handle."

That was exactly what happened. The father was arrested; the mother denied everything and sued for divorce; the girl was placed under probation for counselling. Jerry was told to keep his needs in his pants, and Bill went on to other cases.

Other cases came and went without the irony of Jerry's. As Bill expected, they ran the gamut of different situations from petty street crimes to a bank robbery.

Pretty Boy Floyd would have been proud of that one. The thief almost got away with it. Only a flat tire, the unexpected, laid him up long enough to be caught. As he had hoped, cases then started to come in from California. Among them was a girl charging date-rape. Bill really didn't like that one. A dirty old man, fat and paunchy, wearing a wig, and clicking his false teeth took a young girl out, who should have known better, got her drunk, and took her to bed while she was unconscious. Pawing a girl young enough to be his granddaughter, yech. It was ugly. But he paid his bill, and he was defended. He got off with a warning. The chances of him repeating his obscenity? 100 percent. Bill could see him becoming a repeat customer. Would he give out a discount? Not on your life.

Eventually, Bill's income began to rise enough to make some changes. Also, Jackson was succeeding and was now buying his practice. It was understood that whenever Bill was needed back home, he would be available.

All of this meant that an office and paralegal could be afforded. Sarah Siegal was her name.. She was exactly the type of person for the office that Bill liked. Sarah was about 45, well married with two teenaged boys. She had attended the University of Nevada – Las Vegas so she knew the city and its markets well. For a newcomer in town, her guidance on restarting his life was a godsend for Bill. She had worked for other lawyers and had a strong personality. She knew how to handle prima donnas, set agendas, and find the most obscure legal details that won cases. In short, while he was working one case, Sarah could be managing other cases and researching tough questions of law. Bill ensured she was well paid and not tempted to look elsewhere for work. All of this meant that Bill did better jobs on the cases at hand. Better jobs meant success and more cases to litigate. Life was good.

Still, on birthdays and Christmases, Bill sent cards of good wishes to Virginia and his kids. Why, he couldn't say, but it seemed important even though none of them were answered. Early on, Virginia even returned to sender one of his cards. Still, he sent them and was glad to see them not returned. Maybe one might be answered. What he would do if one were answered was a question for another day.

Not all was work for Bill. He loved to ski and was good at it. He had learned it in Germany during his father's posting there. His first run down a green slope at the G.I. recreation center in Garmisch was enough to make him an addict. One unspoken reason for selecting Las Vegas was its proximity to the western mountains. Texas was OK but with terrain varying in its degrees of flatness, skiing was not something to be pursued. Bill had wanted to take ski vacations, but Virginia hated the cold. Now he had the opportunity to do some big-league skiing.

There was another advantage for Bill's bachelorhood: flying. He had always wanted to do so. Army aviators always seemed to have life with a swagger. But, law school, marriage, kids, and a growing law practice just got in the way. So, if not now, when? Never, and Bill did not want to let this chance pass.

After double checking his income and being assured flying could be afforded, Bill went to Harry Reid International Airport and started flight training. It was in a Cessna 150 with Jim Jenson his instructor pilot. Jim was a retired Marine pilot who was checked out in both fixed wing and helicopter aircraft. He had more hours than time. His hearing proved that fact. Even with Jim wearing hearing aids, Bill learned to speak up when talking. But Jim exuded confidence. It was quiet but there. He would get his students through their lessons safely. That was a strong attraction for Bill.

Jim was also thorough. As he said, "Bill, you take me as on your instructor, you'll be doing a lot of flying and studying before I clear you for any certification tests. You'll be competent in flying, navigation, and cockpit management. Some instructors just want to get their students soloing as soon as possible. Once there, they can be left alone leaving time for other students to fly. With me, ain't so. You're gonna learn to fly properly before I let you go on your own. Any problems with that?"

"Nope. Just what I wanted."

"By the way, what are your ambitions?

"Ambitions?"

"Yep. Just a private license or commercial license, instrument ratings, instructor?"

"Gee, I hadn't thought that far. One thing, though, having access to a plane means I'll have more flexibility for managing my court dates here and elsewhere. I'll use the plane for business travel while writing off the costs from my taxes."

"Sounds good. That means, I think, you'll want to be instrument rated in case you find yourself in the fog unexpectedly. Flying in bad weather is not when you want to learn how to fly on instruments."

"Can't argue with that."

"Good. Then let's take a flight."

Jim was good for his word. He taught the basics of stick and rudder flying to include such things as stall recovery, spins, landings, and take offs. Navigation meant a lot of classroom time learning how to read charts, set courses, and estimate leg times. Emergency procedures were constantly practiced. Often Jim would turn off the engine while in flight. Bill had to go through response procedures until they were done perfectly. As they flew along, Bill had to point out possible emergency landing spots. Jim insisted he do this until scanning the terrain below became habitual. As Jim said, "Bill, handling emergencies have got to be automatic procedures. When they come up, they're always surprises, so being prepared with aforethought means survival."

Much of all this was taught while Bill acted as co-pilot on cross-country runs. He handled the radios, got FAA clearances, looked for other aircraft in the sky, checked for emergency spots. The co-pilot duties just went on and on. Again, Jim said, "Bill, the co-pilot is the airspace manager. A good one just lets the pilot concentrate on one thing...flying the plane. Yeah, when flying solo, pilots can do it all. I did it for years. But learning co-pilot duties well means doing a pilot's job better."

It wasn't until Bill had logged 250 hours did Jim consider him ready for his private pilot's exam. It was scheduled and taken. It lasted about two hours. Bill aced it just as he aced the written portion. Jim congratulated him and said, "Bill, you stuck with me. Other youngsters simply get impatient and leave. But you're ready. Do some instrument flying to bring your skills up to exam speed, and you're there."

Jim was right. Bill aced the instrument exams. He then went to a dealer and leased a Cessna 185 aircraft. It was a straight-forward transaction. Bill only had to show his licenses for the paperwork to start. In the midst, the salesman asked who his instructor was. When Bill said Jim Jenson, the salesman said, "You're set. He's good."

Jim was pleased that Bill had his own plane but gave some other advice. "Bill, you're now halfway home toward being a real pilot."

"What? More?"

"Yep. A lot more. In fact, you'll be studying aviation for as long as you fly. And an important part of it is learning the innards of your plane. So, here's a piece of advice. Make a bargain with your mechanic to be his apprentice. Learn your Cessna inside and out. Knowing it will save your life. Mark my words."

That Jim did. Whenever he made a flight, he checked out his plane before and afterwards for problems . He scheduled all maintenance for his free time. As he watched his mechanic, Jack Rubenstein, Bill asked questions and studied the repair manuals. It wasn't long before he needed this instruction. As he was leaving Las Vegas for Los Angeles, he heard an odd noise that Bill recognized as trouble. He called the tower and told them of his suspected problem and requested space to return. It was granted, and when Bill got the plane back to the hangar, Jack was waiting for him. After an inspection, Jack said simply, "Yep. Glad you came back. It's a simple carburetor fix. You 'll be back in the air within an hour but had you continued on, you might have landed in the Sierra Madres with a fuel starvation problem. Not good."

Bill thought once again, *Thank you Jim.*

Responding to his clients' needs kept Bill flying up and down the Pacific coast. He rolled up hours very quickly. More to the point, he was amazed at how much better service he could provide by being able to make face-to-face meetings on short notice. His clients appreciated it and told others of the service he was able to give. The airplane was expensive, but it paid off.

Bill kept in touch with Jim about his flying. There was always something new to learn. During one such chat, Jim asked how many hours he had accrued. Bill told him almost 500 hours. "You're getting up there Bill. That's good. It won't be long before you're feeling like you're strapping your plane to you instead of you strapping yourself to the plane."

"I am getting pretty comfortable with it. I'm not working so hard with it as before."

"Feel like taking a next step?"

Bill unconsciously looked at his watch. Time was so important; his schedule was becoming tight. But despite his anxieties, he answered, "Yesss. I still have time, and obviously I want to be the best pilot I can be." Besides, it was so much fun flying with Jim. He always had stories to tell and lessons to teach.

"Then get your commercial license and your instructor's certificate."

"Dumb question, Jim, but why?"

"So, you can teach others how to fly. Bill, you're a talented pilot, and you work hard at it. Here's where you can make tremendous strides in your skills. Teaching will teach you more than what I can. Trust me here. Students will ask you questions you can't imagine. They'll also do things that'll scare the socks of you and give you fright lessons that will make you a better pilot. As they say, if you want to learn something, teach it. That adage is so true. It was with me, and I know it'll be true with you."

Bill looked at his calendar and saw if he quit eating and sleeping, he could do it. But what's eating and sleeping anyway? With that assurance, he naturally said, "Jim, I'm in. Let's go."

Those proved to be prophetic words.

Chapter 12
Looking Better

Bill's 40th birthday was good. Life was in order and improving. His law practice had grown. He now had two young lawyers on his staff. Recently graduated from school, they were young and anxious to learn the trade. They were willing to put in long hours to get this knowledge. Eventually, they would be judged, and those with talent would make partner, and the others given the opportunity to look elsewhere for long-term employment. Sarah was placed in charge of their daily activities. That included teaching them about the law, handling their hours, and anything else that young people needed of a strict mother. Sarah loved it.

This staff additions meant time for Bill to handle the big cases. He rarely defended small time violent crimes or drug busts. They were the grist for his young associates. Instead, Bill found himself handling a lot of fraud cases. They could be physicians padding their Medicare invoices or entrepreneurs cheating on their taxes. All this was stuff for which Bill's MBA paid off. Knowing business meant presenting good defenses. It also meant lucrative consulting fees on legal business practices. Once he defended a politician against charges of misusing election donations. His blond girlfriend needed a boob job, and while paying the bill was a donation, it didn't qualify as legal. It was reported however that the lady was pleased with her new appearance. Other similar political cases arose, and while they didn't generate the income that came from defending a past president, it was still for Bill not insignificant.

Having Sarah in charge of the office ensured Bill free weekends. He mostly spent them flying. He had gotten his commercial and instructor licenses punched and now he was a professional pilot teaching flying. It didn't pay much, but it did provide a legal tax deduction for his airplane and other flight lessons he took from Jim. Altogether, he couldn't wait for weekends to roll around.

At one point, with his increasing success as an attorney and his growing use of his airplane, Bill considered the possibility of upgrading to a twin-prop aircraft. But as he thought further about it, he decided against it. While it would be a faster airplane and have another engine during an emergency, seven-figure price tags were eye-stoppers. Also, the extra speed was not important if he were flying a long-distance to a client on the east coast. Bill would be doing just that: piloting, whereas riding commercially meant he could review papers for one client while charging travel time for another. Double-dipping was simply too good of a business opportunity to pass up by flying his own airplane long distances.

What was amazing was receiving a letter from Virginia. After all her silence, Bill wondered cynically what was her evil, or drunken, plot. She was still in prison and would be for several more years before her first parole board hearing. Considering how their relationship had gone down the sewer, her words were hard to believe. He was stunned by them. As a result, he carried the letter with him wherever he went.

Dear Bill,

I know this letter will be a shock for you. Even writing to you would be a novel change in your life. But what's amazing is how I'm now thanking you for sending me to prison. I was obnoxious when I arrived and was quickly separated for the other prisoners. I mean it literally. I wasn't in prison long before I got thrown into solitary. Trust me when I say it was not fun. Twenty-four hours a day of isolation. Nothing else but me.

Those days forced me to look deeply at myself. Who was I? What was I? Where am I? Did I like myself? Obviously, these questions could not be answered during solitary. However, I was asking them for the first time in my life. When I got out, I knew what I had to do. Using everything the prison had to offer and getting answers became my daily goals. Beyond answers I needed to learn how to conduct myself properly. Doing the right thing. So, as you suggested during my trial, I'm attending AA and meeting with a counselor.

I'm still going down a long road. Maybe I'll never reach the end. I really hope I don't. Reaching the end might lead to complacency and a return to a life of confusion. I suspect that getting out of prison alone will extend my time in search of real meaning. To that end, I have started reaching out to ex-con support groups. It takes a con to know one. I don't know where all this is going, but it's a start.

I have also reached out to Jessie's parents and asked for their forgiveness by asking what I can do to atone for my sin. Yes, I used that word. Our correspondence has been like walking on eggs, but progress is being made. At least they're answering my letters. Along that line, I also wrote to my parents about what all has been happening to me. I also asked them to understand that you were doing the hardest job imaginable by asking for my imprisonment. So, I'm hoping they will reach out to you. You, them, and the kids need to gather together.

I could go on but thank you for reading this letter.

Sincerely,

Virginia

While Bill was surprised by this letter, he knew it would not rekindle any sort of close relationship. That had completely ended. But what relationship they could have would be good for the two of them. A different, healthy relationship would also be good for Virginia's parents and his kids. They would no longer be caught in the mid-fire of World War III. So, he answered.

Dear Virginia,

Thank you for your letter. Frankly, I never expected to hear from you given the circumstances surrounding our divorce. But the news you have sent overjoys me. It shows a really strong character in you, one that is overcoming serious setbacks. I wish you all the support I can give you in your quest for redemption. Your courage is admirable. I now hope that our children inherit it from you.

If there is anything I can do to further your progress, please don't hesitate to contact me.

Sincerely,

Bill

It took a while after Bill wrote to the grandparents, but eventually he got a response. Martha was so happy to know what her daughter was doing for herself. She said it brought tears to her eyes. Virginia's father no longer wished him to rot in Hell. Even Susan and George, his growing children, offered short notes that were included in Grandpa's letter. They were shy in tone. *What else could be expected of them when writing to a long absent parent?*

The realization that a lot of absentee time had passed between him and his children really saddened Bill.

However, after a couple of exchanges, Bill offered to fly out and meet them. An airplane ride was part of the deal. George was all for that. Susan, as a pre-teen, had other things on her mind, but she didn't object.

A weekend was selected, and Bill flew back to Houston. It was his first trip. Some things he remembered were changed. The kids were taller, and their grandparents had aged some. The first day was stiff but courteous. Everyone was trying hard, and it showed. Still, the effort was worth it as far as Bill was concerned. He could only hope for the best for everyone else.

The hurdles were flattened with a plane ride. Grandma didn't want to fly. She was afraid of flying. Grandpa was curious. Susan was a good sport. George went nuts. When he got to crank the yoke and make the airplane turn, he was hooked. Flying was in his blood. Grandma thought he had become a fighter ace. Grandpa was quietly proud of him. Susan, like all sisters, welcomed anything that kept her nuisance brother occupied. The rest of the weekend went by with promises to do more cool things. Skiing was among them, and here Susan's interest really perked up. She had seen clips of Mikaela Shiffrin zooming down steep hills and winning medals. That she could relate to and was on Bill's case wanting to know when they could ski. He promised a trip when school was out and grandparents said yes.

Altogether, with some level of reunification in his family, Bill was a happy man and couldn't imagine anything better. Still, he was cautious with his personal life. Flying was his main weekend diversion with skiing being a wintertime exception. Flying to the slopes and skiing down them was the perfect combination. That's not to say he lived in a tree. He did have dates with some gorgeous women. Las Vegas was known for them. But they were all transient affairs. He had come out of a painful marriage and had worked hard to make a fulfilling life for himself. He had been able to reconnect with those whom he had hurt. He was not about to go through another possibility of losing them again. Moreover, one sour marriage was enough. Some of his dates had indicated an interest in marriage, but they didn't go anywhere. When they murmured, Bill ran.

At forty, Bill was also becoming aware of his advancing age. Although he was still trim and athletic, he was not a twenty-year-old. Going out with girls that age palled. Finding interesting women his age was tough. Either they were married, gay, or just coming out of a divorce. Las Vegas was a divorce capital wasn't it? So, celibacy it was.

The life of a flight instructor is always full of surprises, and Bill had one he would remember for a long time. He had an appointment to teach a lady, which was a bit unusual...not entirely unheard of...but since most of his students were male, somewhat unusual. What he didn't expect was a woman in her late thirties, drop-dead beautiful, and ready to fly. As he learned during their introductory lesson, she was also single. What more could a good-looking instructor want? He actually got offers of assistance from other instructors, but he declined their offers with thanks.

The student's name was Glenda Gifford. She appeared to be direct and fully able to handle any situation. When she took the controls, she was surprisingly smooth. Like most neophytes, she was a bit heavy handed, but still smooth. She recovered well. Bill definitely was hoping she would be a long-term student.

When they were on the ground, Bill invited Glenda to the pilot's canteen. There they could chat and become acquainted. He could also give her another appraisal. Her beauty was subtle but arresting. Tall, slender, with jet black hair, wide cheekbones, she moved with a dancer's grace. More was suggested under her flight clothes, but what could be seen was to be appreciated. Perhaps to draw himself away from this distraction, Bill led off with a natural question. "Why do you want to fly?"

Glenda replied simply, "It seems like a cool way to get away from things. Up in the sky, it's just me and the heavens."

"So, getting your private license and being able to fly around the flagpole is your end game?"

"Yep."

"Well, that works for me."

Glenda then asked if flying was his main job. Bill grinned and said, "I wish. Actually, I'm an attorney..."

"That's where I know you."

"Did I do something wrong? I try to be a good one...even honest,"

Laughing, Glenda replied, "No, I just read your name in the paper as the defender of some crook."

"Politician."

"Same thing. But I won't hold it against you. So, you're a part-time pilot..."

"Enjoying flights around flag poles. Yes. I also fly to meet clients everywhere on the west coast. Combine business with pleasure if you will."

Glenda glanced down for a nano-second before replying, "Yes, combining business and pleasure. I understand that."

Bill raised his eyebrows for a nano-second and let Glenda's remark pass.

At the end of the lesson and coffee, Glenda decided. She booked Bill for a lesson every other week. Flying was expensive, and she had bills to pay. Bill understood that and agreed to the schedule.

During the next few lessons, Glenda proved to be as capable as her first flight suggested. After ten hours of flying, she was cleared to take a solo flight around the flagpole. That would be at a nearby air strip where the traffic was very light. He did not want Glenda to become overwhelmed during her first solo flight by the intense activity of a large international airport. When she landed, Bill shook her hand and told her to pull her back shirt tail out. That, in accordance with ancient tradition, was snipped off and handed to her.

"What the hell was that all about?"

"Madam, you have now been inducted into the sacred circle of solo pilots. You may now take this flag home, and fly it from the highest yardarm, and thereafter give it permanent display in your living room. Welcome aboard, Glenda."

Glenda had to laugh. "I was beginning to think this was a strip-tease come-on, and if so, it was the worst one I had ever seen."

Bill straight-faced, "No ma'am. I wouldn't dream of making such a mistake. Gentlemen always ask."

Glenda smiled but then looked at Bill quizzically. Something said through the joke suggested he meant every word. *Well, I'll be damned. And a pilot no less without an ego. Not like others I've met.*

The flight back home was uneventful. After landing, the couple went to the canteen for their coffee. Since this libation was in celebration of an important event, Bill paid. He even brought a cupcake with a candle to mark the occasion. Glenda giggled.

As they were finishing the celebration, Bill asked, "Now, yes, I do ask. And, fair lady, I am asking you for a date."

He takes his time, but when started, he is direct...and I'll be damned again..., he did ask. It was a sincere request at that. Let's go with it.

"We have a choice for the evening. It can be at a restaurant or a simple meal at my place. Public or private.

Your choice. I can assure you that privacy still means safety."

"Safety? My God. This is the best line I've ever heard, and I've heard a lot of them.

Bill noted a blink, and he continued. "Yes, safety. I can imagine a lady with your beauty, and I mean that, gets a lot of propositions, proposals maybe, but I simply can't operate that way. This evening will be about you. In my place, where it's quiet, we can get to know one another without yelling over other people. So, here it is, I'm a good Italian cook, and you will be returned home properly."

"Bill, you're right. I have had my share of propositions, *if you only knew,* but I've never been asked in a manner as your proposal. *Proposal? When was the last time I used that word?* So, yes. Your place. What time?"

"I'll pick you up at 7:30? I have your address, and I know I can pick you up then and home in time for the ragu to be perfect. Dress is casual."

Glenda smiled as broadly as she had in many years. "7:30 it is. "

At 7:30, Bill parked his car in front of Glenda's condo. It was a small, well-kept home. Knocking on the door, it was opened immediately. Glenda was wearing a simple ensemble of a starched white blouse tucked into black chinos. Jewelry consisted of simple gold studs in her ear lobes and a tennis bracelet on her wrist. No rings. Her waist was highlighted with a Mexican themed engraved belt that was clasped by a large silver buckle. Shoes were simple loafers. Stunning.

The drive to Bill's place was a bit stiff. After all, it was their first date and a change from their normal professional relationship. When they arrived, Glenda saw a row of upscale condos that were larger than hers. Going into his home, Bill took her jacket, hung it up, and invited her to the bar separating his dining room and kitchen. In the background was playing an Italian singer who was accompanied by a guitar. No over production, just a simple tenor voice and soft Italian words. Glenda moved to its rhythm.

"You're a dancer?"

"I was once. I actually did back line gigs in the big hotels here."

"Once?"

"Yeah. It didn't take me long to figure out how little talent I had compared to the lead dancers. My God, those girls were so good, and they were just lead chorus girls. But, who's the singer? I've never heard a voice like that."

"He's a well-known singer in Naples, and those songs are folk tunes from the area. His Italian is a Neapolitan dialect, which, in my opinion, is where opera came from. I love their melodies...often melancholy...yet, never without hope."

"Well, I'm impressed. A connoisseur of Italian music. How, pray tell, did you come by this love?"

"My father was a career Army officer, and we spent a tour in Naples. I was in high school there..."

"An American high school?"

"Yes. American forces always bring their schools with them for the kids. Anyway, I fell in love with the whole scene there. One thing led to another, and I met some Italian kids who spoke little English and there I was living the *dolce vita,* the sweet life."

This guy is something. Here he brings a girl into his apartment and leads her into Italy. Yet, he's not bragging about who he is. He just told me simple facts. What else is with him: lawyer, Italian, pilot?

Dinner was served within minutes of their arrival. It started with a few appetizers of crackers, olives, cheeses, and salamis. Then came the pasta. It was a simple recipe of shrimp steeped in an olive oil sauce that was lightly touched with a bit of garlic. The accompanying bread was a sourdough that was scrumptious. This main course was then followed by a tossed salad. Desert was a tiramisu that floated on air. Last came espresso. Bill asked if Glenda wanted it straight or *corretto*.

"*Corretto?*"

"Á touch of grappa or Italian brandy. It makes all the difference in the world."

"After all this, how can a girl not have it *corretto*."

"Buono. Beve. Excellent, enjoy."

I'm impressed. He's putting on a show, but it's so...so real. He has been to Italy without being a snob. Food's worth a second helping anytime.

After dinner, Bill took Glenda to the living room. It was well appointed with comfortable easy chairs, sofa, and coffee table. Side lamps were scattered about. Glenda was escorted to one chair with Bill sitting opposite her on another chair. The singer continued his mournful tunes.

"This guy's not even trying to put on a move. What's next...or not?

Bill deftly turned the conversation over to Glenda. He got her talking about her childhood. Glenda relaxed back into her seat and recalled growing up on a ranch. "Yeah, I'm a cowgirl. My father was a working cowboy on a big Montana ranch. We never had much money, but we always ate. I learned to ride almost as soon as I could walk. Roundups were fun. Everyone running around chasing cattle, castrating them, pruning horns. Yeah. Good days. But winters. You can have them. The cold...not temperatures...cold. That was absolutely it. No other word: cold. But I did learn to ski there. One place was my favorite. Big Sky. Six thousand acres of terrain. I loved that spot."

When the conversation turned to Las Vegas, Glenda sighed, "No cold here. Skiing is available but without the cold. I came here to be warm. I had done some dancing in high school and college that got some gigs here. But as I said...so now I'm in event planning. Here's my card if you want to reach me."

"What did you study in college?"

"Business, What else? With a minor in American history. We westerners have a rowdy history that's fun to study."

Now Bill was thinking. *No wonder Glenda is such a good pilot. Riding horses, dancing, hard work,,,yeah...it all fits. She's also an interesting storyteller. She seems to be enjoying herself here. Not looking for glamour as other girls I've dated.*

The evening went on till late when Bill looked at his watch. "Ooops. I'm sorry but look at the time. You're a working girl who has a busy schedule tomorrow. I know I do. That politician I defended is at it again. I really ought to charge him lower volume rates. God knows, he's a steady customer."

Glenda looked at her wrist in an unconscious glance at a forgotten watch. "Bill, I've really enjoyed myself. You did your deed. We had a quiet evening with a lovely dinner. Let's do this again."

Hot dog!

On the way home, they promised to check their schedules for other evenings. Perhaps directly after flying. When Glenda's doorstep was reached, Bill simply shook her hand and gave a light kiss on the cheek. With thanks, he waited for Glenda to be safely inside and then returned to his car.

Glenda had a strange thought. *He wasn't kidding. I couldn't have been safer in a nunnery. Well, girl, let's see where this all goes.*

Chapter 13
A Curious Friendship

Glenda finished her flying lessons, and as she said in the beginning, she was happy flying around the flagpole. She was renting a cheaper Cessna 150 by the hour. The aircraft was similar to Bill's bird, so she had no difficulty adjusting to it. Sometimes she'd take a short cross-country trip to some remote part of Nevada, get a breath of fresh air, and return. Nothing complicated. Still, Bill felt satisfied about his instruction. It enabled Glenda's goal.

Bill was also happy to be done with Glenda as a student. He enjoyed her personal company, which created different dynamics that felt stiff when she was his employer as a student. Glenda's licensed flying now took over with him on a social basis. They would take his Cessna wherever they wished and for as long as they wanted. Occasionally, they would fly to some other city, enjoy a dinner, stay overnight, and return home the next day. To Glenda's surprise, Bill would insist on separate rooms. It wasn't a big deal; it was just the way it was.

Glenda was curious, as most people are, about Bill's profession as a defense attorney. Bill was open to any questions she had.

"Yeah, I get a lot of questions like yours. Have I sprung a guilty person, one I knew was guilty? Yes, one was even a professional hitman. He made no bones about it. Believe it or not, after he was released from trial custody he hired me as a counselor."

"Why so? He was free. What more did he want?"

"He knew I had been a prosecutor and understood police investigation methods, so I told him. He said he was going to review his planning methods during future executions,"

"How awful."

Bill smiled and said "Not really. He was a professional. It was a business with him. He wasn't psychotic, just a man doing a job."

Bill waited for Glenda to absorb this. Her face showed consternation at the thought of a job. After a bit, he continued. "I remember when I was in Italy, we lived in a community that was sort of gated. That is, the property manager had an office by the entrance, One day, as his grandson told the story, two men came in and asked if 'Nono's name was Giuseppe. When he replied *si'*, the second man took out a photo, looked at it and compared it to *Nono,* and agreed they had their target.' With that they drew their pistols and shot his grandfather, point blank. Note, they didn't shot the grandson, whom they knew would be a witness. He wasn't in their contract."

"My God. Why the assassination?"

"Who knows. Perhaps he didn't pay his quote, taxes, unquote, that is, protection money. By the way, I lived in that community and saw the bullet holes."

A long silent pause until Bill said, "It was just business."

"And you would have defended them if they had been caught."

"Yep. Just business. I won't go into details, but I also defended a child molester. Him I didn't like, but it was a job."

Bill could see how Glenda was having a hard time accepting all this. He then went on. "Glenda, our legal processes are very old, dating back to medieval England when King John signed the Magna Carta. That was a significant occasion because it meant that even kings had to live within the law. Dictators have ever since tried to evade that precedent...Hitler and Stalin come to mind.

We're even seeing it here in our country with ICE raids on illegal aliens. I saw a clip recently where a mother was sitting in her car with her daughter in a quiet neighborhood when a couple of agents in civilian clothes, wearing masks, showing no identification, broke her window and dragged her out. No normal police processes. Just hauled her away like the Gestapo did with Jews. If she had been armed, I believe she had the right to shoot in self-defense. I would have defended her pro bono. But, as it was, she was dragged away never to be seen again leaving a confused child behind. Here is where our Constitutional processes were meant to serve the public."

"I see your point, but it is a paradox isn't it?"

"Yes it is. King Arthur in the musical, *Camelot,* summarized it well when he cried, 'Might for right.'"

On another date, the conversation turned to police brutality. Glenda asked, "You were a prosecutor. What about it?"

Bill didn't hesitate. "Yes, it does exist. Look at the Black Lives Matter cause. I've already talked about ICE. They're simply thugs. I wouldn't defend one on a bet. But, generally, I've found most policemen are dedicated to their work while being underpaid, and facing serious emotional issues,"

"Emotional issues?"

"Yep. Police and soldiers have a lot in common. Both wear uniforms. Both are required to control land against hostile people. Both are armed and required to kill on a moment's notice. Good police forces work hard to train their officers on avoiding such confrontations and what to do if necessary. Make a wrong decision and it's off to prison."

Glenda nodded at that, so Bill continued. "My father fought in Viet Nam and came back to a hostile country where soldiers were hated as baby-rapers. Thank

God that's no longer the case for them, but it truly is for cops. You know that's true."

Glenda nodded silently as Bill mused, "Yeah, and just like G.I.'s, they suffer from PTSD. You'd be surprised how many 'eat their gun' after retiring. No different from the thousands of young men and women who eat theirs after returning home. The military is trying to deal with this syndrome, but it's a hard game to play. Solders or cops having to kill people and then telling them to be nice at home."

Their last conversation on these morbid topics was when Glenda asked what Bill's toughest case was. He answered simply, "Putting my wife in prison."

"What!??"

"You asked,"

"Bill, I figured out a long time ago that you're a straight arrow. But this is really hard-nosed. Remind me not to become your bride."

"Keep straight and you'll have a wonderful husband."

"Well, let's keep the chapel bells quiet for a while. I was married once and not again."

"Me too."

"But seriously, what about your wife? Is she still there?"

"Yes, she is and let me tell you this story. It's a wonderful one."

"I'll bet."

"You'd lose,"

Bill then described his marriage and its need for money. Defense litigation offered more of it. But then Virginia began whining about lost friends and making up for them by drinking. One night, a child died. His story then went on through the trial and how Bill found himself in the center of everything. The law, the Constitution, all that was set to the side. What was the moral thing for Bill to do?

He recited almost verbatim his speech about Viginia's need for prison. "She got 20 years."

By now, Glenda was crying. "Bill, frankly, I've known a lot of men, but your story is one for the records. It's a real tragedy that goes beyond any soap opera I've ever heard."

Bill was able to bring the tragedy to a happier end. He related how Virginia is working to sober up and start a new life that dealt with drunkenness. "She's now got a support group going in prison. She expects to continue with that line of work upon her parole."

"Parole?"

"Yep. That was a stipulation in my plea. If Virginia got her act together, then I'd support her parole. Well, she has done that in spades, and I'm proud of her. We'll never remarry. That can't happen. We're two different people from what we were then. But I can be her advocate."

Glenda was dumbfounded, *Damn, Sam. Every time I turn around, this guy blows me away. Here I am, a beautiful woman who attracts men like flies, and he doesn't move. He talks about law, good and bad, right and wrong, and doing business. Then he throws his wife into the clink. This guy's got more sides than a prism and is throwing light everywhere. I can't keep up with his kaleidoscope of sides. They're always changing.*

Bill crept into Glenda's thoughts as she heard him tell her how he'd like her to meet his kids. *And now he wants me to meet his kids. What is this? I haven't talked to kids other than my nephew for years. What would I say to them? Hi, I'm your father's best bud? Yeah, I'm sure they'd believe that, but damn, it's true.*

Life went on for Bill and Glenda. When they had time, they spent it together. Actually, they did have a fair amount of it, so they had opportunities for flying to new places. Ski trips to new resorts. Visiting cities not seen before. Laughing at jokes heard three times over. But romance. Not a chance and it began to irk Glenda. After all, she was a good-looking woman. Enough men had told her so and spent money doing so. *What was with this guy? Is he made of stone?*

Finally, it boiled over. Bill was giving Glenda her usual goodnight kiss when she grabbed him and gave him a tongue shower. Pulling back, Bill exclaimed, "Whoa, what's this?"

"Bill. Are you a stone? I have been dropping hints of enjoying more than friendship. It's not often that I do so, in fact, almost never. You know why? You are a man of your word, you never push, but damn man, do I have spinach on my teeth?"

Bill took her back to her living room and sat her down. His demeanor would have done a prosecutor justice for being so cold.

He said, "I was wondering when this would come up."

Glenda retorted about nothing coming up in his pants, Bill smiled and replied, "Not that he didn't want to," Then he looked carefully at Glenda and asked, "Do you really want to know the truth?"

"Perjury ain't what I'm about Your Honor."

Bill took a deep breath and said evenly, "Because you're a call girl."

Glenda looked like she had been shot. Her eyes widened into white orbs. Her back stiffened as her hand shot up to her face. "So, you think I'm a slut?"

"Not at all. To the contrary. I think about you every day wondering how I can bring happiness to you. Does that sound like I'm a slut hound?"

"Nooo. OK then. How did you find out?"

"You forget my profession. I get paid by ferreting facts and presenting them to juries. Well, I have seen your work at the office. You're not the boss but a worker-bee. You're being paid well because you're good at your job but not that much to afford flight lessons. You never indicated any other line of work so what was there? Call girl? This is Las Vegas where it's legal. Let me see says I. Click, click, and the answer was there. You're registered. Aha! There are your flight lessons."

Glenda started to get angry now. "So, what else Sherlock?"

"I never said anything because it wasn't my business, but occasionally I've had to meet clients in bars, and not on a few occasions there you were with an older, always older, gentlemen who could afford your time. Anyway, you always looked gorgeous. Drop dead gorgeous. They weren't just social occasions with your uncles."

"So now what? You know what I do. You pulled back from my tongue shower like I was infected. Drop me or hang me on a wall as if I'm a trophy?"

Bill was becoming sad now. Glenda was steamed. He didn't like it that she was. *I really like her. I could love her if I let myself. What to say now?*

"OK, Glenda. Let's start from the beginning. We both like money. It ruined my first marriage and sent a good woman to prison over it. You like it as well. It pays for your flying. Sex is your business that pays for everything."

"And I'm good at it. I bring satisfaction to my clients like you spring yours from jail."

"Yes you are, and yes, I spring guys. But between us, do we want money or love?"

"What do you mean?"

"You answer that question. Sex generates emotions unless it's for sale. Then it's a business. We love flying but frankly it was hard being a professional when I was teaching you. Our lives depended on my being coldly *on safe* when we were together then. When you got your license, I was relieved. Now we could enjoy ourselves and our flying."

"Come on, Bill. Stop beating around the bush. Do you want me or not?"

"Glenda, more than you can possibly imagine, and when you're done with your job, you'll find out how good I really am. Without bragging, I'm good. Why? Because it'll be about you. I'll take you to the stars. But, like flying, I can't mix business and pleasure. You do what you need to do, and I'll wait."

"You mean you don't care what I do professionally?"

"Neither one of us are saints. Our professions have us dealing with shades and shadows. That doesn't mean we have to be depraved devils. It does mean, however, we have to be careful to keep things straight. Simply put, Virginia and I wanted money. We got it. It destroyed us. I'm not going to let that happen with us. It's that simple."

"You mean, we don't get laid until I quit the business?"

"That's it. When you're out, we can fuck and fly."

"Well, that's blunt. *You always have been so.* Meanwhile, you're willing to wait?"

"I didn't stop teaching you how to fly. It was hard, but I done it. Now with your license, we fly together."

Glenda stood up, walked around in circles, sat down, got up, poured a cup of coffee, dumped it out, came back, and sat down. Finally, she said, "My mama always told me men were like cattle. You rope 'em, ride 'em, and brand 'em, but you never let them run wild. They'll leave you in the dust. Bill, so what the hell am I gonna do with you: rope, ride, or brand?"

"You've roped me and are riding me but you ain't never gonna brand me until we get our lives together. That includes me. I got changes to make. Otherwise, we'll fail each other just like I have done before."

"Well sonny, keep your ass tight 'cause one day it'll be branded. And if that ain't a stupid marriage proposal...really, I never dreamed I'd be making it to anyone. No brand was gonna be on my ass, but there it is, all ready for you cowboy."

Bill reached out and took Glenda in his arms and gave her a big kiss. It wasn't a shower but gentle and warm. It lingered on Glenda's lips like a ray of sunshine. He then said, "My branding iron's hot whenever you're ready."

"It'll be sooner than later flyboy."

Chapter 14
A Union

And so, the defender and the call girl were engaged. It hadn't been given as a romantic proposal, but it was real. The parties had been married before, and neither had ever expected to repeat that error. But here they were: a handsome couple approaching middle age who were trying to figure what made life tick between them.

They both admitted to one another that money had been a driving force in their lives. It certainly destroyed Bill's marriage and while Glenda didn't comment broadly about the cause of her divorce, money was clearly a part of it. That issue became understood as a matter of contention. What was enough? How was it to be used? What problems could it cause?

Answering these questions showed another issue to be addressed. Honesty. Had they been honest with their previous partners? Hard question. The answer came up while looking in their mirrors. Did they like the person they saw staring back at them? Glenda said it first. The answer was no. More surprisingly, she saw an urgent need for time to find out who she did like. Bill agreed that was true for him as well, so they both went their separate ways to different counsellors.

Glenda tried out several counsellors, but none clicked with her. They all wanted to say, "I see" and ask if she loved her father. Ugh! How sick. Of course she did. but not what was being intimated. Finally, with the fourth person, a woman, Glenda felt calm, relaxed, and that she was being heard.

Carolyn Jacobs was her name. She was about fifty, married, and short. A bit stocky to tell the truth. Her hair was gray and sometimes a bit frazzled. She wore suits, but they were from the nineties in style. Obviously, she didn't waste money on fashion. Once bought, good enough until worn out. What amazed Glenda was her ability to listen quietly and then ask the most perceptive questions that related directly to what was on Glenda's mind. *This gal can read my mind before I'm even aware of it. I never thought of that. I gotta dig into it.*

It took her some time to dig into her past. She read several books that her counselor suggested and answered the questions that ended each chapter. As she progressed, her answers were presented for discussion. Eventually, Glenda started to compose her answers and give them to Carolyn who took them like a schoolteacher. When returned, they were covered with notes indicating reactions and questions. What she liked, she added smileys . What she didn't like came back with question marks. Either way, Glenda knew her hidden thoughts were carefully read. Not criticized but read. *Such a difference.*

Eventually, it came out that she never felt loved by anyone. Further, it seemed her mother didn't like herself. "Why" would always be an eternal question. No one can fathom a past generation. Her father was nice enough but like many fathers, left home duties to mothers, while he brought home the bread. So, he never became involved, and the ensuring war became one between daughter and mother.

High school was a time of promiscuous experimentation. Did Johnny love her? He took her to bed, but anything else? Nope. Next boy. Nope. Nope, nope, nope until Glenda began to think that men couldn't love her either.

"So, Mom doesn't love me, and no one else does either. More to the point, Mom just checked to see if I was pregnant or not. She actually tracked my periods on a calendar. Heaven forbid that I was a day late. Not that she cared about any baby, but what would the neighbor's say?

"Well, I could see I'm becoming beautiful, and men liked that. So, if they can't love me, then they can pay money to imagine they're with Rita Hayworth for a night. The next morning, to quote Rita Hayworth, 'Men go to bed with *Gilda*, but wake up with me.'" Still, the money was good, and her events planning job gave her many opportunities to practice her profession.

About her marriage, it was one made in hell. For once, she thought there might be love. But he was a pimp. No two ways about it. "In fact he got me started as a call girl. When he first brought it up, he pointed out that I was good in bed, and why not make some money from it? Sounded good until I learned that my fees were supporting his cocaine habit. That was expensive. So next was a Las Vegas divorce court. If I'm earning the money, then it's not gonna go up his nose."

What about Bill was Carolyn's next question. Glenda, after much evasion, admitted she didn't know. "He's a great guy. He always treats me like Gilda, but you know, he's yet to take me to bed. He said sex and money don't go with sex and love. And he's right. It doesn't. So now I'm not taking him on. It's just hard to undo 20 years of playing roles. I'm lost, and here I am wondering where to go."

Carolyn replied, "Will he wait?"

"I hope so, and I try to believe so. But it's hard to believe he's as real as he seems to be. I just can't bear the thought of him seeing me as Rita Hayworth in the morning. But he always says I have just one image and that puts movie stars to shame."

"Let me think about that one,"

"Thank you."

A couple of sessions later, Carolyn asked, "Glenda, you're lost because you're making the problem too tough. The question is simple."

"Simple?"

"Yeah, really. Do you love him?"

"Yes, of course."

"Enough to get out of the trade? Take a chance on him? You might get hurt again, but a worse hurt would be to lose a great guy."

"So either take him up on his proposed standard or leave him alone?"

"That's about it. Fish or cut bait."

Several more counseling sessions later, Glenda said simply, "I'm out."

Bill didn't have any problem finding a counselor that he could trust. He simply called the local VA office and asked for a name. Jeremy James, or as he asked, "JJ." JJ was about Bill's age, a soldier who got his commission through The Citadel in Charleston, SC. Like Bill, he had seen combat. One tour was in Iraq and the others in Afghanistan. By luck, they actually had some acquaintances in common. One problem kept him from making a career of the Army. He was missing an arm. Bill knew not to ask questions about it. If JJ wanted to mention it, he would.

Their sessions started out as many contacts between veterans do. War stories. They are the essence of a soldier's past. Stories come out that are never mentioned to anyone...not even to wives. After finishing one such story, Bill concluded by saying, "That's something I never told to Virginia, nor would I expect to do so to Glenda. She's had a tough enough life, she hasn't gone into details, but I can read between the lines."

JJ just nodded. He had his own stories. He let Bill continue with his life.

"I was an Army brat. My father was a grunt who fought three tours in Viet Nam. He caught Agent Orange and died at an early age. He only had 19 years in when he was medically retired. Shortly after his death my mother met another soldier and married him. You know, wives are as much warriors as their men are. Let no one ever say otherwise, good military wives serve.

"I knew my father well enough for him to teach me character. He truly believed in the Honor Code. I always accepted it while growing up but only when I was in Afghanistan leading a platoon of "leg infantry" grunts did I understand it. You know. G.I.'s gripe, piss and moan, getting dirty, always hungry, seeing horrors, and giving love."

JJ noted that comment into his notes. *Love, a big thing with Bill.*

Seeing JJ note his words, Bill sat back as though this was the first time he had considered them. "Yeah, love. They'll sacrifice their lives for their buddies. You've seen it I know."

Bill just nodded in agreement. He had his own memories.

"So, when I was their leader, I saw why the Honor Code was so important. These guys didn't have much other than their lives, and they were important. If they were to give them, it had better be for something important. Bull shitting them just wouldn't fly. Lie to them, you're dead the next day,"

"So, honesty is important."

"Damn right it is. You know, in my profession, I've seen guys perjure themselves without telling a lie. They were as crooked as a dog's hind leg. But I never saw G.I.'s lie to one another...maybe a civilian...but to each other, never. They'd give their lives for each other but never a lie."

"So, what does this mean to you about Glenda?"

"She'd damn well better not be untruthful, Say the worst honestly, no BS, and I'll deal with it. That was Virginia's problem. She was unhappy but wouldn't confide why. Maybe she didn't trust me...or herself. Whatever, she didn't or couldn't talk to me."

"So, you left her."

"Yeah, simple enough. I couldn't live with the fog we were in. I needed her to get to her points. Maybe if she did, then I wouldn't have left her. Now, it's too late. I sent her to prison where she's making amends for which I'm really proud. She's getting her life in order, and for that, I'll support her. Not remarry her. Too many things have gone on in both of our lives. We're better off apart but as, I hope, I think, true friends."

"Can you say that about Glenda?"

"I hope so. I want to believe so."

"What can she do to prove herself?"

Bill looked at the ceiling for a long time. Then he scratched himself. Took a sip of coffee. Finally, he said, "You know, that's a damn good question. I'm smart enough to know that she needs to convince me but also I have to do something...wait perhaps...I don't know. But if I screw it up with unreasonable expectations, I'll be as bad as anyone."

"Tough place to be."

"Yeah, it is. So far, I do have reason for hope. We've talked some about our past...how I sent Virginia to prison and she about her call girl past. That resulted in our getting engaged, believe it or not."

"Then, if I may make a suggestion, go with your gut. You two have discovered the good, the bad, and the ugly about each other. You've done so with candor, and so far, still wanting to talk...to be open...completely open. Just practice doing that,

Bill smiled. *Yeah, JJ's right.* "Yeah, but I need to know that when, note what I said, when, I can come back and discuss things with you before I blunder ahead. Someone needs to keep me straight and I doubt that person is me."

JJ agreed by saying how he also has heard people lying to everyone and worst of all themselves. "Your father's Honor Code will do you OK. Trust me on this, but yes, practice on me before you try something new on Glenda,"

And talk they did. Once they started, it surprised both Bill and Glenda how easy it could be. Glenda's confession that she left the business was surprisingly easy. As she did, her heart got lighter. Bill then took her into his arms. Glenda felt loved for the first time in her life. She wasn't Gilda anymore. She was Glenda, and it was good.

Not every day was easy. They realized that wasn't possible. Two middle-aged people trying to start a new life together. Lots of junk stood in the way. But they talked.

The first thing they settled were the finances. Amazingly, that proved to be the easiest part of their new relationship. They set up a joint checking account to which both contributed money for mutual expenses. It was understood that big items would be discussed and then money put into the joint account. Getting to that point meant they had to reveal their financial situations. How much did they have in savings and investments? What were their financial obligations? What big expenses did they have? On this latter issue, Bill was better off than Glenda. She liked to fly, and that cost money. So, it became a subject of discussion.

"OK, Glenda. You've left your profession, and you now rely on your events planning job. From what you've told me; it pretty well covers your daily living expenses with just a bit left over for savings. Flying costs money. The question is how."

Groaning, Glenda agreed. "Right on all counts."

"So, how about getting a commercial license? I can teach the exam to you. You have the flying skills. It'll be an easy thing to get. Later on, you can get your instrument and multi-engine ratings that'll let you fly more aircraft at night and bad weather,"

"And what do I get with it?"

"You can fly on other people's money and when you're not, you can deduct the costs off your income tax as enhancing professional proficiency."

"Aaah. Talk more trash to me honey tongue."

"Someone wants a plane ferried. You fly it at a charge plus expenses for your return home. Another person needs a package delivered. You deliver it."

"And you'll promote my business?"

"Your biggest fan."

"I'm in."

Another issue was where to live: your place, my place, or our place. The market was weakening, and Glenda didn't believe she could make money from the sale of her place.

"Rent it out and move in with me."

"You lecher, you. I know your wily ways."

"But I'm right."

"Sadly, yes."

"So, put your house up for rent and keep the rental fees. It also gives you another tax deduction."

"Your mother just covered you with honey didn't she?"

"That she did. Want a lick?"

The only thing that upset Bill was when Glenda held up on talking about something. The subject wasn't important for him. It often seemed to be petty to him. But as he said, "Glenda, I can deal with anything but silence. It destroyed one marriage, and I'll be damned if I go into another one that features silence."

That sort of ultimatum was not what Glenda was used to. Most of her clients had had secrets. They came with the profession, and she wasn't accustomed to someone wanting to air them out. Bill seemingly had none. Any question that Glenda was sure would bring a silent pause never happened. Bill was as open as a book.

This experience became a subject of discussion with Carolyn. Glenda exclaimed, "He's impossible. He's the easiest man I've ever known but try to dodge a bullet and he goes nuts."

"And you've never confronted this type of man before?"

"Impossible. Think about it. Most of my clients were middle-aged married men. That means by definition they were liars. Liars to me, their wives, and themselves. So along comes honest Bill. He's a new one for me."

"And how do you think you want to handle him?"

Glenda took a deep breath here. Handle honesty? What a question. Never in her life was she ever hampered by that attitude. Not once. Never. *But I'm stuck with a guy whose life revolves around it. If he says something, he means it*. With a shaky voice, she asked, "Trust?"

"And what does that mean to you?"

"For the life of me, I don't know. I've never trusted anyone in my life. They've all let me down in one way or another."

"Well, you have made agreements about your finances. We've talked about them. Do you trust those agreements?"

"Yes. I have to."

"Because?"

"I've made financial agreements."

"Glenda, you've answered your own question. Giving trust to him about finances is a big step. We do it all the time with business dealings. Most of your Johns paid you didn't they?"

"Yes."

"So, to that extent you trusted them. Stiff you once, and they never see you again. Right?"

"There's your trust. Do right and I'll come back. Do me dirt and I'm gone."

"The same for Bill?"

"The same for Bill."

With this advice, Glenda got a new look at the relationship she was developing. *What am I seeing? So far, everything Bill has agreed to do, he's done. He's never lied to me. I know I believe what he says. That doesn't mean I always agree, but I know he believes what he says is right. We'll see how he reacts when contradicted. I know one thing about him...don't lie and don't dodge bullets. That's a real no, no for him.*

A real no-no. Glenda sat up in the middle of the night. She stared into the dark until a 1000-watt light lit up in her head. It almost blinded her. She could trust that no-no. She knew this as well as she knew the back of her hand. At that point, the foundation of trust was laid within her. *Just have courage to live with it. Scary but wow, just wow...*

With that thought, Glenda knew she loved her man...completely, wholly. It was a scary feeling. It meant she was opening herself to being wounded. Wounds hurt. She knew that pain well. But this strange emotion, love, drove her impulsively forward. The thought of losing Bill became more painful than any rejection she had ever known. She was hooked.

Bill quickly saw this change in her. It came so fast and hard, it scared him. Virginia acquiesced in his marriage proposal to her. Convenient, warm, but passionate...nooo. That word, passionate, didn't enter Virginia's acceptance.

The difference showed in their lovemaking. Chastity no longer satisfied Bill. He had become convinced with Glenda's departure from her profession. With that he asked her to stay over for the night. Glenda almost lost her teeth.

"Bill, did I hear you right? Stay overnight for breakfast tomorrow morning?"

"Yep."

"Have I gotten rid of spinach from my teeth."

"In a way, yes. Now that they're clean, I want to stay permanently with you, day and night."

"Now there's a romantic picture. Spinach flying out the window. But, yes, I'm stunned after all this time, but yes." Impishly, she said, "I was beginning to think you had taken vows of chastity."

"I earn my living with words, but chastity was never in my vocabulary. Trust me on that."

And trust she did. For someone with as much experience bedding men as Glenda had, their first nights were stiff. Awkward perhaps was a better word. Bedding a man, she loved and respected. *This is a new one for me. Please God, don't let me blow this one away.*

As the days passed in talking, exchanging trust, and becoming acquainted with each other's bodies, the love became better. Bill proved himself good for his word. He was because he focused on Glenda's needs. Patience was his byword until one night a hurricane passed between them. All of her repressed senses, forgotten expectations, came out. Blasts, explosions, bombshells, it was awesome...almost frightening.

Bill sought out JJ the next day. "What happened last night, JJ, was beyond belief. Never in all my born days have I ever experienced anything that came even close to what we experienced."

"I noticed your past tense."

"Past tense?" Then Bill caught JJ's innuendo and laughed. "Yep, in all my life. I didn't cheat on Virginia, but I wasn't a priest after our divorce. I've had my practice. But, yeah, this was in outer space."

"So, she loves you?"

"She always has...huh!..but now she's opened a closed door. Perhaps we both have."

"You can bet on it. Just keep on truckin' my boy."

JJ was full of smiles, and Bill just glowed.

With a lot of big issues on the road to solutions, the couple started to take steps towards a union. Glenda moved into Bill's house and placed her goods into storage for later decisions as to what to do with them. This would entail discussions as to what goods Bill is willing to part with in order to make room for Glenda's goods. At any rate, she was saving housing costs by renting her house and sharing costs with Bill.

Learning to live together was a task. Sometimes it was a funny experience; other times it was exasperating. For example, Glenda liked to clean dishes immediately, while Bill preferred to stack dirty dishes where they would sit until he felt like washing them. Bill had a cat named Kitty who was jealous of Glenda. She glowered whenever she found them in bed. Bill explained how this was a change from being the queen bee of the bedstead. "Tough, Kitty. A new girl is in town," replied Glenda.

Glenda succeeded in passing her commercial flight exam. As Bill promised, it was not particularly difficult. Her flight skills were well up to standards, and Bill prepared her well for the written exam. With this to offer, and through Bill's connections, she started to get paid flight jobs. It wasn't much, but anything to defray flying hour costs was a help. She also kept records for income tax purposes. With this money, and some financial help from Bill, she started instrument flight lessons from Jim Jensen.

Glenda asked, "Why pay money to Jim when Bill was an instructor?" He replied that Jim was a better instructor and two, he was too close to Glenda to have the distance needed to teach flying. "Old axiom, never teach your wife to drive. It'll never work. However, to help you along I have ordered a flight simulator where you can practice on the ground safely. You'll also find later on it can be used for learning new aircraft and flying into new airports. It's really a cool thing, and if saves your life just once, it'll be worth twice what I paid for it."

"Just twice? How about three times?"

"Name your price, it'll be worth it."

Otherwise, life together flowed on from the enjoyment of each other's company. Short flights for dinner or skiing or just flying were frequent. Bill did inform Virginia, her parents, and their children of his new life. Virginia's reply was surprising.

Dear Bill,

I just got your letter about Glenda. I'm torn. On one hand, I'm happy for the two of you. But when I think of what we had, I'm sad. Our marriage had the potential for joy. We threw it away. In that regard, I must accept responsibility for my actions. I have been forgiven by Jessie's family, but it's hard for me to forgive myself. If forgiveness is to be obtained, it'll have to be through atonement.

To that end, as you know, I have started a support group for imprisoned women who have destroyed their lives through selfish actions. Eventually, with your support and that of the Lord, I'll be paroled. When that happens, I will be working to expand the experiences I've gained here in a civil community.

So, while our lives have gone in different directions, I can never forget what you proposed to the judge. It gives me hope knowing you're there supporting my efforts. Thanks are not enough, but they are heartfelt.

Sincerely,

Virginia

Glenda read the letter and said little to Bill. She could only say that it was a tragedy that she needs to reflect on in her heart. *I also understand better who you are Bill. Although you were innocent in the girl's death, you were involved. Now I can feel what you were trying to say when you told me how you imprisoned your wife. What a profound tragedy. I can also understand your standards for honesty. This would have been something to hide for most people.*

Bill didn't press. He had learned from JJ how silence doesn't always mean hiding. Truths often need to be coaxed out from fear. He was willing to wait for Glenda to come out from her heart's shelter. *This has been tough for Glenda to take but she's been strong. She takes these things on the chin and carries on. She doesn't cave in. That's a real test of integrity. So, let her have her space. What she has to say will eventually come out.*

Finally, wedding bells began to ring. A date was set at the Chapel of Crystals. Bill sent out invitations to his kids and Virginia's parents. Susan and George agreed to come. They were curious about Glenda, and Susan was dying to be a flower girl. It was sooo romantic, George said OK to being Bill's ring bearer, but he wanted to fly. However, their grandparents passed with a courteous note and well wishes. Jim Jensen, JJ, and Carolyn were invited guests. A private room at a nice restaurant was rented for the after-ceremony party.

True to custom, Glenda kicked Bill out of the house 24 hours before the ceremony. "It's bad luck, and I've had enough of that." Bill boarded at Jim's place. On the day, Bill saw it was worth the wait. They met in the anteroom of the chapel ready to walk down the aisle. Bill wore a blue suit, white shirt, and red tie. His shoes were spit-shined to a mirror finish. Glenda was simply gorgeous in a bright, off the shoulder dress. It was cinched tightly at the waist. Its rose color set off her hair and complexion perfectly. Besides, as she said, "Roses are for love."

When the first chords of the wedding march chimed, Bill took Glenda's arm and marched her to the altar. The officiant, Mac Smith, was a fatherly man. He was about sixty, slightly round, and smiled with bright blue eyes. His voice, an announcer's baritone, said, "Gentle people, we are gathered here..."

After the ceremony, the party went to a restaurant by taxi. Champagne would be in abundance, and Bill wanted everyone to enjoy themselves. No private cars were allowed before, during, or after the party. They would all be taxied home.

The meal was everyone's choice from the menu. For this sized party, and catering to everyone's taste, menu choice was easiest. The cake, however, was a real bridal treat. It was cut in a traditional manner by the wedding couple with small pieces stuffed into each other's mouth.

Susan loved being Glenda's flower girl, and she hung on to her. Everywhere Glenda went, Susan was sure to follow. She just adored her new stepmother. Glenda responded with joy. As she told Bill later, "She just blows me away. I never dreamed I could be so caught up with a youngster."

Bill understood and thought, *Maybe your mother never got caught up with youngsters*. He said, "Here's a youngster who wants to get caught up with you."

With that, the couple knew one another biblically.

Chapter 15
A New Life

In the months following their wedding, Bill and Glenda became busy with their marriage. It was one thing to make decisions while living apart; it was another thing to do so while living together. Not that there were earthquakes. They had done a lot of work beforehand to learn about each other and how to talk about things. Furniture in Bill's old home now had to be rearranged to accommodate their house. Kitty Cat had to learn about this new female in her house.

Both Bill and Glenda continued to visit their counselors. Each had ghosts from past lives that needed to be confronted. Both were dedicated not to repeat past mistakes. It was a new marriage, and new mistakes were called for.

Bill and JJ continued to deal with communication. Bill's position was having an open window where everything could be seen. Being patient with Glenda's ghosts took time. Was Virginia given enough time? It was a question that haunted him. But he was seeing how patience brought progress.

"JJ, I have to say things are going well. I find myself surprised by things."

"How so?"

"Well, this marriage is like an artichoke."

"Artichoke?"

"Yeah, artichoke. You know how their leaves are hard and bitter?"

"Yes."

"Well, as you peel them back, each new layer is sweeter than the one before."

"Nice metaphor for exploration. But you're right. Just remember, these first discoveries are just the first of an eternal search each bringing forth new insights. When a couple quits looking is when they need me. But, Bill, a word of caution. Be patient. Not every discovery comes easily. Don't pull the leaves before they're ripe."

Glenda had other issues.

"Carolyn, I'm truly happy. For the first time in my life, I'm happy. Bill is proving to be a man whom I can trust. His demand for no secrets has been hard for me after living a lifetime of filling moats around my castle. But I'm draining them."

"Wonderful. Tell me more."

"Well, not every discussion is a UN meeting. Most of it is nickel and dime, but it accumulates. Where should we put this chair? Who needs the airplane today? What needs to be budgeted? Discussions like this are open. There are times where continued negotiations are needed. Disagreements arise but we aren't afraid. At least I'm not. I'm not...anymore. What a wonderful feeling."

"Sounds normal to me, but practice does make perfect. There is one thing, however, that I need to clear up in my head."

Now Carolyn sat up a bit straighter and held her pencil a bit closer to her notebook. "Yes?"

"It's babies."

"You're pregnant?"

"No and getting so isn't the problem. Deciding whether to get pregnant is the question. Obviously, I don't want to surprise Bill with something this big. That would destroy the confidence we're building in each other."

Carolyn nodded appreciatively and then waved her hand for Glenda to continue. She did. "First, do I want babies? I'm pushing 40, and that's a late start. I've never had any urge for them probably because there was never any love in my home. Being a loving mother never occurred to me and especially so given the men I knew. None of them would have wanted a baby. Their wives had them, and that was enough for them.”

Carolyn murmured, “So the years went by.” This was a statement and absolutely not a question. Glenda nodded absently.

“Yes. You’re right. Now I’m married and in a loving home. Having a baby wouldn’t raise a public eyebrow.”

“But, what about your eyebrows and those of Bill’s?”

“Bill, I’m certain would accept his responsibilities. That’s the sort of guy he is. Would he like it? Uhhh, that might be another question that I really don’t want to make him answer.”

Glenda paused here to gather her thoughts while Carolyn waited until finally, she asked, “Glenda, has Bill indicated a desire for kids?”

“No. Not at all. He’s so funny. He doesn’t say anything, but it’s obvious how he’s trying to be patient with me. He wants an open door between us, yet he knows he may have blown it with Virginia. He doesn’t want that to happen twice. He’s so cute.”

Glenda giggled at the image then continued. “All this wouldn’t have come up if I hadn’t met Susan, his daughter. Children simply weren’t part of my life. Then here comes a young girl who’s just fallen in love with me...and to tell the truth...I love her too. We exchange texts every day. It’s sad in a way that this is so.”

“Sad? How so?”

“Well, Virginia pushed Susan out of any relationship with her father. Then she gets thrown in the clink. Now where is this young girl? Her grandparents, who seem to be very loving and caring. But they’re an older generation. Is that the same as a parent generation raising a daughter? I don’t know. However, I have no intention of disturbing her grandparents’ lives with her. That would not be fair to anyone, least of all to the people who have accepted two children under forced conditions, and who are doing a good job."

Carolyn offered a suggestion. "You're right, and congratulations on being so perceptive. But you can be a favorite aunt."

Glenda brightened up at that idea as Carolyn continued, "Yes, favorite aunt. You know, under the best of circumstances, children and parents have secrets. Adults come to me with problems. Children seek out favorite aunts for similar reasons. Listen to her. Let her prattle on. Let her discover her life through all the upcoming changes that she will be enduring through her teen years. It's a tough time for kids, and favorite aunts are a big help."

Glenda nodded wistfully. "I wish I had had a favorite aunt."

"Here's the bottom line. Neither you nor Bill are ready to have kids. If you did, you'd be pregnant by now. That decision to have some may never come, and at your age, don't be stupid. If you have kids it should be because you really want to have them...I mean really with a capital R. You've not indicated that desire, but you are responding as a favorite aunt role. So enjoy it, and then in the future, if you and Bill want a child, then have one, but not before. Push it, and you might raise another Glenda."

Glenda winced at that thought. *No, under no circumstances do I want to create another Glenda. What I went through I wouldn't wish onto my worst enemy...never being loved. Now I've got it. I ain't letting it go.*

Good counselors are a godsend. Glenda continued with her flying and eventually got all of her licenses and started flying more commercial flights. Bill continued his teaching and resumed his defense work.

Then, as happens in all marriages, the unexpected happened. The honeymoon couple was happily asleep when Bill started crying. It wasn't a weep, a mewing, or a sniffle. It was a full-blown crying from his soul.

Glenda was awakened to nothing. She looked about in the darkness. Was a thief in the room? No. She looked at her husband to see him asleep but writhing. His sheets were being twisted into knots. Their blanket had been thrown to the floor. Bill's head was churning from side to side. His feet were thrashing like scissors.

They had been bed partners for about six months, and nothing like this had ever happened before. Glenda was dumbfounded. What does a girl do in these circumstances? Not knowing, she did nothing.

The next morning, Bill got up as though nothing had happened. Yet, when Glenda looked into his eyes they were so tired. When asked how well he slept, Bill merely shrugged his shoulders and went on preparing for his day.

Glenda thought, *H'mmm. Well, we can all have nightmares*. Then she went about preparing for her day.

It wasn't long before the nightmares reoccurred. Again, Bill didn't seem to remember them. As before, he only looked tired. It was during the third episode that Bill started to shout the names of his children. This repetition of nightmares and now Susan and George's names being called out began to bother her. Should she say something to Bill or not?

Rather than call Bill's attention to his dreams that he didn't seem to remember, Glenda conferred with her counselor, Carolyn Jacobs. She had been with a lot of men in her life but she had never been through these dreams. Rather than make a mistake, Glenda sought guidance.

"Good morning, Glenda. What brings you here?"

"Good morning, Carolyn. It's not for me. I'm happy as a bug in a rug. But Bill has been having a series of horrible dreams. The next morning he looks tired but remembers nothing about them. In his latest episode he called for his children. That really concerned me. We can all have nightmares, but when children are involved, I get nervous."

Carolyn recorded some notes, looked at an item in her computer, and then said, "Yes, I expect you are nervous. How long have these dreams been occurring?"

"I don't know. We've only been living together for a short time. Perhaps they hit him before when I wasn't around. If I were to ask him, he'd probably not remember them. I don't think he's lying. He just doesn't remember."

"That's not unusual. I suspect...well, let's see. The human brain does a lot of dumping during sleep and something in Bill's past is being jettisoned. At least, that's what I would think. Are things OK with his children?"

Glenda thought a long time about this question. *He's been separated from his children. Their mother is an imprisoned drunk. They are being raised by their grandparents*. Finally, she related these issues to Carolyn.

Carolyn listened carefully while taking notes. "Are there any signs of violence in Bill's dreams?"

"Well, to the extent that the bed is torn apart from his thrashing about. He doesn't scream about violent actions. Otherwise, I don't know."

"Has he talked about any violent time in his life?"

"If you mean war experiences, no. Absolutely not. At most, he makes jokes about his service time."

Carolyn let that statement hang in the air. She knew about Glenda's call girl profession. Did she have any dealings with other men who had nightmares? When she asked, Glenda simply said no. Again, Carolyn let things hang.

A long silence ensued until Glenda began to think back about the men in her life. *Most of them were businessmen out for a romp with a young woman. Perhaps reliving lost yearnings. Most of them would talk about their hobbies or what they did in college. A lot of them complained about their wives. If asked, they would discuss their professional lives. The G.I.'s in her life. Some of them not so much. This was especially true of guys just back from combat duty. They might drink like fish or screw manically, but they would not talk about their tours of duty other than jokes. Bill was a G.I., is there a connection there?*

Glenda then described this difference between her civilian johns and soldiers. "The civilians might feel a bit guilty, but the soldiers not so much. Those just back from Iraq or wherever, were wired. That's the only way to describe them."

"Please try to be specific. Any details here could be very important."

Glenda talked about their frantic, nervous behavior. Once, she remember a guy diving under the table when a tray of dishes fell and shattered loudly. "He apologized and made a joke of it. I didn't think anything of it other than 'that's weird.'"

Carolyn slapped her notebook closed and muttered to herself, "Sounds like PTSD."

"PTSD?"

"Yes, I would be willing to bet on it. I'll bet he's seen some horrible things happen to children during his tours. He's now conflating them with the horrors his children are experiencing as they suffer through their wars with their parents. I'll bet he feels guilty about what has happened to both the Afghan kids and his own kids. To him, they're all one."

Glenda was horrified. "My God. Is there anything I can or should do?"

"Does Bill have a counsellor? An ex-G.I.?"

"Yes, he does."

"What's his name and phone number?"

Glenda told him, and Carolyn immediately called him. She had a long discussion with him and upon hanging up, turned to Glenda and said, "I made an appointment for you with Bill's counsellor. Jeremy James is his name, and he's a former soldier. He's missing an arm. That most likely means he's seen his share of combat. Now when you talk to him, he will not disclose anything Bill has said. Rather, he will talk only as an expert about PTSD and how it affects soldiers. You're going to find they are a tough, tender, stoic breed of people. Your job is to learn how to deal with them. You won't cure them. You can only deal with them by giving endless love."

Glenda arrived as scheduled for her appointment with Jeremy. As warned by Carolyn, she noted Jeremy's missing arm. He greeted her warmly, and welcomed the appointment made for her. "Glenda, it's wonderful you've come here. I know Bill well, and I know he hasn't said a thing to you about his military time."

Glenda nodded silently. She was really wondering what she had gotten herself into. Her gesture reflected her question, and Jeremy immediately caught it. In response, he said, "Glenda, you're not the first person to ask that question. Frankly, I don't worry about you or others like you. It's the ones who don't ask who concern me."

The next several minutes were devoted to introducing each other. Glenda described their courtship and how they learned to trust each other. "It was particularly tough for me given my background. Carolyn has been an angel of help in that regard. But, as God is my witness, I trust Bill with all my heart. He taught me to be open with him as I had never been my entire life."

"And he is open to you?"

"Yes, as far as I know. When we have issues, he insists on our talking them through and when appropriate, accepts responsibility for his actions. I have never caught him trying to be evasive or lying."

"But he's never talked about Afghanistan?"

"Other than funny stuff, no."

"And I'm sad to tell you he'll never tell you."

Glenda was almost shocked to hear this. "What? If there's one thing he's adamant about is openness."

Jeremy let that comment hang in the air. *She needs to understand what's coming. She can't be rushed.* Then he continued. "Glenda, G.I.'s are a strange lot. You've seen their handsome uniforms and listened to their bravado perhaps. Certainly their jokes. But underneath it all, combat vets have seen stuff that no one should see."

Glenda's shock was now approaching horror. "And they don't talk about it? Why not?"

"Glenda, Bill was an Army brat. He was taught to live by a strict honor code...to accept orders and responsibility...and when shit hits the fan to suck it up. That's their credo. Yes sir. No sir. No excuse sir. It all goes in and never to come out. Perhaps to others from his unit, but otherwise, no."

"Not even you? You're a combat vet."

Gesturing his short arm, Jeremy nodded and said, "And you know what? I've seen things I'll never tell him. We just suck it up and wonder why life goes to hell when we come back to civilian life."

"And that's where you come in."

"Yep. That's where I come in."

After this clinic, Glenda started doing some research on PTSD. She learned that soldiers have an extraordinarily high suicide rate. Just like Bill said about cops eating their guns. Jeremy said it was a symptom of the internal stresses of holding crap inside without no relief. She then investigated the history of wars that modern soldiers have had to endure. From 9/11 until several years ago, a whole generation of young men and women have known nothing but war. Twenty years of it. Twenty years of being separated from family. Twenty years of seeing beloved friends dying. Twenty years of seeing children being blown to bits.

This last thought about children disturbed Glenda. *Children. We see news clips every evening about them...until we're bored and turn to a different program. Is that why Bill shouted for his kids? To protect them?*

Glenda didn't tell Bill about these sessions with Jeremy. She was learning too much to share it. The information almost overloaded her senses. Yet, as she watched Bill do his daily tasks, he seemed so calm...so much in control. *My God, man. Let it go!* But he never did.

Let it go was Glenda's question. "Jeremy, why do soldiers endure such horrors? Why do they return to fruitless battles year after year? Don't they have a choice?"

Jeremy was straight-forward in his answer. "No, they don't. None. When they became soldiers, they took on an obligation no civilian ever endures. They give up their families, their wealth, their friends, their lives...everything but their honor. That is never allowed. So they suck up stuff and trudge on to meet their duties."

"Surely, someone must see the folly in all of this?"

"If you mean politicians, no. They're the last to see it. Trust me on this."

Jeremy waited for Glenda to absorb this conundrum of serving and suffering through idiocy. Finally, he summarized their situation by reciting a poem that Rudyard Kipling wrote over a century ago:

> It's Tommy this,
> And Tommy that,
> And Tommy, damn your soul.
> But it's the thin red line that marches,
> When the drums begin to roll.

"So Glenda. When you see a G.I. uptight or perhaps see some who are alcoholics, just remember this poem. These guys today are marching in a long line that extends back through centuries. Your Bill is among them, and he'll never leave."

Glenda needed several weeks to work her way through the complexities haunting this man she loved and wed. Jeremy had pretty well convinced her that Bill was carrying a lot of baggage. Furthermore, she doubted it would ever be shared. Perhaps at best it would be an oblique reference. Were his dreams such a reference? She needed to explore this idea. So, it was back to Jeremy.

As usual, Jeremy was upbeat and glad to see Glenda. She was happy for it. *He has such a way of welcoming you...making you feel good about being here.*

"Jeremy, I've gotten through what you've told me, but where do we go from here?"

"Meaning?"

"Well, his present life. His wife is in prison. His kids haven't seen much of him. He's here with me."

"Are you feeling guilty by all this? Perhaps feeling you're holding him back from his kids?"

Damn. Another thought. Glenda reviewed it and tossed it out. She said so by saying, "No, I don't. He was a free man before he met me. He courted me properly, and I've learned to trust him. You'll have to talk with Carolyn for details there. So, no, I'm not holding him back. If anyone is holding him back, it's him, and I don't see him thinking that way."

"Good enough. That is an important question that a lot of people fail to address honestly. So continue. What's bothering you?"

"Bill's a litigator. Litigation is a form of warfare that does not often address morality. It's ethics at best as they are described in a canon, whatever that is. He's good at it. But he must get tired of it."

"Consider this. You're right. Bill is a litigator, and that makes him a warrior fighting battles. He's been well trained for this profession. He really doesn't know anything else."

"Well, no. Not entirely. He knows flying. He loves it. It's so clean for him. As one of his students, I can well relate to it." After a pause, Glenda dove into her question. "He left the Army and its combat. Why not leave the law with its combat?"

"Think about your question. I believe your answer lies in there."

Glenda did indeed have to ponder the question until another session was scheduled.

"Jeremy, you always leave me hanging. But your purpose was good. To find answers for myself that I can live with. So, yeah, he has said that he's had enough of it...and..."

"And...what?"

Snapping her fingers, she saw it. "He just traded one uniform for another. He wanted a civilian life with marriage and children and that meant earning a living. Combat, litigation was his strong suit. So, as long as he feels the need to support others with enough money, he'll continue soldiering on in courtrooms."

"Bravo. You've just cracked Bill's code. Knowing this, when would you guess he'll leave the law?"

"When he thinks his job is done? That is, when his kids are secure? Maybe Virginia?"

"And then?"

"He'll want to fly the pure skies of heaven."

"Let me know when that happens."

Glenda needed time to digest this lesson about her man. It made sense, but one question was left to be answered. Why did he cry out for his children in his nightmares?

Jeremy didn't answer her question directly but rather asked her what sort of work Bill did in the Army.

"He was a lieutenant in charge of infantry soldiers. What exactly that means I don't know but I imagine he had to lead them."

"Yes, that's right. And it was in combat wasn't it?"

"Yes. I suppose so. I really don't know."

"But, combat meant danger, perhaps death, didn't it?"

Another horror for Glenda. Seeing war movies always disturbed her. They featured such senseless dying. "You're suggesting he had to...had to..."

"Finish your sentence."

"Lead them into deadly...?? Oh God, such a burden for such a young man."

Jeremy replied sadly and softly, "Yes, he did. He had to hold them as they died. Write to their families about the death of a loved son or father. Now if you had to do that about a child you were charged to attend, how would you feel?"

"Oh Lord. Responsible beyond anything I could imagine."

"So, is Bill responsible for George and Susan?"

"Of course." Again the light went on. "You mean he worries about them even if he doesn't say anything?"

"Is that possible?"

Glenda was crying by now. "You know I've never had children. I've talked to Carolyn about it. My life never allowed for them, and now it's too late. But I used to see cows tend their calves and bawl when they were taken away for slaughter. Those mothers would cry for hours for the pain they're feeling. And Bill feels that pain?"

"More than you can imagine. Of course, he can't express it. Soldiers don't do that so he suffers dreams."

Glenda murmured softly, "My poor man. So confident. So capable. Always ready to solve problems. Yet feeling helpless about his children living apart. Such agony he must be feeling. And yet, you say he'll never acknowledge it?"

"Never. The Army has an adage: 'Take care of your horses, your men, yourself, in that order.' So, that's where Bill stands in his personal pecking order. Until he knows his people are safe, he'll never rest."

Glenda sat silently until Jeremy said, "Glenda, get a recording of *Taps*. Listen to its plaintive notes while you read its lyrics. When you understand its meaning and absorb it into your heart, you will finally and completely understand your man."

Chapter 16
A New Case

Glenda never discussed her counselling sessions about Bill. She played *Taps* until she knew every slur of every bugled note. She actually dreamed about it one night. Her insights were kept tightly in her heart just as tightly as the torments her husband suffered each day. However, she used them subtly to keep Bill happy and especially when he dreamt or had concerns about his responsibilities. And they kept coming in.

One morning, a call came in.

"Mr. Ginn."

"Yes. How may I help you?" "We haven't met, but you may have heard of me. I'm Giuseppe Bisognio."

Indeed Bill had. Mr. Bisognio was a legendary character around Las Vegas. He supported the careers of many strip stars. He opened doors for them that would have been closed otherwise. It was also said around town that one did not ask questions as to how Mr. Bisognio said, "Shazam." He was never convicted, never even tried for that matter. But the police knew him. He was a man of respect. One didn't screw with such men.

"Yes sir. I have heard *of* your reputation. It's not one I thought would ever need my help."

"No, I haven't. But my nephew does, and I have told him to come directly to your office. I promised him you'd be happy to help him."

Bill thought, *For a man with your respect, I can hardly say no.* "Yes sir. Will you be coming in with him?"

"Not now. It is better I do not hear what he has to tell you."

"Of course." You can't be held as an accomplice, and it protects your nephew's client-attorney privilege of omerta, the good Italian word for silence. Zip your lips Bill.

Mr. Bisognio continued, "At some time later, when you think it is appropriate, I'll come in to discuss my nephew's plight."

Mr. Bisognio is no fool. I don't know where he studied, but he's well educated and not stupid.

Bill heard his secretary/receptionist, Julie, talking to someone, and while waving for her to admit the man, Bill replied, "Sir. I believe your nephew just arrived. With your permission, I'll ring off. When we're done, I'll call you. No details will be told to you, but we will be able to discuss how you want to help. Will that be OK with you?"

"Yes. Thank you." The phone went dead as the nephew entered his office. He was a large man. Standing six feet two inches, he weighed in around 225 pounds without an ounce of fat. He knew what a weightroom was. The suit he wore was immaculately tailored to his build. His shoes were brilliant. What was most arresting were his eyes. They were dark brown and dead flat. As the client reached out his hand, Bill noticed a college ring.

"Hello. I'm Richard Bisognio."

"And I'm Bill Ginn. Please have a seat, and may I offer a cup of coffee?"

"Thank you sir. That would be nice."

Bill asked Julie for a pot and a couple of cups. When he stood to take them, he whispered to her, "I expect this will not be a short meeting." Julie nodded and exited to her desk where she cleared his morning calendar.

Until the coffee was served and doughnuts offered and refused, the man just sat there. He was neither uncomfortable nor impatient. He just sat there. *Not much for small talk.*

Richard said simply, "I've been charged with murder."

Now that's a flat statement. No more emotion than saying he got a parking license. Bill had defended his share of murderers before, and he had learned to remain calm. "OK, Mr. Bisognio..."

"Richard, please."

"Richard, it is. I'm here to see that you are well defended..."

"Thank you. My uncle thinks highly of your work. You have defended some of his colleagues."

"I'm glad to hear that. Now, let's start at the beginning. Perhaps an introduction on both of our sides. Sound fine? Oh yes, you've been charged and arraigned? Bail posted?"

"Yes sir."

"Good. I'm Bill Ginn and like you, Bill is fine..."

Richard nodded silently.

"I've been a defense lawyer for a number of years. Before that I was a prosecutor, so I know both sides of a trial."

"Yes sir. Perhaps you don't remember me, but I was a student at one of your conference tutorials. I must say. You know your stuff. I learned a lot from it. "

Bisognio, Bisognio..."Bisognio...that name rings a bell besides your uncle."

"Yes sir. My father, Ricardo Bisognio. You put him in prison. He has been very upset by it. He thinks he got a raw deal and has worked hard to get out."

"I've read some of his appeals. He may have some points but frankly, I was doing my job and the facts, as I saw them, landed him in jail. But I must ask, will your father complicate my defending you? "Please think carefully about this matter, I know you came to me on your uncle's advice, but your father swore he would get me. From your comments, I take it he still wants to do so?"

"He does, but frankly, I don't really remember him. He has been in and out of jail since I was a youngster, and he's never really reached out to me or my mother. In truth, Uncle Giuseppe has been my father and his wife, Maria, my mother. My mother dumped me on their doorstep one morning, and I haven't seen her since."

"That's a sad story."

"Well, we're Italian, and families take care of their kids. My mother was Irish and never understood us."

"I can see that, and I understand how kids can be deserted. Believe me on that point."

"Yes sir."

Bill motioned to Richard's ring and said, "And Uncle Giuseppe sent you to college?"

For the first time, a stoic Richard smiled, "Yes sir. University of Nevada – Las Vegas. I'm the first member of my family to get a degree. Papa, excuse me, my uncle...father to me...is very proud of this. If there's one thing I always try to do is make him smile." *Who says gangsters can't be human with passions of love?*

Bill smiled at that. He was really touched. Richard felt that and went on to talk about his college career. He played *calcio, soccer.* First string defense four years in a row. Got his degree in logistics management on an athletic scholarship. So after graduation he got married and had two children: Joseph and Catrina. Like any proud father, he dug out a family photo that displayed a wife with jet black hair and two chubby infants.

Taking the photo, Bill looked at it carefully to give family respect. "They are lovely, all three of them."

Taking his photo back, Richard laughed, "My wife, Anna, is Sicilian. I'm Napolitano. When she gets angry she spouts her dialect that is impossible for me to understand. I just know she is upset about something."

"Wives," replied Bill with an understanding smile.

This chat went on for another quarter-hour. Bill found it best to create a personal relationship with clients. Without it, no trust can exist, and good defense lawyers need it like air if they are to get their clients to be honest. Honest means being forthcoming with facts. Good, bad, or ugly, they needed to be on the table. Otherwise, a good prosecutor will know something and use it as a surprise to win his case.

Eventually, all discussions get down to business. Bill asked, "You work for your father?" His choice of father was deliberate, given what he had just learned.

"Yes. As you know, all businesses need to take of their material side. Supplies, personnel, information, contracting, all of that. I'm in charge of it. If done right, a lot of money can be saved, and if I say so myself, I'm good at it."

Here was a thorn for Bill. Richard talked about logistics as a legitimate part of a legal business. Giuseppe had never been convicted but not without effort on the part of the police. What to do? Bill thought carefully about this conundrum. Some clients became belligerent when the subject was raised. Others were evasive. Some simply clammed up, and all trust was lost. How would Richard react? Given the trust offered by Richard so far, Bill decided to be direct,

"Richard, I'll be direct with you. The truth between us must be sacred. I won't tell anything you say to me to anyone except as we both agree it will help your case. Are we clear on this because if you have reservations about it, I can't be your defender. That's the way I work."

"Yes sir. No problem."

"Good. Now we can go forward. Next, I will only ask questions about issues that pertain to your trial. I do not want to know anything about your family business except as it, again, relates to your trial. So far, so good?"

"Yes sir."

Bill nodded and smiled. "To be honest, I am saying this because your business has the police interested. No question about that. So, without suggesting anything, what I don't know can't be spilled. The police can take the slightest hint and turn it into a big deal. By not knowing, I can't *spagliare,* make a mistake."

Richard said only, "Your Italian is very good...and very appropriate." *Ho captito bene. I understand what's not being said.*

"But here's the question: what happened that has the police on your case?"

"Do you know Benny Jacobs?"

Bill searched his memory and came up blank. "Can't say that I do, But he's the victim? What was his racket?"

"Yes, he's the victim. From what the police indicated during their interrogation with me, it was a professional hit. Why? Who knows? Maybe he shortchanged someone. But generally, he' was a nickel and dime grifter. He dealt in small fraud rackets mostly with tourists."

This wasn't a new story for Bill. Small time crook knocked off during petty gangland spats. Still more information was needed. "So, why come after you?"

"It wasn't for motive. I wouldn't be bothered with a small-timer like him. And no, I'm not a contractor who kills for hire. Listen, I've not been an angel all my life. No details, but during your lesson, you emphasized getting out of the rackets. If in, do so for specific ends, and once done, get out. Now, I'm completely legit. I work for my father, and everything is done by the books. Our tax returns aren't cooked either. I routinely ask the IRS to check them for accuracy. Papa says he sleeps better as a result."

"So you didn't do it, but again, why you? What attracted the police to you?"

"Right, back to your question. It was a gun I own."

"Have you got a carry permit?"

"Yep. Here's the details. The police found some brass by the body. They had my fingerprints. No question there. The fingerprints were traced back to my carry permit, and that was enough for the police."

Bill was writing notes as fast as Richard cited his facts. "And they came to your door?"

"Yes. They wanted to know if I had a .38 automatic pistol, which I did and showed to them. They took it as evidence. They also wanted to know where I got my ammo. I told them I had handloaded my rounds with stuff bought from Jakes Gun Shop. It's down on the far end of the strip."

Bill noted it and nodded for Richard to continue. "And they wanted to see it?"

"They did, which I did. They photographed everything and left with me in handcuffs."

"You've been arraigned with what?"

"Murder."

"What class?"

"Second degree for now. Without a motive or proof that I took a job they can't yet prove capital one. Let 'em get some stuff on me, and it'll be for the death penalty."

"Here's the $64,000 question. Did you do it? Be straight with me. Some lawyers don't ask this question, but I do. It makes a world of difference for my strategies if I know what I'm dealing with."

Richard simply said no. Bill summarized his notes, and then Richard continued. "Since I got straight and working to improve Papa's business, we're making a lot of money. It's legal, and my family is well supported while sleeping at night. They've got no worries. I'm not gonna screw all this up for a couple of grand."

"I believe you and not having a motive, the police will have a hard time proving a capital one case. They'll try to stick you with a second-degree charge."

Bill continued to organize his notes. Then, another question. "Did they present a warrant when they first contacted you?"

"No. They identified themselves, explained their reason for the inquiry, and asked if they could come in and talk about things."

"But they didn't come in and directly arrest you?"

No was the answer. Richard then took some time to reflect on earlier times. Bill waited. It was important to let him review his thoughts. Press a client and important thoughts may be pushed back where details will get lost. Lost details can lose cases.

Finally Richard sat forward. He knew what he needed to say. "Bill, you know the police have long been interested in my father. They have come at times trying to pin something on him. Papa always told Mama not to worry. He could handle it, and he did. I'd watch him deal with cops barging in. He treated them with respect. Questions were answered promptly. No haggling for a lawyer. Whatever was requested was produced. When I asked why he acted so deferentially, he said 'Don't put up barriers." It only makes cops want to dig deeper, and if there's something to be found, they'll find it. It becomes a point of respect for them."

"So you followed your father's advice?"

"Yes."

"Good idea. It makes life easier for me. If I appear respectful, the police deal with me more easily. They don't get their danders up. Still, here's a point. With me, are there things I should know that you haven't told me?"

"No. I've been straight."

"I know that, but anything forgotten? Keep pushing your memory and if anything, no matter how foolish, tell me. OK?"

"Got it."

Bill sat back in his chair and relaxed for a moment while looking at his watch. "Richard, this has been a long session, and I know you're tired. So let's call it a day. If you see my receptionist, she'll have some papers for you to sign that say you know what my services entail, what my standards are, and what my hourly rates are. Meanwhile, I'll be visiting the police, hearing their side of things, and then I'll get back with you. I suggest you talk with your father about our visit. He'll be anxious to know what's happened. Then, anytime he wants, I'll be happy to talk with him. Finally, thank you for being candid and honest with me. I can't say that to a lot of my clients."

Richard in turn, got up, shook Bill's hand with thanks, and then went out as instructed.

Chapter 17
Discovery

When Richard left, Bill gathered his staff for a meeting. This case would be a hard one that would be sucking up his time. When everyone was gathered, he reviewed their work schedules. Commitments were evaluated and where possible, simple ones were turned over to lesser skilled people. Changes or problems were to be presented to the office manager, Sarah Siegal, for direction. She had worked with Bill long enough to know how he wanted things done. In fact, she was better at such things than her boss.

When this task was done, he called Ralph Turner, a private investigator whom Bil had used for other cases. "Ralph, you know Giuseppe Bisognio?"

"Who doesn't?"

"Well, he wants me to represent his nephew and foster son, Richard, on a murder charge."

"Murder? The Bisognio family?"

"The same one. So, obviously, we need to do this one right. In fact, it's only been after a short interview, but I do believe he's innocent, It's not often I can say this, but nothing else makes sense,"

"That's a change."

"Isn't it though? But, when I get enough details, I'll be wanting you to research them. Find out what Richard was doing at the time of the murder, and what the victim was doing at that time. Pretend like you're a prosecutor sending out detectives."

"Got it."

"Thanks."

After that, Bill made an appointment with Mr. Bisognio for the next day. Obviously, he would be paying his son's bills, and being who he was, careful consideration about the case would be needed. Having one Bisognio angry at him was enough for any defense attorney.

When he got home, Glenda had just gotten in from a day's event planning session. It was to be held at the Venetian where money was no object. Glenda would get a good bonus from it if it went well. She was tired. However, when she learned of Bill's new client, she became very attentive. Bill repeated most of what he had told Ralph. With that, they were a tired couple who wanted only a quiet dinner and an early bedtime.

The next morning, Mr. Bisognio came in. Hot coffee and doughnuts were waiting for him in Bill's office. When they were comfortable, Bill led off. "Mr. Bisognio, I had a long interview with Richard. The good news is I'm happy to say, I believe he's innocent."

Mr. Bisognio nodded in surprise. *Of course he's innocent. Why else would I hire you?*

Bill noted his body language and said, "I'm not being facetious, sir. I've been in this business a long time, both as a prosecutor and a defense lawyer. Jails are full of quote innocent people unquote, but Richard's different. He is innocent. I truly believe it, and frankly sir, I find this to be a pleasant change. I can play Perry Mason for once in my life."

Mr. Bisognio smiled and relaxed as Bill continued, "The police do have some damning evidence that I'll have to deal with."

"They are?"

Bill explained how Richard's pistol had been identified and matched to the bullets that killed the victim. He also went on to say how Richard had done the right thing by being cooperative with the police. "Being a bastard with the police gets you nowhere. It makes my job harder to learn from them what I'll need to know in order to defend him to a not guilty verdict."

Mr. Bisognio understood perfectly. After all, he had had his own issues with police investigators in the past. Bill went on to explain his strategy that included hiring a detective who would track down all relevant details. Finaly, he suggested that Mr. Bisognio review everything Richard had signed. "Mr. Bisognio, I won't lie to you. This will not be cheap, but I'm confident we can beat the rap. Please note, sir, I said, 'we.' It's very important that the three of us work together. In reality, we are all we have against the entire resources of the police department."

Mr. Bisognio sat back, took a sip of coffee, and said, "Mr. Ginn, I knew I had a good man when I called you. Yes, I know it will be expensive. You will be running up expenses in pursuit of the case. You also earn your living from your work. So, charge me what you must. Next, I like your approach to your work. You're open to me and Richard. That builds trust, and believe it not, people in my business operate mostly on trust. Words among my colleagues must be stronger than any written contract."

Mr. Bisognio, I hear you very clearly. I will never betray your trust. You may not like what I say to you, hopefully you will, but I will not screw you. Life could become very difficult for me if I did...especially with your brother who already hates me. I can't have two of you hating me.

"Sir, I believe I understand you better than you might think. A long time ago, I was an infantry platoon leader in Afghanistan. My soldiers trusted me with their lives so long as I was honest with them. Betray them and my life was toast."

Mr. Bisognio said nothing, but his eyes blinked slowly in understanding. He was satisfied that he had gotten the right man. With that satisfaction, he took his departure with thanks. *Funny. Mr. Bisognio has seen the worst in men, yet he is still a human who has values. He loves Richard like his son, and when someone stands by him, he's thankful. Remember that about him, Bill.*

Bill then went to the police station to talk with the chief of detectives in charge of this murder case. That man was Lt. Mike O'Connors. Yes, he was an Irish cop. So was his father. Together they had seen generations of bad guys, yet he wasn't crooked. He was a straight shooter. That really didn't surprise Bill. During all his years of dealing with crime, he had found most cops were serious about their work. They believed they were making a difference. They weren't stupid. That was for TV programs that pitted wise-cracking private eyes against blustering fools.

But Bill didn't just rely on those impressions. He worked hard at gaining their respect, When he first set up shop on Las Vegas, he introduced himself everywhere and to everyone. He asked them to check him out by contacting John McElroy. "He was my boss and mentor who taught me a lot. He and I also clashed when I became a defender. He'll give you an honest appraisal."

As a result of these overtures, Bill slowly earned their respect. They could trust him. He would fight hard for his clients; that was a given. But he didn't cheat. Consequently, they would talk to him. He could get information from them that other lawyers couldn't dream of getting. It was all about attitude. All this not to say that some cops and prosecutors didn't try to do him in. Bad mistake. They were quickly crucified in public during trials. Bill was always prepared with the winning details and a smart nose for stink.

When Mike saw Bill, he got up from behind his desk and extended his hand in a warm greeting. Just because they had courtroom conflicts didn't mean they had to hate one another. That was just doing their jobs. "What can I do for you?"

"The Bisognio case."

"You got it?"

"Yep. And I'd like to hear your side of the story. What tagged Richard?"

Just like Bill. He'll get our side and if it's airtight, he won't waste time. He'll just plead it out as best as he can for his client. Where there's room for doubt, he'll drive a truck through. "It was the ammo. It was a handmade job, custom load. We tracked it through various gun shops looking for buyers. Richard's name came up. We followed up to his house. One thing led to another and asked to see his gun and ammo. They matched, and we arrested him."

Bill thought a bit about the scene and asked, "Did he give you any trouble?"

"No, he didn't. Very cooperative by answering every question and request. For instance, when we asked for his gun, he showed it. The same thing for his reloading shop. Very impressive. Obviously knew what he was doing, He even volunteered his concealed carry permit."

Bill nodded approvingly. "Good. Getting testy just makes you testy and that ruins things for everyone."

"I just wish everyone understood things like that."

"Well, it's common sense. But I do have some questions. Did you read his Miiranda rights to him?"

"Orally during the arrest. At the station we repeated them, asked if he had questions, none were offered, and then, he signed the statement. Again, he was very cooperative."

If it was a contract job, who paid him? Where's the money? Incidentally, if it was a hit, it was a sloppy job. I'd have used a cheap throw-away ,22 revolver that made less noise and harder to trace.

Bill asked, "What kind of pistol was it anyway?"

"Colt Gold Cup National Match,"

Bill whistled, "That not a cheap hit gun,"

Mike could only agree, Bill continued, "If it was a grudge shot, what's Richard's beef? He says that while he knew of Benny, he had no business or other dealings with him. Blackmail? That might work, but it has to be uncovered to strengthen your case."

Mike could only agree again. Bill was on target there, "All this tells me your case is getting weaker. Another question: are you sure he was the shooter?"

"His fingerprints were all over it including the ammo clip and the rounds. I did see a partial fingerprint that we couldn't attribute to him because it was so smudged. But otherwise.,.,"

"Where was the partial?"

Mike replied, "On a round."

"The smudge doesn't prove anything, but it does indicate the possibility that someone else handled the weapon."

"Can't argue with you there,"

Bill thought some more while Mike sipped his coffee. Finally, Bill got up and said, "Mike, I won't waste any more of your time but thank you for giving it to me. I'm going to investigate this some more like a prosecutor. If I find anything I'll send it over to you,"

The two men shook hands while Mike did some thinking. *Just like Bill, asks a couple of questions and my case is blown out the window. Yet, he didn't gloat. Just did his job. And to send his findings to us voluntarily, that's class.*

Bill went back to his office to think and give directions to his investigator, Ralph Turner. "Ralph, OK. I've got a job for you. It'll probably become a bit extended so keep track of your hours and expenses." He then went on with instructions to track down Richard's life during the month prior to the murder and do the same for victim, Benny Jacobs.

Ralph asked, "You want to see if there's a connection between the two men?"

"That's right. Was Richard anywhere near the victim and was there any connection between the two. If anything interesting pops up, don't hesitate to follow the lead."

"Gotcha. I'll keep you posted."

"Thanks."

Now about the fingerprint smudge. Mike indicated it wasn't Richard's, but he couldn't be sure. No matter. The question he should have been asking, if not, who's? There is a possibility that someone else had access to the gun and used it to assassinate our grifter, Benny. Another thing, Richard's innocent of this charge but his father intimated he once had not been clean. He had gotten out of the rackets apparently after my broadcast lesson at the conference I once held. Probably being married with kids helped his decision. Whatever. What is important is surely that Richard would have known how to do a neat hit. Leaving cases behind? Use an expensive pistol? No way. That was the job of an amateur.

With those thoughts to guide him, Bill called Richard. "Hello, Richard. This is Bill. Listen, can I come over to your house today? I want to ask you about your gun. It's about a fingerprint that doesn't belong to you. Two o'clock? Perfect. See you then."

At Two, Bill knocked on Richard's door. His wife, Donna, a perky brunette with two youngsters in tow answered. Bill introduced himself, and he was invited in. Donna called ahead for her husband, who appeared from the kitchen with a sandwich in his hand.

"Bill, I'm here with my gun and anything else you want to know about it. You said something about fingerprints?"

"Yeah. Let's go into your library. You don't have the gun I assume? "

"No, the police have it."

"No matter. Here's what I was told. Your fingerprints were all over it, the clip, and its ammo. There were a couple of shots missing from the clip that had been filled with the brass. They had your prints except for one that had a smudged print. It was pretty well smeared by your fingers. But, that smudge...did anyone have access to your gun?"

Without hesitation, Richard answered, "Sure. My friend, Arturo, Art for short, Francesco. He and I would take turns shooting targets at the Frankie's Range. We both enjoy punching holes in targets."

"Would he reload your clips?"

"No, but he would pick up brass after we were done shooting. Frankie's fussy about that. She likes her place kept clean."

"You also would want it for reloading as well wouldn't you?"

"Yeah."

"Got any empty cases around?"

"Yeah, as a matter of fact, Art returned some from his last shoot."

"Last shoot?"

"Yeah. He's borrowed my gun on occasion. He can't afford one like mine, and he's a good friend, so he'll go down to practice. He's not a bad shot."

"When was the last time he took it?"

"About two-three weeks ago...My God, that was just before Benny got shot,"

"When did he return your pistol and cases?"

"A day or two afterwards. I didn't think anything about it at the time because the cops hadn't arrested me. When I was arrested, I was too busy to think about it. Lending Art my gun was like lending him a lawnmower.

"Some other questions just come to mind. What does Art do for a living?"

"He's a driver."

"For?"

"Mostly a laundry pick-up."

"Anything else?"

"No. Not that I know of. I never asked him about anything else,"

Bill considered that answer carefully. *Don't ask so you can't give answers. Richard ain't stupid whatever else he is.*

Bill started to feel a tingle. This bag of empty shells opened up possibilities. They would contain fingerprints of the last man to handle them. Art was a that man. Now where was he, and what's he been doing? He had a final request, and that was some of Bill's loaded cartridges. *I just might have something, and I want to have absolute proof that Richard's gun was used.*

Bill's next call was to his investigator. "Ralph, this is Bill again. Hey, listen. I've got another job for you. Can you do a search on an Arturo Francesco? He lives in the area somewhere. I know because he is a good bud of Richard, my murder client. Also, as you check, go to Frankie's Range and see when, or if, he last shot there. This is an important issue 'cause if he came alone, it may have been to check Richard's pistol for a hit."

Ralph understood completely. "I'm on it. I'll keep you posted."

Bill then left the office and went directly to see Mike O'Connors. He was greeted with a handshake and a cup of coffee, Then he asked, "So, OK, Bill, what brings you here?"

Bill presented the bag of empty cartridges. "Requesting a favor. Two actually. One, could you research the fingerprints on these cases? They may belong to my client's friend who may have touched the case with the smudged fingerprint,"

"So, the smudge might be the friend's print?"

"Yep. It seems like the guy, Arturo Francesco, borrowed Richard's gun when the murder occurred."

"And Art may have done it?" Mike thought a second and said, "Sounds plausible but Richard doesn't get off on just that. Until I do, Richard's my man."

"No problem. Now, my second request. Here're some cartridges that Richard loaded. Could you do some firing tests with them using a variety of pistols? I don't care what they are. I just want to be absolutely sure that Richard's gun did the trick."

Mike chuckled a bit and replied, "Man, you just can't get out of the prosecutor's office can you? But, yeah, I'll do it. No harm there as it confirms what I already know."

Bill agreed while saying, "Mike, every once in a while, a defender gets to feel good about his work, and this is one of those times. I hope it'll be true with you as well. So, many thanks."

"I'll let you know what I find."

Bill would have to wait for several days before he got anything from Mike. In the meantime, he kept Richard and his father informed as to his suspicions and actions. "If what I believe becomes fact, there may be no need for a trial. The police will have the right m an."

Mr. Bisognio was very pleased. Richard was relieved. Bill was elated enough to take Glenda out to a wonderful weekend in San Francisco. Airplanes were wonderful for getaways.

Monday came early with news from Ralph. He had talked with Frankie and her records showed Arturo as shooting on the range two days before the murder. Ralph now paused a bit in his recitation before continuing. It was possibly an important point. "Here's something interesting. She also said he had to be reminded to pick up his brass. Arturo was courteous in doing so. But Frankie also said he was careless in this respect. She had even hung a large sign for shooters to clean up after themselves. It just seems that Arturo needs constant reminding. Are you thinking what I'm thinking?"

Bill didn't need another question to direct his thoughts. "Yes, the brass I expected but being careless is a real break. If Arturo was careless on the range where he had plenty of time and no pressure, then forgotten brass at the site of a murder should not be too surprising."

"Those are my thoughts," replied Ralph.

"Next question. Where is Mr. Arturo?"

"Don't know. I asked Richard for his address and went there. No luck. The landlady said he'd been in and out for the past several weeks or so. Ditto at his workplace. His boss is about ready to fire him for being so unreliable. At any rate, he's not in now. I'll keep a watch for him at work and his home. OK if I hire a spotter to do that? It'll free me up to do other things for this case."

"Yep. Go for it."

"Thanks. I'll keep you posted."

The next day, Mike called to report his findings. "Bill, you must be a magician because both test results were positive. The empty brass consistently had Arturo Francesco's fingerprints. They were first class images. Since they came in a single bag, I'm assuming he was firing alone. Also there's no doubt about Richard's gun being the murder weapon,."

"I believe so, but I've got Ralph, my investigator..."

Interrupting, Mike said, "I know him from when he was a cop. Good man."

"Good. I always thought so. Anyway, I had him visit the range where Arturo and Richard shoot to see if he did some shooting in or around the time Benny was shot. In fact, he had been there alone during our time of interest. He also was sloppy after shooting. The range owner had to tell him to pick up his brass. I'm now having him search for Arturo. No news yet on that score. Whatever I find, I'll let you know."

"Many thanks, Bill. Good luck." This information got Mike to thinking. *H'mmm. This Arturo had possession of the gun when Benny was shot. He also did some shooting by himself at that time. He can't be found now. If more stuff like this comes out about Arturo, I might ask the prosecutor to slow roll Richard's trial. Going to court for someone that might not be the bad guy is not a good idea. Makes us look bad.*

Bill then passed on his findings to Richard and Mr. Bisognio. "I've also been keeping the police informed of this information as it appears relevant and helpful for our case. Mike is a good cop, and he sees where I'm going. Get enough convincing evidence, and I'm sure he'll let you go, Richard, and then tag the right guy. Now, here's something important. If Art calls in to you, let me know. Try to find out where he's located. I need to talk to him...possibly have the local police bring him in for formal Miranda Rights questioning. He's certainly becoming a person of interest."

Both Bisognios were pleased with this update, and they promised to keep Bill informed of anything they learn.

Fire In The Hole

Chapter 18
Thoughts and Reunion

The next two months saw the investigation of Richard's murder case stalled. Arturo was nowhere to be found. Mike definitely accepted him as a person of interest and until he was found and questioned he would remain so. But he did not cancel out Richard as a suspect. As he explained to Bill, "Just because there is strong evidence that Arturo is the perpetrator, I can't release Richard. After all, they could have been working together. However, it's hard to imagine that a son of Bisognio could have been so inept in committing a murder. "

Bill could not argue with Mike's logic, and that's what he reported to his clients. At least Richard wasn't being tried now. His trial was being delayed until Arturo was caught and questioned. The Bisognios didn't like this situation but recognized how protesting would be fruitless. As Mr. Bisognio said, "It's better than being convicted of a bum rap."

While everyone was waiting for Arturo to be caught, life went on. His staff were handling smaller cases that made rain for the office. Most of them were DUI's, petty theft, confidence games, and the like.

This left Bill and Glenda time for attending the growth of their new marriage. Glenda had been promoted to senior director at her events planning agency. That brought some more income, which pleased her, but she was noticing a new turn in Bill's attitude towards his law practice. She wondered what was happening.

Bill replied, "Oh, I don't know. Things are going well, but other than teaching flying, I'm bored I guess."

Things were left like that. Glenda was worried but said nothing directly. She knew Bill would eventually come clean on his concerns. *He's got some 'cause I've noticed him spending more time on his finances.*

Bill was doing exactly that. He had made a nice profit from the sale of his Houston practice. Occasionally, he still got some consulting work from them on knotty issues. That work generated more income. The money from the sale had been invested in mutual funds that tracked the various investment averages. This ensured a steady rise in his portfolio's value. It wasn't sexy investing, but it worked with little effort on his part. Just stay the game. He had talked to Glenda about her making similar investments, and when he explained what they meant, she took her savings from a money market fund and followed Bill's lead. She was pleased to see her portfolio climb in value as the Dow Jones and S&P improved. The value of Bill's house was also climbing to become a significant investment. Altogether, their combined net worth was nice.

As Bill reviewed his finances his thoughts wandered. He was bored. Yes, he was. Why was the question. Was there something else?

At this time, Bill had to fly back to Houston for a consulting job at his old firm. When done, he hopped into his Cessna for his return flight home. The flight home was uneventful. The air was clear with no turbulence. There was little traffic to see. It should have been an easy bus ride. Still, something was bothering him. Actually, as he wandered through his musings, nothing was evident. Work was going well. His flying was fun. Glenda was happy. But what was stuck in his craw? The time spent flying a boring run prompted his mind to wander over this question.

Flying from Houston to Las Vegas required refueling. Albuquerque was his favorite pit stop. It had a nice restaurant where he could get a decent hamburger and cup of coffee. As usual, he stopped there. While munching his lunch, he reviewed his thoughts some more. *Things are great...on the surface. I can't complain. Then what do I want? Glenda and flying with some skiing thrown in the side. What's missing?*

Then it hit him. When he listed his wants, being a lawyer was not there. What was the law to him? A job. A paycheck. As it has always been. Nothing more. *I'm not John McElroy who loves his work.*

The name of another person who loved his work popped up. *Amos, my God, it's been a long time since I thought of him. Wonder how he's doing? The last time I saw him he was studying to be an auto mechanic, and he was happy. He had a future doing a job that he actually liked. He wanted to go to work.*

As he reviewed Amos's success, he recalled how he and Joe helped it happen for him. *Yeah, we did it right. We got a kid off the streets and led him to a great future. How often has that happened to me? Not often.*

Thinking on it, Richard was his only other case. *Twice in 25 years of practicing law. Just twice. Hell, I get that good feeling twice a day with my students. And it ain't the money. I earn more in one hour of law than my pay from giving an entire flight lesson. And the law isn't nearly as much fun. H'mmm. Maybe I need to talk with my advisor, Jeremy. He knows me better than I know myself.*

The second half of his flight went by quickly. As Bill flew his Cessna, a dim excitement began to poke through the clouds. *Do I need more money? No, not really. Do I need to feel alive...without complications...dirtbags, what all? No. What I need is more time doing exactly what I'm doing this instant.*

When Bill got home, he made an appointment with Jeremy James. It had been a while since he had unburdened his soul. Leaving the law was definitely a big step. He'd talk to Glenda. He always did that. First, though, he wanted to get some neutral advice. *Glenda will support me in this decision. No doubt about that. I just want to be certain that it's a good decision for me to present.*

Jeremy, as usual, was upbeat about life. He welcomed Bill into his office with a jovial, "How goes it Bill?"

"Actually, fine. Really fine"

"What brings you here then?"

Bill stroked his chin, hummed and hawed a bit, and then replied, "Well, I've been giving a lot of thought of quitting the law to concentrate on Glenda and flying . You know, do things that are fun for a middle-aged man. My question is simple. Is this a pipe dream, a mid-life crisis, or something sensible?"

"Tell me the details."

Bill then described his sense of unease and how practicing the law wasn't really a lot of fun. Nothing like the charge he got from teaching flying. He then related how his finances were in good shape. He had only his home mortgage to pay off. He could sell his Las Vegas practice and add to his investment portfolio. Glenda was working as a senior events planner and making good money. Her portfolio was growing. Of course, he had to pay child support, but his monthly budget was well-accommodated to that responsibility.

Bill concluded by saying, "So you see, there isn't any real reason for me to continue lawyering for an income, which is the only reason I ever did it. Teaching will bring in some mad money for fun things, but otherwise, Glenda and I are set financially. Now, does it make sense for me to make a change?"

Jeremy thought a second, made some notes, and then answered with a question. "What would Glenda say? Would she support this change?"

"I think so. In fact, I know so. We met through flying, and she knows how much I love it. But I want to present to her a sensible proposal that can be sustained. Selling a pipe dream is not sensible."

"Then, if she'll go for it, then I'd do it. You've obviously done your homework for the facts and defined what you'd like your future to look like. You're meeting your financial responsibilities both for now and into the future. So, why not? It sounds sensible to me."

With those words of counsel in his ears, Bill started to double-check his finances. Glenda waited for about a week while noting how Bill continued to analyze his financial situation. Finally, she asked, "Dear husband, seer of all things financial, what intrigues you?"

Bill pushed back from his computer, turned to his wife, and replied, "Fair lady, I am busy wondering how long I must practice law before I can do other things."

"You mean fly?"

"And chase you around the house."

"Ooooh, I'm not very quick so be gentle when you catch me. But, seriously, what's on your mind?"

"Well, the law has only been an income source for me. Some people like my friend, John McElroy just love it. I never have. It has been a financial source and not much else. Now, I am happy to be on the track of finding the real killer of Benny Jacobs and getting Richard off the hook, but that's an exception to the rule. Most of my clients are guilty. Some are real slimeballs No other way to describe them. But they all get their day in court, and I have been successful in putting their best foot forward."

"But now you want to fly."

"Yeah, that I really love. I know it won't bring the money that practicing law brings, but if it covers expenses and a bit more, then I'd be happy. So, now, dear wife, I am earnestly seeking an answer to my question: can I quit and do what I enjoy doing? You know, last Tuesday I had an appointment with Jeremy to run this idea by him. After reviewing what I presented, he advised me to tell you. It was a sensible change. So, right now, I'm double-checking our finances, and if what I see continues to be accurate, I want to go for it. More than that, though, we'll make this decision together. OK?"

"As long as I'm in on the decision, yep, I'm good with it." This answer was cool enough, but inside, she was excited. *Jeremy, old boy, you were right on. Bill's feeling like he has met his responsibilities and can leave the combat of litigation. Hot damn!!*

With that support, Bill continued with his law practice by day and reviewed finances by night.

While all of this was going on, Bill occasionally got letters from Virginia. Her last one brought some good news.

Dear Bill,

I've been in jail now for about five years. It's been a long time, but a fruitful one. My work as a group leader has been rewarding. Not only have I been able to help others, but I've also learned a lot about myself. Listening to the problems of other women has given me perspectives I would have never seen before. I don't want to get into details, but it's true.

Now Texas law imprisons DUI drivers who have caused fatalities for a minimum of two years. I'm well past it and have told the staff here of my desire for a parole. They know my record here and my projected plans. I want to continue with my group efforts in a local jail while working for MADD. I'm a real example for them. It's almost funny. A drunk driver working for Mothers Against Drunk Drivers. Who would have thunk? But the Houston chapter has heard of my work and offered me a job. All this is important information for parole boards as they make their release decisions. Will I be steady and productively occupied upon my release? That question is always on their minds.

Anyway, my parole hearing comes up in a month, and I'm asking for you to attend in my behalf. You testified at my trial that you would do so. I'm hoping you remember. I'll send the appointment date and time when I get it.

Virginia

Bill was happy to hear this news. The kids have been without her for a long time. Occasionally, they visited with her in prison, but that's a far cry from having a daily mother. Undoubtedly, Virginia would stay with them until she got herself in order. So, yes, he would be very happy to vouch for her. But, first, he needed to discuss this with Glenda.

When he explained what he wanted to do Glenda had no problems. She was secure in her marriage to Bill, and she had seen enough of the shady life to know how women can get caught up in things beyond their control. Bill asked if she wanted to visit.

"Thank you so much for thinking of me. But I think not. This is Virginia's time to reconnect with her family. While you're married to me, you still have a relationship with her and the kids. Children make it so. You have chosen to have a good one to preclude Susan and George from becoming lost sheep during a world war they didn't start. That says a lot about you. So, go, and do your mission. Then later, when the dust has settled, I can come and be introduced to everyone."

"Thank you. This will be tough, but it'll mean a lot to some good people.

Dear Viginia,

Your letter was a joy. It's the proper ending for the work you've put into your life. Of course, I'll come. Just give me the time and date. Then I can fly you home to your parents and kids. They are really excited at the prospect of having Mom home.

Bill

About two weeks later, Bill learned when Viginia's hearing was scheduled. He blocked off a couple of weeks from the office. Everyone was given their last assignments. If something important rose about Richard, he would attend to it but, otherwise, his thoughts were about a family reunion. After that, he called the Bisognios and told them of his plans. He assured them that he would be following their case while he was gone and if something came up, he'd be on top of it. The Bisognios wished him well.

Viginia was imprisoned in the Christina Melton Craine Unit that was located in Gatesville, Texas. Its location was not too far from Ft. Worth. Knowing George would love to get a flight, he decided to fly his Cessna. Besides, that was always fun. He could also use it to transport Virginia back to Houston. So, when Virginia's hearing came up, Bill was there.

The hearing was conducted by a board consisting of the warden, a staff psychologist, and several lawyers. Anyone testifying was seated in a waiting room where he or she could sip coffee and wonder what would be the prisoner's fate. Small talk was made but it was stiff. Minds were elsewhere.

When It was Bill's turn to testify, he was called forward to the hearing room. When he entered, he saw Virginia seated to the side. She had aged some. Where she was once a blond, streaks of gray were seen. She had lost weight and no longer the obese, bloated woman she once was. Her uniform was a short-sleeved international red jump suit. Her name and serial number were imprinted over her left breast. On her right arm was a tattoo of a lost child. It was prison ink but not bad. The artist had some skill. When she saw Bill her hand flicked a wave but otherwise, she remained stock-still.

The board was chaired by the warden who had a stack of papers in front of her. They contained Virginia's entire record at the Craine Unit. She was in her mid-fifties, very thin, and white-haired. Her voice was surprisingly deep for a woman. Probably came from hours commanding prisoners. She asked, "You are Mr. Bill Ginn, former husband of Virginia Ginn?"

"I am, ma'am."

"Your profession?"

"Attorney."

"And what brings you here?"

"To testify in behalf of Virginia Ginn. It keeps a promise I made to her during her trial."

"Please proceed."

Bill talked for about five minutes. In that short time, he related how he had testified in behalf of the prosecutor during the sentencing phase of her trial. He emphasized how he would be here if she turned her life around.

"I'm now proud of what she has done. She has used her time to develop her inner self by helping other women with their problems. Her plans now are to be an employee of MADD and to work with imprisoned women near her home where she will be with our children and her parents."

With that testimony, Bill was excused with thanks for coming. He was assured he would be hearing the results of the hearing shortly. Upon his departure from the hearing room's office, he left his contact information.

From the prison, Bill returned to his Cessna and flew to Houston where he would spend his time until he could return for Virginia. While en-route, he got to thinking about his future. Being an attorney was profitable for him, but it didn't light his fire. Question: how much money did he need? Obviously enough to be responsible for Glenda, the kids, and next Virginia until she gets her feet under her. Lay aside some for retirement and emergencies. After that, how much is enough? *Is it worth my time* and by time, he didn't mean just an hourly rate. It meant time for life, Glenda, the kids, his flying. Things of importance for which an extra hour of work making rain doesn't equate.

From his review of his finances, he knew he was near that overflow point where he could move into new waters of independence. What would it take to push him through the rapids? Answer, a couple of hundred thousand. Question: where could that money be found? Answer, selling his Las Vegas practice is a possibility.

Sell the practice? He had talked about it with Jeremy. He had studied his finances with that in mind. Would Houston like to expand into my new territory? I would insist on his senior associate, Jeremy Miller, be promoted to partner. The other associate, Gene Caplin, could be promoted based on his sustained performance. All of them would need MBA's to be successful partners. Knowing business was as important as knowing the law. Of course the firm would pay the tuition fees. Investing in people was always a good practice. Good business...Bill had to laugh at that image: lawyers and business. Who was the crook? Sarah, his paralegal, would get a permanent associate promotion. She wasn't a lawyer, or otherwise he would promote her to partner, but lacking that, she should benefit from her skills, dedication, and talent. No question there: absolutely none.

The question confronting this idea was the sales price. He didn't really know what the financial strength of the Houston office was. He knew the sales price he'd have to get in order to make things work for himself. As he mused through these ideas, they began to sound better and better. Well, let's see what happens if I make the proposal.

When he landed at Houston, Virginia's parents and his kids were waiting for him in the General Aviation terminal. Frank Krupka was not much different from the angry man who cursed Bill to Hell. He offered his hand without saying much. His wife, Martha, was a plump housewife who followed her husband without question. She gave Bill a brief hug. Susan stood by until it was her turn to greet Bill. She gave him a hug and asked about Glenda. She had grown a lot since their last visit. She was now a full teenager at five and a half feet tall, blonde bob cut hair, blue eyes, and blossoming figure. George was a tweener with a cracking voice. He wanted only to know when they could take a flight.

"How about tomorrow?" replied Bill.

"Cool."

After dinner, Frank invited Bill to the living room for a shot. This surprised Bill a bit. Not that he didn't know Frank liked a nip but that he was invited to have one.

"Thank you, I will." It was a bourbon that went down smoothly.

A few minutes passed without comment. Frank was not a talker but eventually he opened up. "Bill, when you sent Virginia to prison, I really didn't like you."

"That's ancient history."

"Ancient yes but not done. You've surprised me. What you said at her sentencing, you've done. It has included child support and support for Virginia. She has written me often about how you have supported her. Now, here you are, testifying as you promised at her parole hearing."

"I did simply what I promised. Virginia's life became a tragedy that will never be entirely healed."

"I know. I have maintained some contact with the girl's parents, and they have forgiven her. That's something I doubt I could do, but they showed me what true compassion is all about. Reaching out to feel pity for Viginia, who killed their daughter, is something most people couldn't do."

"I agree. Yet, Virgina made it possible by accepting her responsibilities and the pain everyone has endured. She's a strong woman as well."

Frank thought about that and took another sip. Finally he said, "Bill, we've never been close, you and I, even before Virginia's going to jail. But I have thought long about your divorce and going to Las Vegas. You've found a new wife."

"Glenda, yes."

"Well, I don't know what happened to cause your divorce, but I must say that you have proven yourself a better supporter than many husbands I know who stay married while making life miserable for their wives. I'm now glad to say I know you."

"Thank you sir. That is...well...I can only say I feel...well...complete...that's..."

"Never mind. I know what you're trying to say."

That evening, just before turning out his bed lamp, Bill called Glenda and told her what all had happened. He emphasized his conversation with Frank. Glenda was very pleased with this report. Nothing special had happened back home but she missed her man and was counting the days until she saw him again. At the end, Bill wrapped up his impressions of the day and then turned over feeling better about life and his profession than he had in a long time.

The next morning was Saturday and that meant Bill and George went flying. This time, he started teaching his son a lesson. Starting with an inspection of the plane, a review of departure procedures with the tower, and then take off. Bill let George do some simple taxing and when off the ground take the controls. They shot some landings around the tower and then went off to do some sightseeing in the area. Over the ocean where space was empty, he let George fly fairly close to the ocean below. Altogether they spent about three hours in the air. After parking the airplane, he had George do a post-flight inspection of the plane. The boy was enthralled with it all. For a kid of twelve, George did a good job. His hand-eye coordination was good and consequently could keep the airplane pretty well centered during turns. Bill was a very proud father. He told George so during lunch. When they returned home, Bill had George tell everyone what they had done and what he had learned. Bravos and applause followed.

The afternoon was spent with Bill just chatting with Frank and Martha. A lot of stressful time had passed among them, and they all felt the need to talk, to become reacquainted. Of course, Virginia was a center of discussion. They exchanged understandings of what her plans were. Her relationship with the kids were another important topic. For most of their lives, Susan and George had not seen much of their parents. Gramps and Gramma were their real parents for all intents and purposes. Martha talked about Susan's expected response. Cool was a good word to describe it. Susan was doing well in school and had a number of girlfriends. No boys were yet in sight. But her upbringing as compared to her friends was different. None of them had a mother in prison. So, she was distant. Making friends was not an easy task for her. This being the case, Susan's making friends with her mother would probably be fraught with difficulties. Hopefully, they could be overcome.

That evening, Susan agreed to go to dinner with Bill. As he had seen and heard from Frank and Martha, she was a reserved young lady. But Bill hadn't been a defense attorney without learning something about bringing people out from their shells. He started with simple questions about school.

"OK, I guess."

"Any classes or teachers you do like?"

"Well yes. Sort of."

"OK. Clue me in."

Susan started talking about her English teacher. "He's so cool. He really understands the stories of young people." Perhaps because he wasn't much older than the kids in high school. He had been out of college for just a couple of years, which had him just short of being an old fuddy.

"Anything else in school you like...plays, clubs, the like?"

"Clubs?"

"Yeah, like French Club, Science Club, Thespians...the like?"

Susan replied, "I wouldn't know. Most of my friends just hang out and text when they have something to say. Anything else is Googled."

"Isn't that a bit lonely?"

"No. Why?"

By dessert time, Bill noted that Susan had little interest in what her father did. Flying was just, well, flying. What's cool about that? Glenda's glamor, however, was another thing altogether.

"She's a Hollywood model or could be if she wished," she squealed. "I'd love to grow up like her."

Bill agreed one hundred percent. No argument there.

That night, Bill told Glenda how she had a fan. "Susan wants to grow up as glamorous as you. I could only agree," he said.

Sunday was devoted to church and Sunday dinner. The afternoon was devoted to football. No team like the Texans. Any opinion to the contrary would have brought an argument. Bill chose to agree heartily. That night, as always, he call Glenda to say night-night.

"Tomorrow I'm going to my old Houston law firm to say hello and be able to write off some expenses of this trip off my income taxes. Who says that being lawyer doesn't bring in money?"

"That's my dear. Always thinking."

The next morning saw Bill keeping his promise. As he walked into the office, a number of old-timers recognized him and greeted him with hellos and hugs. It was good to be home for a day. He asked, "Is Jackson in? I know this is unexpected."

A deep voice came through the door of his office, "If that's Bill Ginn, tell him I'm out."

Bill retorted, "And I'm the big bad wolf who's here to huff and puff and blow your door down."

"Come on in. The door's open. No need to get huffy.."

Bill did just that to see a big man, about six feet four inches, weighing 250 pounds, wearing a black suit, white shirt, and a large silver bolo tie. He was just rounding his desk as Bill came through. Jackson had been Joe Brady's replacement at the firm who then bought Bill's practice.

"And what I can do for you?" asked Jackson.

Closing the door behind himself to provide some privacy, Bill replied, "Well, to see old friends while I'm here testifying at Virginia's parole hearing."

With that, Bill explained how Virginia was about to be released on parole. Her plans were described and how her family was happy for her return home. Meanwhile, Bill was also reconnecting with his kids. Jackson took it all in very happily.

After some small talk following this explanation, Bill got to the point of business.

"Jackson, would the firm be interested in buying my Las Vegas practice...perhaps under the same terms you bought me out here?"

"Well, damn, you are a man of surprises aren't you? What brings you to make this offer?" was Jackson's question.

"A lot of things but basically I want out of the law. It's provided a good living, and I've saved up enough to seriously think about doing something else that I would love to do."

"And that is?"

"Flying. I love my part-time job teaching flying. With retirement from law I could do full time." Bill paused here to collect his thoughts, then proceeded. "Yeah, as I said, law has done well by me financially, which was the reason I became a legal beagle. But, I never liked it as say, John McElroy does. It was always a job that has me defending scumbags, deviants, and industrial liars who cheat on their people at every turn. Yeah, we do it because we can...the Constitution demands that someone do so...but it's not fun...not like flying."

"And you want fun?"

"Exactly. I'm also thinking that freedom to fly would let me come back here more often to see my kids."

"Well, here's the bottom line. How much do you want?"

"About the same as what I asked for this office. Same terms. Yeah, I want to fly but I do need this money to let me do so. Teaching won't bring in a lot of money, and my income would mostly be from investment returns."

Jackson more or less understood what Bill was saying. Defense lawyers were needed, and it paid good practitioners well, but it wasn't a positive work experience unless one was a rabid dog about it. Jackson enjoyed it. He loved battling John McElroy and others. Getting people was a kick no matter what others may say or no matter how the clients repeated the offenses on innocent people. That was just part of doing business. He had once defended the son of a wealthy parent...got him off...only to learn the next day he was caught trying to rape a three-year-old girl. Ah, another day in court. What a life.

Jackson said, "Well, yeah, I'm interested and I'm sure the partnership will be as well, so long as the returns are worth the investment. So, send me details. I'll present them and we'll see."

"Sounds great. You'll have them shortly after I return to Las Vegas and can crunch the numbers."

With that Bill returned home to learn that Virginia's parole had been approved. She would be released after several days of out—processing. Bill was there at the gate awaiting Virginia as she exited. She was wearing the same suit she wore at her trial. It was old and hung loosely on her frame but did the job. She wore the same garnet ring and tennis bracelet. She was carrying a small satchel containing some extra clothes and release papers.

As she came out, Virginia looked around and blinked in the sunlight. It had been almost ten years since she had seen freedom. It was almost too bright to bear until she saw Bill standing by a taxi. With him in sight, she smiled broadly and came over. He reached out and gave her a warm hug.

"It's good to be here seeing you get out."

"I can't believe it's true. After all these years."

"Come on. Let's get out of here."

With that, they went directly to the airport and Bill's airplane. Virginia said, "I knew you were flying but this is very nice. I guess you like it?"

"Love it. It doesn't bring in much money but there's a purity to it that the law doesn't give me."

"Maybe we should have made different plans when we were young."

"Maybe. That's water over the dam though. Let's concentrate on what's left of our lives."

The flight back to Houston took a couple of hours, which gave them some solo time to talk. Bill delighted Virgina about his new relationship with Frank, Martha, George, and Susan. "She's a lovely girl but very reserved. I think she's lonely and certainly cautious about people."

Virginia took out her hanky and wiped her eyes. "Yes, having to deal with a cold world that has judged her mother is a tough thing for anyone. It's always the innocents who suffer the worst."

"And Susan has. But please give her space and time. With it I believe she'll come around.

"God, I hope so." It was a fervent prayer followed by a long period of silence.

About half-way through the flight, Bill let the Cessna down for a lunch period. It was a small club airport that featured a lunchroom that was quiet. He knew this would probably be their last chance for private time, and for some reason, he sensed that something was still on Viginia's mind. Her quietness was disconcerting, and he wanted her to have some time to perhaps get something off her chest.

He was dead right. After finishing hotdogs and ice cream sundaes, Virginia asked if coffee was available. Bill instantly looked for some. Coffee was not something that Virginia liked, so asking for it could be seen as an excuse for some more discussion.

Virginia stirred her coffee haphazardly. Bill waited. He had learned patience by now from Glenda. People will talk when they're ready.

Finally, Virginia asked, "Bill, have you ever looked in the mirror and not liked the person you're seeing?"

"Yes. There have been times."

"Well, through all my time in prison, while I was getting people organized into support groups, I kept seeing myself and not liking the image looking back."

This surprised Bill, and he said, "Really? From the glowing reports the warden has been saying about your progress, getting dry, helping others, and developing your plans after being released, I would have thought you would have come to a sense of serenity about yourself."

Virginia answered ruefully. "One might think so but all that was a reflection of what I had been doing all my life."

"Doing what?"

"Manipulating people. Not now in a harmful way. I meant what I said about getting myself straight there. But what about me? Why had I become a drunk? Why couldn't I answer your questions when we were in counseling? As I was succeeding with others as I had done in my sorority and in the community, and now in prison, why did I fall apart when I was rejected were questions that seemed to have no answer."

"Until?"

"Until five years of hard work digging through the trash in myself. My psychologist, an angel if ever there was one, kept pushing me to dig deeper. Trust me, it was five years in coming but in the last six months it finally began to make sense."

Bill was now getting excited. This was a confession that he never expected from Virginia. But from having learned from Glenda, he was patient and said nothing while unconsciously leaning forward in anticipation.

Virginia continued, "As I looked back over my college days, I had learned how to deal with people and to enjoy partying. This carried over to our married time. You earned the money, and I dealt with people. When they deserted me, I was marooned...lost...with only a bottle for comfort. I didn't know who I was or how I was to act on my own."

Bill had seen some of this in Glenda, so he remained quiet and let Virginia continue. She did. "With no one to validate me, I only had my gin bottle for support. Sadly, even after being married to you and having two kids, I really hadn't learned how to talk to you about us...about me. I couldn't even talk to myself about me. As a result, I dug a huge hole and pulled the gin bottle in with me."

By now, Virginia was crying. Bill offered his handkerchief that she took to wipe her eyes and blow her nose. "I could play a game as I always had done, but that little girl would always be looking at me. How her parents have managed to forgive me is a blessing beyond understanding. Yet, from the strength of their hearts, they have done so. There was something inside them that I didn't have. Remember how I blasted you after your testimony? It wasn't me at fault. It was you. It was everyone but me. But their forgiveness taught me this lesson. Live within yourself. Be true to yourself. Accept yourself first. Friends are important but only so far. Beyond that, it's everyone's inner self that must accept responsibility and give yourself a sense of love."

Virginia waited for a second and then snorted bitterly. "Gin's fine, but it makes for a lousy friend. I was blessed by her parents, it wasn't enough. I needed a better friend than gin who was always true." Blowing into her hanky, she continued. "You know who that friend was?" Bill shook his head. "It was Jessie, the little girl I killed. She came to me in a dream saying how she could forgive me if I took that responsibility for what I had done and to accept what happens in the future with love."

Bill was shaken by these words. *Take life with love. Such words from a child.*

Then, she turned fully onto Bill and said, "It took me five years of the hardest work I have ever done, but I have learned that lesson...from Jessie, the little angel I killed. I know she has forgiven me, and how she looks over me every day. I have written a letter to her parents with thanks for their blessings that I didn't deserve. So, Bill, this is my big lesson in life taught in the Big House. Thank you for listening."

Bill did not relate his counseling sessions. Now was not the time for another war story. He simply took Virginia's hands and held them for a long time. He did remember her story for the rest of his life as an abject lesson in humility and honesty. Whenever possible thereafter he tried to use it for helping others, Glenda, and most of all, himself when he didn't like his reflection.

Arriving home was a warm reunion. Bill stayed in the background to let Virginia bask in her parents' joy. Susan and George reacted as all kids do in new situations. They stood back and watched until they felt room for themselves. Then they came forward. Virginia was crying at that point.

Bill called home that night. He really didn't say much about the day. It was very private, and he needed to absorb it before relating it to Glenda. She didn't ask for details. The next morning, Bill bade everyone farewell with promises to return and then got into his plane. It was good to be going home after a difficult time away. He promised himself to tell Glenda all the details.

Chapter 19
A Homecoming

Bill arrived home from Houston in time for dinner that Glenda had already prepared. It was his favorite: steak, medium rare, baked potato, and green beans done *al dente*. Most importantly, she greeted him with a big welcome home hug and kiss. Altogether, Bill was as happy as he had been for a long time. Virginia was out of prison and embarking on a new life. His kids were doing well under Grampa and Gramma's care. He had made an offer of his firm that was not refused. Maybe, hopefully, he could turn his life onto a new direction with Glenda at his side. He was smiling with joys of happiness.

Glenda asked, "OK, lover boy, I know I'm beautiful, and I cook like a dream, but what else has you all fired up? Over dinner with a good bottle of chianti going with the occasion, Bill related all that had happened. Glenda listened attentively without comment. Finally, Bill concluded with the thoughts that had been running through his mind during his flight home.

"Glenda, until I got into my plane to come home, I never realized how unsettled I was. Not you. You've been a godsend, but in general with my life. Legal work was bringing in a good living. Occasionally, seldom but occasionally, I actually got to help people. Otherwise, no. I didn't enjoy prosecution, but it was a living. I went into defense for the money. It led to my divorce from Virginia and separation from Susan and George. There were just two candles in my life: you and flying."

Raising a glass towards Glenda, "Thank you flying for bringing a dream into my life."

Glenda smiled broadly and replied, "Thank you flying for bringing my savior into my life."

Over a dessert of strawberry shortcake and ice-cold sauternes, Mike and Glenda sighed happily at their good fortune. Then, Bill laid on his sales proposal. "Glenda, you remember earlier when I said I'd like to leave the law and go into flying?"

"Yes. I also said I was good for it as long as I was in the decision."

"Well, you are. If all goes as planned, I think we can do it."

With that he explained his proposal to Jackson. "You may remember him. He bought me out in Houston, and now I've offered to sell this practice to him under terms similar to before. Well, he said he'd have to run my offer by the other partners, and if it looked promising a deal might be made. I'll have to give him the financials and case load information to see if it would be attractive. But, with all this, now I can concentrate on chasing you around the house and fly."

Glenda snorted and laughed saying, "Yeah, with me and my job at the events shop, you have a sugar mama and a plane. Now, tell me, which do you love more?"

Bill giggled and said, "You, but don't push it babes."

A towel was thrown into Bill's face almost spilling his sauternes.

After the fun, Glenda did ask to see the figures. Not that she distrusted Bill, far from it, her point was that joint decisions involved joint review of the facts. Bill was pleased to oblige. Here was a woman who would talk to him. In the end, a joint decision was made for Bill to become a full-time pilot if he could sell his practice.

Glenda just thought, *Dear Soldier, wounded and tired. Your battles are about done. It's time to lay down arms and live in peace.*

Monday morning saw Bill coming into the office. Julie gave him a cheery welcome back. Bill replied he was happy with both his time away and his return. He then got a cup of coffee and as he was stirring in some sugar, he asked Julie to have the staff come in for an office meeting after he had talked with Lt. O'Connors. "Right, sir."

The telephone rang. "Lt. O'Connors here."

"Mike, this is Bill Ginn. I'm back in the office calling for an update on the Bisognio case."

Mike replied happily, "Good Bill. I have some encouraging good news."

"Richard's been sprung?"

"Not quite that far but his bail has been returned, and he has been downgraded to a person of interest."

"OK. That's progress. What 're the details?"

"Well, we caught Artie boy. He was in Michigan working as an Uber driver. Of course he denied anything to do with Benny's murder. But he had a hard time explaining lots of details."

Mike then described the investigation work that had been underway when Bill left for Houston. "We went through Richard's finances. His bank withdrawals were for legitimate purposes, and you know a contract killing will be expensive. Nothing resembling such a payment for a hit job. Richard claimed he really didn't know Benny...heard of him but that's all. A check with his friends and colleagues backed up that claim. Finally, downright motive. We check for infidelity, past activities in the mob, other things that could be good for extortion. Again nothing. Richard did have a shady past...even his father admitted that but nothing that brought charges. Then it seems he listened to your pitch of getting out of any rackets, and that's what he did. He's been a clean businessman since. So no motive. Summing up, he didn't have the pistol during the time of the murder. He didn't know Benny, and he was clean. Arturo, on the other hand, did have a beef of some kind against Arturo. What sort, his friends didn't know, but being sore Arturo was. He had the pistol, and he was known to be looking for Benny shortly before the murder. Then leaving town without reason or notice looked suspicious. Incidentally, about the pistol, your request to have it fire-tested against other pistols was a clincher. It proved beyond any doubt that it was the murder weapon and knowing that Arti had been using it at that time means no one else was likely to be the hitman. Good work, my man."

"Mike, I'm just your humble servant, but what's next?"

"Getting Benny extradited as a person of interest. His lawyer has been making the usual fuss, once even claiming his Miranda Rights reading was invalid because of a typo that transposed an e for an i. The judge dismissed that claim with disdain. I won't repeat what he said, but it wasn't complimentary. Actually, Michigan did the Miranda drill perfectly. When Arturo was brought in for questioning the first time, there was a lawyer already present. Every encounter was taped. Each time Arturo was brought in he had to sign and date the Miranda statement indicating he understood it."

Bill whistled appreciatively. "Wow! That's thorough. So, he's coming in shortly?"

"Be here tomorrow."

"Good work, Mike. Many thanks."

"It couldn't have been done without your coaching Richard to cooperate."

"Hassling the police makes for good TV drama, but it doesn't help a client's case."

"You're right there."

With this good news, Bill called the Bisognios. They were delighted with the progress that had been made during the past week. As Mr. Bisognio said, "In the old country, police were like lice...always crawling up your back and itching. But, I must say, Bill, your work with them has been very productive. *Mille grazie, Amico.*"

"I was just doing my job, sir, but thank you. I'll keep you posted of details as they come up."

Hanging up, Bill called for his secretary, Julie, for everyone to meet in the conference room in about a half-hour. When he arrived, everyone scurried in because Bill hated meetings as a waste of time. So, if he called one, it must be important. As they came in, they welcomed their boss back home.

Once seated, Bill looked around at his staff. There was first his office manager and para legal, Sarah Siegal. She was his first employee and had proven herself to be a powerhouse. She came from an impoverished family that had scraped up enough money to put her through community college. She had worked in various firms learning the law by dint of reading legal tomes without end. Next, was Julie. She was a pretty young lady who was recently married to a dealer in a hotel on the strip. Her interest was family, but for what Bill required, she did a good job. How long she would remain with him was to be answered by when she delivered her first baby. She made no bones about the fact that being a good mother was her life's ambition. No problem there. His senior associate was Jeremy Miller. He was a graduate of Penn State's Dickenson School of Law. He had come to Las Vegas because that was his wife's hometown.. Jeremy became known to Bill through Joe Brady because he was his replacement. He had left for the same reason as Joe. He couldn't make partner at the firm. He was ambitious and seemed to enjoy defense work. Finally, there was Gene Caplin. He was a local lad just graduated from Las Vegas law school. He worked hard but whether he would stay or not was problematical. Like most young people, he was feeling his way into his life's career and new opportunities could attract him at any time. They didn't have to be in the law. Well, time would tell with him.

Bill led off with thanks to everyone for keeping the office going during his absence. He was happy to report that life back home was in good shape. It also gave him time to think about where he would like for the office to go. Essentially, it was to move away from just violent criminal law. The bigger money was defending corporate crooks and politicians. They could afford to appeal bad verdicts and that meant more rain. Perhaps a flood. Jeremy cheered. Gene sat quietly absorbing what was being said.

"This means that we have to be smarter in business matters. I had actually been going in that direction when I was in Houston. Lots of oil people there who needed help. Recognizing that meant I had to understand how they worked."

Bill looked around as he talked to see how people reacted to his comments. Sarah looked concerned. She was good at digging into law books, but corporate work? H'mmm. That was something else. She was clearly doubting her qualifications.

Bill continued. "So here's the deal. Anyone wanting to get their MBA can get it. Sarah and I will set up a continuing education fund to cover those expenses."

Then looking directly at Sarah, he said, "Sarah, that covers you as well. You have your AA now; next stop is your BS in business. After that, what you want to study is up to you."

Sarah smiled gratefully. Her work was being recognized, and she appreciated it immensely. She said softy, "Thank you, boss."

"But we're not done Sarah. As of now, you are the newest associate in here. You're getting this in recognition of all the valuable contributions you've made to resolving tough cases."

Sarah's mouth just dropped. Never in her life could she have dreamed of this. Everyone applauded her. What a story she'd tell at home this evening.

At the end of the meeting, Jeremy immediately told Bill he was enrolling the next semester. Gene said nothing as he departed for his work. Sarah was still speechless but nodded with tears when Bill just repeated softly what she meant to the firm. Julie gave her a hug. When all was done, Bill asked Julie to stay behind.

"Julie, I know your heart is in your home. That hasn't stopped you from doing whatever it took to make things happen, and I appreciate it more than you can believe. But understand this if you want to advance here, just come and talk with me. Sarah might surprise us and go to law school. Perhaps you could take her office manager's job. Bottom line: your future here is in your hands. I'm here to help you get what you want."

Julie replied quietly, "Thank you sir, but as nice as these opportunities arc, the biggest thing you've done is tell us that you care. That means a lot to us."

Bill thanked her while thinking, "Take care of the troops, and they'll take care of the mission. How true that is. Thank you, Pop, for another good lesson in life."

Over the next week, life continued its usual course. Eventually, Arturo was returned to Las Vegas. He was accompanied by a couple of Las Vega's finest. When they got past the TSA exit, Mike was there to greet him with an escort service to the police station and more questioning. He made sure Arturo had a lawyer at hand and a copy of his Miranda rights. Camera lights lit up the video camera.

As he told Bill, "He tried to pawn the murder off onto Richard, but the more he talked the deeper he dug his hole. His lawyer told him several times to shut up, but Arturo was not very bright. Eventually, I decided he was our man. He did the job on his own and very ineptly at that. He didn't admit to the crime. His lawyer wouldn't let him do that, but he almost had to sit on him. So, we'll have to go to trial."

"So Richard is clear?"

"Clear as rainwater."

With that, Bill called the Bisognios again and told them the good news. "There'll be a trial, and you might have to testify. That'll be up to the prosecutor. I know I will to confirm the detective work that I did. Mr. Bisognio promised a nice bonus would be under Bill's next Christmas tree. Bill thanked Santa Claus very much.

For once in his career, he felt good about his work. As he told Glenda, "Can you imagine that; I did my best job defending someone by helping the cops? Who'd a thunk it?"

Glenda was very happy and not simply about the case. *Bill, you don't know how much of a man you are. You take care of your troops. You ensured your wife, who could have been a bitch, got a new start in life. You took in a whore as your wife and gave her hope. How you have managed all this while wading through the crud of life without even a whimper is something I'll never know. I just hope, pray, you can leave it all the crap of life behind and fly into the purity of what life can be. Thank you, my dear, for being you.*

Glenda gave Bill a long tender kiss and took him to bed. It was time for a night-night reward.

Chapter 20
The Trial

So Arturo was cited for the murder of a low lifer by the name of Benny Jacobs whose profession was a grifter or a fraud hustler of unsuspecting dupes...usually tourists. Bill's client, Richard Bisognio, was released. Bill was in an unusual position as a defense lawyer by having to testify on behalf of the prosecution. In all of his career, he had never been required to give testimony of any sort. It was a strange feeling for him.

This strange feeling amplified the satisfaction he got from knowing, for once, that his client was actually innocent. That Perry Mason still lived. Defense lawyers could actually do good for society. Not often, but when it happens, it's a thrill.

Because he was only required to testify, Bill could direct his attention to the affairs of his office. Other clients needed his help. He wanted to sell his practice. Getting it evaluated for Jackson took time. He worked closely with his accountant to get that information. As it came around, Bill decided to approach his original flight instructor and now part-time boss, Jim Jensen, about his becoming a full-time part of that company.

All of this was possible because trials are slow processes. Unlike TV shows where the crook is caught today and tried tomorrow, there are lots of preliminary steps that must be taken. The prosecutor must provide the defense team with the information they will use in the trial. If either side wants to block certain information from being presented, there must be a hearing where the presiding judge will render rulings. If the hearing does block information, then that team will ask for time to revise their trial strategy. It really becomes a long ping-pong game before a trial date is set.

In the case of Arturo, three months passed. This gave Bill time to send off a proposal to his old Houston office. It essentially aped the sale of that office to his old partners. With that out of the way, Bill's next step was to approach Jim about working full time as an instructor. If a partnership could be arranged that was profitable for both men, Bill would listen to it as well. Instructor pilots don't earn a lot of money. They do it either for the love of flying or building hours for a commercial airline seat. Bill flew for the love it, but anything that would increase his income as a pilot would be welcome.

Jim was a retired Marine fighter pilot. He had amassed about 3,500 hours of flight time during that time while recording 400 carrier landings. He also did a tour as a flight instructor that prepared him for his FAA instructor certification. This was typical of such pilots. Fighter pilots do not normally accrue a lot of flying hours because of the short duration of their flights. Consequently, they think more in terms of sorties and all the repetitive experiences they provide. Also, military pilots can generally count on just ten years of dedicated flight time. As they rise in rank, Jim retired as a lt. colonel, staff work creeps in that diverts them from the cockpit. This staff work includes a lot of schooling. In the course of things, senior leaders are expected to be leaders of young pilots, which involves a different set of skills. Leadership and management are required for them. With all this, Jim was actually well prepared to start his flight school retirement job.

Jim looked up from his desk as Bill knocked and entered his office. "Bill, it's good to see you back. It's been busy here and I always need a good instructor around."

Bill smiled. It was good to be back. There was something wonderful about flying and the people who do it that attracted him. After all, how else could he have met

Glenda? Following Jim's nodded invitation to take a seat, Bill first outlined what all had happened during his absence. Details were not included, but his story had a happy ending, which was its point. "Now I'm ready to start thinking about teaching full time. Jim, can we make it happen? It'll be a while before my practice is sold but I'm fairly certain it'll go through because it'll be a good step for the buyers. I really believe that, and I'm not asking for the moon...just enough to make ends meet for me and Glenda."

Jim always needed more pilots that wanted to stay with the job. Turnover among them was high because most of them looked at teaching as a steppingstone to other things. To find a dedicated instructor was a godsend. "Bill, this is wonderful. I competed for a gig teaching Air Force ROTC cadets at Las Vegas University how to fly. The Air Force sees this as a good way to attract future officers and weed out those who won't have the talent to fly its airplanes. Military pilots must meet high standards, and my school is a fairly cheap way to weed out those who don't have the talent. For those who make through my school, they get a private license and a lot of good hours of preparatory time for the Air Force school."

That was all good news for Bill but was there anything more that he could do was his question. "That's great, but is there anything else I can do? I'm not in this strictly for the money...God knows that's not the case...but what I can earn will be helpful for meeting bills."

Jim sat there and thought. *Bill has been a loyal employee. A good one as well. He's a passionate instructor that keeps him going without too much regard for money. He's also able to connect with his students. After all, he married one didn't he?*

Turning full on towards Bill, Jim thought further. *He's a lawyer. Been both a prosecutor and a defender. That means he can sift through details to find his truth. He can also write or otherwise he couldn't present briefs to judges. As owner of a law firm, he must know something about personnel management.*

Yep, his mind was made up and Jim asked, "Bill, how would you like to be my senior Air Force instructor? You would be managing their program."

Bill asked what it would entail and as Jim described it, he became more excited. It took his lawyer skills and put them to good use. "Jim, you got a deal. I'm really turned on by this prospect."

The two men shook hands to cement the deal. Then Jim went into details about his ideas. He wanted this program to be good. It offered too many benefits to screw it up. He wanted success. That meant his instructors had to be qualified and good communicators. They had to fire up the candidates who would bring good stories back to their commander. They also had to be able to determine who had the talent for Air Force flying and render their reports accurately enough for Bill to finish the evaluations thoroughly. After all, his reports would go the Air Force, and what he said would determine who would be sent on to jet training.

Bill went home to Glenda as excited as a boy on Christmas morning. She was immediately attracted to whatever was on his mind. When she heard what had been offered to Bill, she too became excited. *At last, Bill's got what he really wants. Get out of the law and on to flying. Moreover it'll have a purpose.*

Without telling details to Bill, Glenda had had a number of military clients. Most of them were married but OK. They were still humans needing something. Some of them related stories about their careers. That included situations of life and death under conditions that civilians could hardly imagine. Yet, they stayed the course. They may have been alcoholics, skirt chasers, or lonely bachelors in need of a woman's presence for an evening. Whatever, the military held them as closely as a woman in bed. She had seen that attachment in Jim. He would always be a Marine. So, letting Bill work with future generations of these dedicated servants would give him a sense of positive accomplishment that he hadn't felt in many years or perhaps ever.

Glenda turned to Bill and gave him a warm hug. "Flyboy, you've found a home. Now go and make it yours."

About a week later, Jackson called Bill and asked if he could fly to Houston. "We like your proposal, but like everything else, we gotta cover the details."

Bill said he'd clear his calendar and be out the following Monday. That night, he and Glenda celebrated with a good dinner and a long evening at home. The next morning, he called his staff to tell them of the good news.

When they were gathered around the conference table, Bill came directly to the point. "People, I will be taking next week off for the purpose of seeing whether I can sell this firm to the people who bought my operation in Houston."

There was a sense of shock that floated around the table like a ball of St. Elmos' fire. Bill expected it, and so he continued with words of comfort. "Actually, I've been thinking about this move for some time. Anticipating your needs, I held our last meeting to ensure you would be taken care of."

Take care of your horses, your people, yourself...in that order was an old Army maxim about leadership.

"Yeah, seriously. I set up the education program in preparation for you to take over everything. The Houston firm would own this operation. Maybe they would install a senior management partner...I don't know...but you are the people who built the success we've enjoyed here. So, by getting your MBA's, and in Julie's case, her BS, you'll be prepared for this change. You will all be retained. That's part of my bargaining demand."

Turning to Jeremy Bill said, "Jeremy, you came here in hopes of becoming a partner. You knew it'd never happen where you were. Well, as of this instance, you're a full partner with all that comes with the title. You will continue to be a partner under the new management. I'll negotiate as much as I can that you be the senior partner here. After all, you know the business here and it will only save money by not bringing in someone from outside to run things. I can't guarantee it after I'm gone, but you need to have your chance. You've worked for this opportunity."

A round of applause followed with Jeremy standing up and addressing himself to the group. "Guys, gals, this means the world to me. I did, in fact, come here looking for an opportunity. Bill's given it to me, and this is a promise...I'll work my fanny off to fill Bill's shoes. It'll be hard, but that's the challenge...to be good as the best."

More applause followed. It was followed by a celebratory bottle of champagne and lunch. Afterwards, when Bill was in his office, his junior associate, Gene Caplin, knocked on his door. Looking up, Bill smiled and said, "Come on in Gene. I guess you want to talk about something?"

"Yes sir. I do."

The tone of Gene's voice told Bill this would not be an easy chat or a discussion about a fine point in law. The young man sitting before him was slender, of average height, and blond thinning hair. Owl glasses rested on his nose that he was constantly pushing up. "So, what's up?"

Gene's body language showed he was deeply distressed "Well sir, I'm not sure how long I will be staying here."

"Frankly, I've been seeing this of you. Now, first, remember, what you say here stays here. As long as your work is acceptable you will be eligible for promotion. You do understand that don't you."

"Yes sir." That's absolutely not the problem. I've worked in other places, and you've been a wonderful boss. As a result, the work atmosphere is excellent. The issue is mine...not yours."

"Well, I'm glad to hear that because I have tried to be fair and supportive. So, what's tying you up?"

"I'm not...I...well, I...it's hard to say it but I don't think I like defense work. It's not what I dreamed of in law school."

Bill understood old dreams. Every law student dreams of being a Perry Mason who saves the world against injustice every Saturday night. "Well, Gene, let's start at the beginning. How you came to be a lawyer. And, as you tell me, listen to yourself talk. Hear yourself think. OK?"

"Thank you sir. Well, my parents were working people. On the assembly line every morning...good union members...paying down a house. Family has been a big issue. But I guess I wanted something more."

"Money?"

"Well, yeah."

"Sounds familiar. Go on please."

"So I got through school by working extra jobs and student loans."

"That you'll be paying off forever."

"You got that and my parents. I paid for most of everything, but it was a financial strain for them as well, and I owe them...big time."

"So you have a lot of debts, moral and financial, and you took the first job that offered a decent salary."

Gene brightened. Bill was listening hard, understanding well, and he had heart. "Yes sir. And you've been generous. I have enrolled in school as you suggested. God, it's good to be going to school and not racking up bills. I owe you sir."

"No you don't. Just do your job. That's all I ask."

"Whatever sir...but..."

"Well, Gene, I know you're seeing a middle-aged man sitting in front of you who has it made." Waving off Gene's gesture of protest, he continued, "Well, you're right. As of now I do have it made. But let me tell you my story, so you can see a parallel to your situation."

With that, Bill related how he flunked out of college, joined the Army, went through officer candidate school, got an infantry commission, pulled a couple tours in Afghanistan, got out, went to law school, and then became a defense lawyer for the money. "Now, here's the tough part, I got the money...enough that I don't have to worry about it...but I paid a price in terms of family. I lost it entirely and have only now been able to patch things together. That was one goal I had when I just went back to Houston."

Bill waited a minute for Gene to absorb everything he had heard. When he saw Gene's eyes blink in understanding, he continued. "Now in retrospect, should I have stayed in the Army? I dunno. I know I got tired of seeing people getting killed. I knew I didn't want to do that for a living. So, I became a lawyer only to find myself putting people in prison. Was that what I wanted? Not really, but it was a living until my wife and I decided we wanted more money. Do I regret making that change? No, not really. Do I like defending slimeballs. No, but it has been financially good. In hindsight, would I have done anything else? Again, I don't know. But I do know I want to teach flying, and that's what I'm gonna be doing for a long time. Maybe I'll regret it, but I don't think so."

Again Bill waited for Gene to catch up. When he did, Bill said, "Gene, you're a young man with a big heart and heavy conscience. Never regret that. Instead, find what you like to do...something that fits your values. This choice doesn't mean you must abandon the law. For example, family law? There you can create lifetime relationships helping people make good life decisions. I dunno. That'll be your choice. Just don't be afraid to make it."

By now, Gene was smiling. He could see that the man he respected, the man he thought never had a regret, had his own history. That this man could lay it all out on the desk like a hand of cards, well, that was something. It meant he wasn't trapped. He did have choices.

While Gene was thinking about this, Bill wrote down his counselor's name and phone number. When he finished the note, he handed it to Gene saying, "Here, take this. It's the name of my counselor, Jeremy James. He's a cool dude who has helped me get through my problems. You'll find he'll help you frame your issues realistically and work to help you find good solutions for yourself and everyone in your life. If there is anything I do regret is not having known him earlier. If I had, I might have taken a different course that might not have been as sad as what actually happened."

Gene was now a much brighter lad than he was an hour ago. He shook Bill's hand like a pump handle while thanking him for his understanding and guidance. Bill just accepted it and patted Gene on the back as he left the office. *Maybe there I've done something right for someone. Well I certainly hope so.*

Over dinner that evening, Bill related this discussion with Glenda. She began to cry as she heard the story. Bill got anxious and asked, "Glenda, did I screw up? Please tell me."

"No, you dummy. I just wish I had had you as a boss when I was Gene's age."

"But then you couldn't have married me."

"No, but you did listen to me and help me get my life straight. Marrying you was just a side benefit...a perk from a wonderful instructor."

"Come here. Let's hug and have you teach me what I need to do."

Work at the office continued. Bill took his flight to Houston where he visited his family and negotiated the sale of his firm. The terms of the sale were similar as those of the earlier Houston sale. Bill would remain on a consulting basis. He was pleased with that because it would provide extra income needed to make up for what flying didn't pay. Also, he was available to the staff for problems such as Gene had brought forward. Altogether, he was a happy camper.

But first, before leaving, Bill felt obligated to finish the Bisognio case. Here it meant he was defending Richard by working for the prosecution. Strange switch that always felt awkward, but it did do the job. He was finishing a full and effective defense of his client. That was pleasing.

The trial date eventually drug forward in front of everyone. Mr. Jacobs was being tried for second degree murder. A jury was selected and convened. Opening statements were presented. The prosecutor and the defense lawyer presented totally different personalities to the jury. The prosecutor led with his witnesses. The police told how they first thought a different person, Richard Bisognio, was the culprit because of his fingerprints on the gun. The defense tried to stop further questioning once the police talked about the fingerprints. The judge said the prosecutor had the right to continue with his presentation. Overruled was his final word.

Next came Bill. He and the prosecutor, a seasoned lawyer, who knew both the law and courtroom tactics well, had rehearsed his answers. Again, like working for the prosecutor, giving testimony felt odd, but it was the truth, and that, after all, was presumably the whole point of a trial.

"Mr. Ginn. Would you please tell the jury your relationship to this case?"

"Thank you sir. I was asked to represent Mr. Richard Bisognio, during the early part of the police investigation. As I first heard his story, I, frankly was dubious about his chances."

"What made you change your mind?"

"As Lt. O'Connor's indicated it was the smudged fingerprint on an empty cartridge that caught my eye."

"What did you do?"

"Several things. A smudged fingerprint by itself might not mean much, but it did mean someone else had access to Richard's pistol or at least his bullets. When I asked Mr. Bisognio about it he said the defendant was his friend and had borrowed his gun during the time when the shooting took place.

The defense tried to object stating the smudged fingerprint couldn't be used as evidence. The judge overruled him. Bill continued, "Then, voluntarily Mr. Bisognio brought out a bag of empty shells that the defendant had returned to him along with his pistol. I took them down for fingerprint analysis. They were a perfect match to the defendant."

"So you assumed the defendant was the perpetrator?"

"No sir. I learned long ago never to assume anything. Rather, I left the cases with Lt. O'Connors and continued to have a private investigator do a review of Richard's finances and his whereabouts and whether he knew Mr. Jacob."

"Why did you do that?"

"To see if there was any collusion between the two men in the murder of the victim."

More objections followed, and most were denied. Enough were sustained that Bill could continue his story.

"And what were your findings, sir?"

"That Mr. Bisognio and the defendant were friends and that no connection existed between Mr. Bisognio and the victim."

"How did you act on this information?"

"I presented all the information to Lt. O'Connors for use as needed."

"And that was all?"

"Yes sir. As a private citizen, I had no power to effect a format investigation. That remained with the Las Vegas police department. But, when information came forth, I immediately offered it to them for use as they saw fit."

The defense countered by asking whether Bill was a professional investigator. His reply was, "No, I'm not. But, prior to being a defense lawyer I worked as a prosecutor for five years. So, I am well versed in proper sleuthing processes. In any event, I simply offered information. It was up to the police to use it. They did."

The defendant asked various other questions that Bill answered. During them, the prosecutor objected on occasion, but the interview went fairly smoothly. At the end, Bill was excused.

Testimonies dragged for a couple of days after which both sides rested their cases. Summary statements were then presented to the jury by the opposing counsels. The judge gave final instructions to the jury and excused them to begin their deliberations. Since it was already late in the day, they asked to be excused until the next day when they would begin deliberations. It was a short deliberation. Their decision was made within several hours of deliberation.

The jury took their seats. A note was passed to the judge by the bailiff. He read it briefly and returned it to the jury foreman.

"Have you reached a decision?"

"We have your honor."

"Will the defendant please rise?"

They did.

Turing back to the jury, the judge asked for its verdict. The foreman intoned, "We the jury find Mr. Jacobs guilty of second-degree murder."

Mr. Jacobs sagged a bit against his lawyer. A murmur arose in the courtroom that was squelched by the judge's gavel. He said, "Bailiff, please take the prisoner out for confinement where he will stay until sentencing is pronounced. Ladies and gentlemen of the jury, the court thanks you for your diligent search for a truthful verdict. You are excused."

That night, Bill, Glenda, Mr. Bisognio, Richard, and their families celebrated. It was a quiet, elegant restaurant where prices were not posted on the menus. They were read only for information about what was to be served. Full five course Italian meals were presented with fresh bottles for each course. This simple repast was finished with *café corretto* meaning it was spiked with a potent Italian brandy, *grappa*.

At the end of the meal were offerings of thanks for Bill's work. Bill modestly tried to say it was his job, but the pro-forma objection was waved off by Mr. Bisognio. He came before Bill and asked him to stand. When up, Mr. Bisognio took Bill by his shoulders and kissed him while saying, "*Bill, nella la mia casa e' tu mio figlio.*" Richard whispered a translation into Glenda's ear, "This brings you into our family forever. My father told him, 'Bill, in my house, you are my son.' Trust me, he means that."

Chills went down Glenda's spine.

Chapter 21
Justice

Following the trial's conclusion, Bill wrapped things up at the office. That took a month, but it was a busy time. He had to fly back to Houston to sign sale documents and establish lines of communication. This was an important issue. Houston and Las Vegas had to know one another for trust to grow between them.

"Jackson, here's the staffing. Jeremy Miller is the senior member. He is a partner. He is the man you'll want to liase with. He's been in the business for a long time, and he's good. He's now working on his MBA so he can do a better job at fraud defense. Sarah is my right-hand girl. She's been an up-by-the-bootstrap success. She works as the office manager and para legal. She really knows the law better than most lawyers. It's amazing the details she pulls out that save cases. I have made her an associate for the value she brings to the office. Gene is a work in progress. He's a young and capable associate, but I suspect he'll be moving on to another line of law that will be suiting his temperament. Finally, there is Julie who is my receptionist and secretary. I can tell you that when she gets pregnant, her days at the office come to a close. Being a mother is her ambition. Finally, for everyone, they have full insurance coverage, leave benefits, and tuition assistance. At some point while I'm still in the office, I think you should come out and be introduced. You'll find them all to be good people."

Jackson promised that he would come out. This promise was kept two weeks later. He spent a lot of time talking to everyone. This ensured a sense of continuity. The policies Bill established would be honored. Everyone felt better for the visit.

On his final day, the staff took him to lunch. Although he would continue on as a consultant, his daily presence would be gone. They told him how he'd be missed. The farewell was closed with promises, toasts of thanks for the past, and toasts for the future. Bill was satisfied that things were being left in good hands. Although he was happy to leave defense work, he still was attached to the people who had supported his energy and ideas. From there, it was out the door.

Bill then became a full-time instructor pilot. The Air Force ROTC program did mean a lot of business for Jim's school, and he was happy to have Bill direct it. Bill loved the management of the program and flying with the cadets. They were eager to learn in anticipation of flying jets.

After getting the program fully organized, Jim said, "Bill, you're a good instructor. You have talent, but it's time that I make you a real pilot."

Bill was surprised. "Uh Jim, I'd never challenge your judgement. After all, you taught me everything I know. But..."

"No buts. Listen, you're teaching future jet jockeys, and I want them prepared for their Air Force flight school. It's tougher than anything you have ever experienced, so you have to learn jet jockey flying. It's a point of honor for me. What I learned in the Marine Program saved my life on many occasions, and I want these kids to live and fly another day. Got it?"

"Yes sir. When do we start?"

"Now."

Later Bill reflected on this conversation. *Yeah, I got it. What the Army taught me, and what my sergeants taught me, kept me and my soldiers alive. He wants me to keep these youngsters alive.*

Jim took Bill out that afternoon for an orientation flight. Using Bill's Cessna, he turned it inside and out. Bill never imagined that this simple airplane was capable of such maneuvers. Frankly, the ride scared the socks off him. Jim promised to teach these skills to Bill. But that wasn't all.

"Bill, the next thing for you is to visit the maintenance shop where we get our airplanes fixed. That includes yours by the way. Your job is to learn the innards of every one of them. That means you'll be spending a lot of time with their chief mechanic, Jill Bessard. She's a small thing, but tough. She knows her stuff and you're going to learn it and teach it as much as possible to your cadets. When an aircraft acts up during a flight, you gotta understand it and know how to fly around it. Got it?"

"Yes sir."

"Finally, I know you understand the basics of navigation. You mostly use your GPS to do that work don't you?"

"Yes."

"Well, what happens when it craps out?"

"Then I get out my whiz wheel and do it manually."

"And when was it last used?"

"During training."

"So you don't know squat. Now you're going to learn. Why? Because your cadets will be flying long distances in bad weather, hostile conditions, and lord knows what all. We're going to teach them how to navigate manually when their GPS's crap out. Now here's your application for a navigator school. When you're done there, you'll take your FAA navigator certification test."

"I didn't know such a program even existed."

"Well, you do now, so be prepared to study. While you're doing all that, you'll be directing your instructors who are good enough to start the basic flight course for your boy scouts. As you learn your stuff, you'll teach it to your instructors. They won't come up to your capabilities, but that's not important. What they learn will make them better. Who knows? Maybe it'll save a life. So, any questions?"

"Nope. You want your school the best the Air Force can have. I understand that and I'll get it done."

"Carry on."

Bill almost saluted.

Bill did become a better pilot. It took hours of practice but eventually he satisfied Jim. He became a certified navigator. Again, what he didn't know amazed him. His hands got greasy from fixing planes. Eventually, he even got his airframe and power, A&P, certificate. His cadets got rave reviews from the Air Force. Jim was pleased. Bill never had so much fun in his life.

Life with Glenda was fulfilling. She was a partner who lived her life but supported Bill. In turn, Bill gave her everything he had. As the years passed, their lives settled into a routine that was filled with hugs and kisses. As he often said, "My job every day is to make Glenda feel like a queen for a day. How have I done today Ma'am?" Glenda just purred.

One day, he got an email from Jackson that Ricardo Bisognio was coming up for a parole hearing. The next minute Jackson got a call.

"Jackson, this guy was a dumb, psychotic soldier in the local mobs. His final words to me, when he was hauled away to prison, was how he would get me. I have no doubt of his intentions to do so. If he can't come after me, there's no reason why he wouldn't try for Virginia or the kids. In short, we gotta stop this."

"It's gonna be tough because from what I've heard, he's been a model prisoner."

"Only to get parole."

"Yeah but tell that to the board."

"What does John McElroy say."

"He agrees."

"Good. I'll give him a call."

The call went through to John's office. "McElroy here." The voice had aged. Bill thought quickly how John must be pushing 70 now. Still putting bad guys in prison.

"John, this is Bill Ginn."

T from Jackson you've left the law and become an instructor pilot. The legal profession lost a good man when you quit."

"Thank you John. It's good to hear your voice, and yep, I'm a pilot. Loving it too. But this is a serious call. What have you heard about Ricardo Bisognio? I'm concerned because of the threat he made to me when he was hauled out of the courtroom after I convicted him."

John became serious instantly. "Yeah, I assume you're talking about his coming up for parole. Yep, it's true. From what I've heard, he's been a model prisoner and has a good chance of getting out."

"Well, I'm going to come in and argue to the board that he's a clever psychotic and should not be released. As one person he threatened, I think I have a stake in their decision."

"Can't argue with you there."

"Well, keep me posted on what's happening. Meanwhile, thanks for listening."

"Will do. Bye."

Bill then called Mr. Bisognio to inform him of his brother's parole hearing.

"Bill, this is distressing. I know he's my brother, but he's also a killer. Before he was sent to prison, he was a low-life errand boy for the bosses in Houston. My family used to have dealings with them, and it was only through that connection that Ricardo got any jobs at all. Otherwise, he caused more problems than what the jobs were worth. What makes all this so difficult is that Ricardo has one talent."

"And that is? It's important that I know so I can counter his tactics."

Mr. Bisognio thought carefully for words that described the talent that his brother had and used to help himself. "Ricardo is a chameleon. When you first meet him, he can be very charming. He figures out what a person wants to see in him, and bingo! There you have him...the perfect image of what you want. In prison, the warden wants to see a model prisoner, and that's what Ricardo gives to him. It'll be hard for you to deny this long-term image that he has projected around the guards and the warden."

"Thank you for your appraisal of him as it confirms my opinion. Now, I'm not sure you know that when I prosecuted him, he promised to get even with me. Now, that can be a direct threat or through family members still living in Houston."

Mr. Bisognio's tone became intensely grave at this information. "And who are your family members, Bill? Also, where do they live?"

"My ex-wife, children, and parents in law. They're all living in Houston."

A long sigh and then Mr. Bisognio asked, "May I come with you to testify at the board hearing?"

"Oh thank you sir. That would be most helpful and is so kind of you to volunteer."

"When is the hearing?"

"Next week on Wednesday, the 29th."

"Then I'll accompany you."

"I'll have my airplane prepared for us. It'll be an easy four-hour ride."

"That'll be fun. I remember that you're a pilot."

"And a good one if I say so myself."

"Then, let's go."

Bill's next job was to review Texas and Nevada's self-defense laws. Although variations in the two codes existed, it was clear that when a clear and present danger existed, particularly to being killed, self-defense was justified. With that, Bill applied for a carry permit and bought a .22 caliber pistol. He did not want a higher-powered weapon for fear of ancillary harm from a bullet flying in directions unknown. A small caliber would work fine for his purposes.

That evening when Glenda saw the gun, she asked with some anxiety, "What's this?"

"A guy I once prosecuted threatened to kill me if he ever got out of prison. Well, his parole hearing is coming up, and if he is sprung, I want to be prepared. I'm going to advise Frank about this as well since the thug is a Texas problem."

"Oh dear, should I be worried? What if...?"

"I'll be sticking to you like glue if need be." Gesturing toward his pistol, he continued, " I don't like doing all this, but if I must to protect you, I'll do it."

Glenda knew of Bill's military service, and she understood what he meant. She shook a bit in fear of what all could happen. Bill saw this and said, "I'm going to the hearing next week with Mr. Bisognio, who's the prisoner's brother, to testify against the release. Hopefully, for everyone's sake he's sent back to his cage."

"God, I hope so."

"Me too."

Bill met Mr. Bisognio at the general aviation terminal. They went out to his Cessna, safety checked it. and took off. During the flight, Bill tried to make conversation, but Mr. Bisognio was very quiet. He was obviously preoccupied with the purpose of this journey. This was a hard place for anyone to be having to testify against one's brother. So, Bill let his passenger have an opportunity to think about what he was about to do.

When they landed and arrived at their motel, Mr. Bisognio asked if he could borrow their rent-a-car for a while. "Of course, sir. Is there anything I can do for you?"

"No thank you but that won't be necessary. I should be back in a couple of hours."

"Take your time sir."

Upon Mr. Bisognio's return, they went to a nearby restaurant for dinner. Again, Mr. Bisognio was almost deathly quiet. Not a word crossed between them. Bill just continued to leave him alone.

The next morning, Bill went to Frank and Martha's house to fill them in on the purpose of his visit. He had already called ahead to alert them of his arrival.

Frank greeted him with an outstretched hand of welcome. "Bill, welcome home. I presume this is not for fun."

"Sadly it's not."

With that, Bill related everything to his parents-in-law. They listened with horror. When done, Frank asked what should they do to prepare for the worst.

"Call Mr. John McElroy and establish contact with him. He's a friend of mine, my prosector boss actually, and he can provide police protection until we see what's happening. If this guy is released, he'll probably be out in about 10 days. John can confirm that. Now he won't be surprised by your call as I've already discussed the case with him. I just want you to make your own connection with him."

Frank and Martha promised to do that as Bill gave them John's phone number.

The next morning, Bill and Mr. Bisognio were at the prison's waiting room. A number of other people were ahead of them to testify. Mr. Bisognio remained quiet. Bill was finally called.

The board consisted of three men and two women. The head asked for Bill's name, profession, and contact with the prisoner.

"Thank you for having me. I am Bill Ginn, formerly a prosecutor for the Houston area county. I prosecuted Mr. Bisognio and during that time, I came to believe that he was a very dangerous man. I won the case, and when he left the courtroom, he promised to get even with me."

"And how did you interpret that?"

"He'd kill me or someone I loved. I still believe it, and I'm worried because my former wife, her mother and father, and my two children live in Houston. It would be an easy thing for one or all of them to be killed. I am truly in fear for their safety."

The board asked a number of questions of Bill then he was excused. Mr. Bisognio was invited next. He stayed in conference with the board for about 30 minutes. When he came out, he didn't say anything to Bill. In fact, Bill was never told what was said during that latter interview other than to hear what he had been told. Specifically, if the prisoner was paroled he would be released in about a week. From there he would be escorted to the Houston, his hometown, and placed under a parole officer's care. Neither Bill nor Mr. Bisognio were happy with that prospect.

A subsequent call to John McElroy summarized what all had happened and that Ricardo would be returned to Houston if he were released. John groaned. He didn't need to hear that news. He promised to keep Bill informed of any developments and Ricardo's final situation.

With that, Bill said goodbye to Viginia's family along with instructions again to stay in touch with John. They promised to do so. From there, Bill and Mr. Bisognio left Houston early the following morning. Late in the afternoon, they arrived home.

Glenda saw Bill and recognized the stress of this trip. She made just a light dinner and sat quietly until he had finished eating and was ready to talk.

"Well, Babes, it's done. Mr. Bisognio and I did all we could to keep his brother in jail. This has been terribly hard on him because he had to testify against his brother. Family is important to him, but he values my relationship with him so much that he is going against his brother."

Glenda thought a bit and it hit her. She exclaimed with insight into Italian ways, "You're his son and your kids are, in effect, his grandchildren. Now I understand what Mr. Bisognio meant when he pronounced you his son." She shook her head. "Something that could only exist in an Italian family, I guess. Certainly I have never seen it with anyone else."

Bill just sat in silent thought until Glenda came over and gave him a hug. He responded with a sad, but welcoming smile. *This gal is always here for me. Thank you God.*

About a week later, John McElroy called. Bill held his breath. "Bill, what can I say? In spite of your testimony and Mr. Bisognio's, the board indeed paroled him. They weighed your remarks against his prison record and decided that past threats were just that. Ricardo had learned his lesson and could be released into society as a productive member."

Bill groaned loudly causing Glenda to stir in apprehension. John then continued. "He was released yesterday with instructions to stay at a nearby motel for further transportation today for Houston. Well, when the police came to his room, he was found dead...lying on his room's floor. He had a bullet hole in his forehead and two in the back. It was a professional job with a .22 pistol and nothing left behind." A pause was given to let Bill absorb this information when John continued, "There will be an investigation, but I can't possibly imagine a culprit will ever be found. It was too good a job." John also thought to himself, "It ain't likely that we'll be looking too hard either. Good riddance to a scumbag."

Bill straightened up with joy. He didn't like death but in this case, there was justice. There was also no possibility of any danger to his family.

"Thank you John for your call. Frankly, I feel a lot better."

"I can well imagine."

Glenda asked what the good news was. When she heard, she cried, "What an irony. A killer is killed."

Bill just let things stand. *This was not irony. It was Italian justice. On the other side of the bar between a courtroom and a back street. One modern; the other ancient. One by a set of written rules; the other by an unwritten code of honor.*

Bill called Mr. Bisognio with the news. He offered his sadness about the entire matter but nothing else. Mr. Bisognio gave thanks and hung up. *Mr. Bisognio has done his duty; the hardest thing in his life. That poor man...to bear such a burden.*

After Words

Chapter 22
A Final Word

Bill lived until he was 85 years of age. He never litigated another case. Instead he flew until bad eyesight grounded him at 78. The cause of death was simply due to complications of old age. Fortunately he died in his sleep with Glenda at his side. She reported feeling him turn over once, and then he remained quiet. Glenda died a month later. Her health had been excellent, and there was no medical reason for her demise. It was said that she simply died of a broken heart. Virginia continued to live with her parents until their passing. She remained active in her women's issues. Sadly, she died of a drunk teenager driver. Such a cruel joke. Susan became a litigator specializing in women's rights. In effect, she combined her father's and mother's professions. George made flying his career. He attended the Air Force Academy, got his commission, and after flight school became a C-130 pilot. Why he chose that aircraft reflected his early training. "I chose the Herky-Bird because it's fun to fly, and it's really the only airplane left that must be flown. All the others are computer driven, and they're no fun." His father and Jim Jenson would have approved.

His legacy was a lifetime of dealing with the morass of morality and its application. He threw some people in jail, and some got sprung. Beyond that, he taught a thousand bright-eyed students the mysteries of flight. Some became military aviators; others flew for the airlines; and others just flew around the flagpole. Bill cheered them all on to their goals.

In the end, Richard Bisognio, the man who was kept from prison by Bill, summarized Bill's life. "Bill was a complex person as we all are. He followed truth however he saw it. Sometimes he made mistakes, and tragedy occurred. Most of the time he hit it right. However, when all is said and done, please know he was a good man."

The End